The Myrtlewood Grove Revisited

BY

Royal LaPlante

BLACK FOREST PRESS
San Diego, California
March 2000
First Edition

The Myrtlewood Grove Revisited

BY

Royal LaPlante

PUBLISHED IN THE UNITED STATES OF AMERICA
BY
BLACK FOREST PRESS
P.O.Box 6342
Chula Vista, CA 91909-6342
1-800-451-9404

Other Novels by Royal LaPlante:

THE MYRTLEWOOD GROVE 1994 and 1998

PENALOMAH, THE EAGLE SOARS 1997

COTTAGE COVE,
A CHECHAKO IN ALASKA 1998 and 1999

UNCLE JACK'S CREEK 1999

Printed in the United States of America
Library of Congress
Cataloging-in-Publication

ISBN: 1-58275-015-7

Acknowledgments

The author acknowledges the advice and support of his wife and partner, Joanne, who served as typist, proofreader, and editor in preparing this manuscript. His mother, Margaret, provided encouragement and positive critique for the story.

Converting the manuscript into a published book was a task shared by colleagues at Black Forest Press. The professional work of Dahk Knox, Keith Pearson, Mary Inbody, and Dale and Penni Neely is much appreciated.

Family friend, Roy Stevens, shared his knowledge of Port Orford geography and history. A special thanks is warranted for the contribution of June (Knapp) Angel, whose family memoirs lent historical and anecdotal integrity to the final draft of *The Myrtlewood Grove Revisited.*

Prologue

Scott McClure leaned back against the solid base of the Cape Blanco Lighthouse, basking in a bright July sun as his thoughts drifted in peaceful reverie. His fleeting gaze swept the Pacific reaches to the western horizon, settling on a distant barque approaching the Port Orford Heads under full sail. Not many of the old sailing ships called at the port these days, steamers having replaced them during his lifetime.

An enigmatic smile creased the stern lips of his seamed face as he recalled his first visit here in 1851 when the barren promontory had been all but untouched by the hand of man. While the lighthouse was being built in 1870, he wandered over in curiosity, prepared to hate any structure which might scar the pristine landscape. Instead, he found a place suited for his lonely meditation. The cares of family and problems of Curry County could be put aside while he pondered his life and its meaning in solitude. The lighthouse keeper understood Scott's need to be alone and seldom interrupted his privacy.

His wind-seared countenance showed the age of a pioneer farmer who had endured the Oregon coastal weather as well as years of labor carving his Myrtlewood Grove ranch out of the Sixes River wilderness. A painful grimace accompanied an unconscious shift of weight to ease the pressure on his cantankerous right knee. Lifting his wide-brimmed hat to brush sweat from his brow with a sleeved forearm, he exposed matted gray hair sparsely covering a glistening scalp. As Scott replaced the venerable felt cover on his head, he chuckled softly to himself and sank deeper into his reverie.

I feel every one of my fifty-three years. Damn joints are always aching. I keep telling my children when the weather is due to change based on that nagging right knee. Missy used to laugh every time I predicted the weather — God, how I miss her. Buzz gone in the '68 Demon Fire, and then my beloved

Melissa dead from pneumonia in '74. It's been a chore being mother and father to Richard, Anne, and George, even though they are fine youngsters. Hmph! Mighty fine adults is what they've suddenly become, and as independent as their parents were at that age.

I hope Anne will be happy living in Salem. She seemed so young at her wedding last week, and she looked so much like Melissa at our wedding twenty-one years ago. My daughter made a fetching bride, and Albert's a lucky man, as he repeatedly told me that day.

He bears a strong family resemblance to his uncle, John Lee, both in temperament and looks. Albert's prospects are excellent, being a lawyer and junior partner in the Salem firm of Lee, Gerbrunn, and Lee.

I sure enjoyed seeing Kurt and Kurt, grandfather and grandson, and Johann, too. All three Gerbrunns seemed happy talking about living in their big old family home. It's been over a year since Inge and her daughter-in-law drowned in the Willamette River, that tragic ferryboat accident near Oregon City that claimed several lives.

Scott chuckled aloud as a stray image flittered through his head, Grandpa Kurt's wistful expression in talking about his three granddaughters and an expected baby back in Salem. Uwe and Angela couldn't attend the wedding because their fourth child was due any day. Kurt lamented to his old friend, "I love the girls and my lawyer-to-be grandson, but Uwe needs a son to carry on the business."

A rifle shot echoed through the clearing south of the lighthouse, the aging farmer's melancholy interrupted by that sound and the sight of the keeper running through coastal shrubs in pursuit of a wounded deer. As the man disappeared from view, Scott's thoughts refocused on his family concerns.

What should I do about Georgie? He's so young to make a decision for life. Even though he is determined to be a Catholic priest, I have my doubts. He's been thinking about a life of service to the church for years. Where did he get his religious bent? Most likely from his mother, or maybe from Father Francis Blanchet on that trip to Jacksonville.

Well, he's got a mind of his own, that's for sure. When old Cougar died last year, he knew just where to bury him–next to

Buzz in the family plot. So they could keep each other company, he told me. George's injuries from the forest fire may have crippled his body, but it left his mind healthy and his intellect continually growing.

"He'll make a good Jesuit, but will he be content?" Scott muttered aloud.

"I think Georgie will be fine, Dad. He loves his books, particularly those written by the great philosophers, and he hasn't been satisfied at home since Mom died. I'm afraid you and I are too practical in our conversations, he'd prefer arguing with Plato, Rousseau, or Webster about the meaning of life. I never could understand what difference it makes if a falling tree in the forest makes a noise when no one can hear it," Rick rambled to a close as his father smiled.

"Well, it looks like the Myrtlewood Grove will be yours, Son. Anne and Albert got the land I bought east of Salem, and George needs all our cash to travel to San Francisco and meet Vicar-General James Croke. You know, I remember a bustling priest baptizing the Hermann boy, and George thinks he was Father James here to set up a chapel at Cape Blanco. Anyway, I told Albert to prepare a partnership agreement between you and me. You're my farmer-son and will have to carry on the ranch business."

A moment of silence was broken as Richard gasped air, surprise and pleasure mixed in his response, "Phew! Thanks, Dad, I love the Myrtlewood Grove, and I'll always preserve it. But gee, you're still young. You'll be around for years, making decisions and running the ranch."

"No, we'll manage as partners from now on, and some day maybe there'll be a grandson to help us," Scott teased. Digging his elbow into Rick's ribs playfully and then throwing his arm over his son's shoulders, they turned easterly for the trek up the Sixes River to their home.

Chapter One

Wind-whipped sea spray struck Richard McClure's pallid face again, his younger brother George chuckling unmercifully at Rick's discomfiture. The older brother grinned sheepishly in bravado, moments before lunging forward to lean over the rail, succumbing to the seasickness caused by the rolling motion of the barque, *Eliza Ross*, outbound for San Francisco.

She was the same ship he and his father had observed from the Cape Blanco Lighthouse just yesterday afternoon. When George was given permission to study with the Jesuits, he was determined to leave on the next ship out of Port Orford. The two brothers were aboard the *Eliza Ross* in the early morning hours as she stood out to sea, Captain Nathaniel Monroe wisely clearing the harbor in fair weather. By mid-morning a summer squall had enveloped the sailing ship, its offshore winds a boon for the crew eager to reach home port, but an upsetting experience for one of the two landlubber passengers.

George was enjoying the stimulating voyage, not so secretly pleased at besting his brother by avoiding any queasiness, his twisted gait somehow suited to the tilting deck. But when a deckhand laughed tauntingly at Rick's position over the rail, George was quick to censure the sailor, "Leave my brother be, friend!"

The wiry but muscular young crewman stopped before the lad and muttered threateningly, "Shut up, boy!" just as the mate called the man forward.

"I'm all right, Georgie. Don't go fighting with the crew. After all, Dad sent me along to look after you," Rick declared in a broken voice, followed by another round of retching.

"Ha! Ha! Some escort you are, big brother," George teased, but sobered to offer solace, "Captain Monroe says we'll make as good a time as a steamer with favorable winds."

"Favorable?" croaked Rick, giving his little brother a dirty look and bemoaning his condition, "I'm sick and you're laughing. Pshaw!"

"You're just mad because I'm a better sailor than you. Do you want a piece of venison jerky?" George asked playfully as he drew a morsel out of his pouch.

Big brother lost interest in any retort as he shivered and shook over the rail, drawing another cackle of laughter from a deckhand nearby. George swiveled about to meet the glare of the heavyset older man, who laughed again with a touch of malice crossing his bearded countenance.

The young sailor who had accosted the McClure brothers earlier chimed in, "Hey, Jake! Pretty boy doesn't look so tough, does he?"

"Harry! Jake! Get back to work and don't bother our passengers," Captain Monroe bawled in no-nonsense tones and then smiled as he waved good-naturedly to George.

Rick stood ensconced at the *Eliza Ross* bow rail, right knee braced against solid wood and fingers grasping the rigging tightly. He viewed the beauty of a California sunrise, beams of light streaking through mists nestled in green hills flanking the Golden Gate. The barque would be in port before noon, and the young man needed a moment with his thoughts.

He was up early this morning, already having washed and shaved while Georgie slept on, their cramped cabin limiting activity, its headroom insufficient to house his muscular six feet without a bruised noggin. A square chin and aquiline nose made his face seem rugged and harsh, but his mother's lucent blue eyes and his father's wistful smile softened the look, auburn-tinted locks framing his face. Not a "pretty boy" as that oaf Harry had said, but still handsome enough as the girls of Curry County would attest.

Large calloused hands were his most noticeable physical characteristic, size coming from his father, and the calluses a direct result of hard work on the Sixes farm.

From the corner of his eye Rick observed Jake staggering unnecessarily across the deck and held his place solidly as the big bruiser fell into him.

"Oh, excuse me, Pretty Boy," the insolent sailor offered for the benefit of the mate on watch. At his signal, Jake clambered aloft with the other hands to furl sails.

Rick curbed his irritation, reflecting to himself, *I'll have to talk to Georgie about those two would-be bullies. A good punch in the nose is what they'll get if we meet them ashore.* He studied the bay and city, looking over the multitude of ships gathered ahead, and thought, *I'd better round up brother George and our gear. We'll be going ashore soon.*

✶ ✶ ✶ ✶ ✶

The McClure brothers shook hands with Captain Monroe as he stood at the head of the gangway, George exchanging pleasantries with the skipper while Ricky waited patiently with his question. During a break in their conversation, he queried, "Thanks for putting up with this landlocked farmer, Captain. When are you sailing north again? I'll be going home in a few days."

"Not for several weeks, Mister McClure. I just received sailing orders to Monterrey and a cargo bound for Hawaii. However, I can recommend the *Empress Trader*. She's anchored over there," Monroe stated as he pointed to a steamer lying offshore. He added with a co-spiritual smile, "Captain Drummond is an old friend of mine. Sailed with me as a deckhand on this ship over thirty years ago."

Rick nodded with interest as he asked, "Is the *Empress Trader* headed for Port Orford? When does she sail?"

Captain Monroe pointed across the dock to a small group of people gathered around a big dark-haired man and suggested, "That's her mate over there, name of O'Keefe, a tough Irishman. Why don't you ask him?"

With a casual nod of thanks and a friendly salute, Rick hoisted his duffel bag over his left shoulder and hurried down the gangplank, George shadowing him closely. As the tandem approached the gathering, the older brother paused in wonder at the sight of a beautiful woman standing before O'Keefe, her lilting laughter carrying across the pier.

Under close scrutiny, Rick decided the young lady was perhaps sixteen years of age, a girl but with considerable poise.

Her fair complexion was enlivened to a gentle blush by the breeze blowing in from Alcatraz, as well as the mate's attention. A pert white hat crowned long brunette hair, and her lavender-blue eyes flashed humor as she laughed once more. The girl was slender and lithe, her stance naturally graceful as she turned toward the approaching McClure brothers.

Rick met her eyes as a thought flashed silently through his mind. *She's sure pretty, but Mom always said it was impolite to stare.*

He nodded a bit jerkily and forced his glance upon her three companions, their close resemblance to one another marking them as a family. The older woman illustrated how maternity would mature the girl, her features still beautiful and her demeanor very ladylike. A husky lad about George's age exchanged greetings with his brother while Rick waited for the gray-haired father to conclude his conversation with the officer, "We'll see you on Saturday, Mister O'Keefe. I hope we'll enjoy fair weather up the coast. My wife and children have never sailed before."

"Aye, Mister Madsen, it will be much more pleasant for all of us if this weather holds. I'll send a pair of hands to your hotel for your luggage. We'll be docked right here after the *Eliza Ross* departs. Good day, sir!"

"Thank you, Mister O'Keefe. I believe this young gentleman is waiting to talk to you," the well-dressed gentleman said with a smile at Rick, taking his wife's elbow to lead her aside.

"Thank you, sir, ma'am," Rick stated courteously, his gaze lifting to meet the mate's eyes as he continued, "Captain Monroe said you might be sailing to Port Orford at the end of the week, Mister O'Keefe. I'm seeking passage home."

Equally polite, the mate smiled ruefully and replied, "Port Orford is a port of call, sir, but both our passenger cabins are booked. We don't have two more bunks available."

"My brother is remaining in San Francisco to attend school, so I'll be alone. Oops, except for a palomino mare I'm picking up for my father. Could I bunk with the crew? Is there room for the horse?" Rick queried.

Mister Madsen was within earshot and spoke out, "Mister O'Keefe, this gentleman's horse is welcome to keep my mare company in the hold."

Stepping forward to offer his hand, the volunteer introduced himself and his family, "I'm John Madsen, and my wife's name is Hazel. Julie and Fred are our children."

Rick smiled at each member of the Madsen family in turn, Julie getting extra attention before he replied, "I'm Richard McClure, and my brother here is George. He's going to…"

"Why, pardon me, lad!" the mate fairly shouted as he stated gleefully, "You'd be Scott McClure's eldest child. Your daddy is and old and dear friend, and the only man who ever beat me arm wrestling. Why, your dear mother let me hold you on my knee when you were a wee babe. How are your folks?"

Rick nodded slowly, confirming his father's friendship before answering his final question, "You'd be Bos'n Mate O'Keefe. Dad has spoken of you often. It is good to meet you again, sir. Father hasn't changed much, except he's a mite older, but Mother's been gone three years. Caught pneumonia after Christmas and passed away. Dad misses her terribly—as we all do."

O'Keefe's tough image cracked a bit as a tear flowed along a wrinkle in his weather-beaten face, and he sniffled, "Agh! Such a lovely lady was your blessed mother. Every man in Port Orford was in love with the schoolmarm, and your father was the lucky man she chose as her husband. God rest her soul. You and your father have my sympathy."

"Thank you, Mister O'Keefe. I'll pass along your regards and feelings to my father."

O'Keefe's countenance brightened as he declared, "Better yet, lad, you can bunk with me on the voyage home, and I'll tell Scott myself. It's time we had a good visit anyway."

Standing leisurely on the boardwalk in front of a busy fisherman's market, Richard watched the Madsen family boarding a carriage, smiling at Julie as their glances met. George nudged his brother in mock impatience, grumbling, "Come on, Rick, quit staring at the Madsen girl and let's head uptown."

Rick laughed cheerfully and winked at his brother as he replied, "Sure, Georgie, but you have to admit Julie is the prettiest girl in town. Well, let's go!"

Swinging his duffel bag over his left shoulder one more time, he spun on his heel and strode south, exchanging a comradely grin with his brother as they continued their adventure—their last day together. Rick had no doubt that George would be a successful student and theologian, and hence, pursue the career of his choice.

Suddenly sad at the thought of losing a brother, perhaps never seeing him again, Rick was oblivious to Jake's appearance on the sidewalk until the bully shouldered him aside. A nasty laugh accompanied the antagonistic affront as Rick looked into the sailor's sneering face.

The young man's mood continued its metamorphosis from happy-go-lucky to sorrow to instantaneous rage in those brief moments of suspended time. Without conscious thought, Rick threw aside his bag and struck out with his right fist, using this momentum to knock Jake off his feet into a pile of trash.

Harry charged toward him along the sidewalk, but George was ready, tripping the second culprit and shoving him into his partner. The brothers stood over the garbage-splattered bullies as bystanders gathered to watch the fight. Both sailors hesitated to rise, evoking laughter from a man in the crowd. As Jake struggled to one knee, Rick stepped forward with fists clenching threateningly, and the seaman sat back down in the trash, accepting his ignominious defeat without further contest.

Rick's heady feeling of victory soon lost its flavor as a carriage passed the scene, and frowns of disapproval were reflected in the faces of Julie Madsen and her mother. George followed his brother's glance and murmured, "So much for your white knight image, Rick. But it was a fine fight, if somewhat short. Come on, Brother, cheer up, you can impress the girl with your stalwart qualities on the trip home."

"Ha! Ha! You're right, George. We should never take ourselves too seriously. Besides my appetite has been whetted. Let's find a Chinese restaurant and pamper you with a feast before I turn you over to Father Croke. I bet your school meals will be staid."

George smiled as he retorted, "I think a better word to use is spartan, Big Brother, but I expect you are correct. After lunch, I'd like to buy Father a gift, which you can deliver for me, a watch to remember our time together. I know how difficult it was for him to let me go. It's hard for me to tell him how much I love him."

"Dad knows it, George, but I'll tell him for you when I get home. Now let's make the most of our day," Rick concluded, leading George uptown toward his destiny.

Friday arrived for Rick as a ray of sunshine struck his eyes through the impractical lace curtain adorning his window. Missus Arbogast served the best food on Market Street even if her rooms were decorated for girls. Her daughters were all married, and their unchanged rooms provided the Boston lady with a tidy income.

Rick's first thought for the day was, *Where is our San Francisco fog? This is the first morning I've seen the sun before noon—except for the Alameda ferryboat ride. I bet it's a scorcher today, and just when I've got a bundle of errands to run.*

A half-hour later, filled with flapjacks, fried eggs, and fresh orange juice, he hurried off to the jewelry store. Hans Schweizer had promised the brothers George's gift for his father would be inscribed with the lad's personal sentiments and ready for Rick to pick up this morning.

The old craftsman and his brother had struck up a friendly and lengthy conversation after Hans mentioned his acquaintance with Kurt Gerbrunn of Salem. The two men had met in Portland years ago, and in the manner of kindred souls, the two new Americans, formerly a German and a Swiss, had maintained cordial ties through the mail. Rick had left George and Hans to their own devices as he stepped outside to verify the sight of Mister and Missus Madsen walking down the street, eventually disappearing from view around the corner. His hope of catching a glimpse of Julie was a failure.

Entering the small shop on this bright and cheerful morning, he was greeted warmly by the old man, "Hello, my young friend! Isn't it a beautiful day? Did George meet the Vicar-General as planned?"

Smiling with a trace of regret, Rick replied, "Yes, and of course, George was accepted as a student. I knew he would be. Father Croke's secretary had compliments for you when George handed him your letter of reference."

"Well now, my wife is devout, and I pay my tithe. I expect the Catholic church to approve of us, and I am happy to help such a fine young man," Hans lauded George as he produced and open leather box containing a simple but elegant silver watch.

Rick lifted the timepiece carefully by its small silver chain and studied its face before placing it upside down in his left palm. Engraved in tiny flourishing handwriting was George's message to his father. Rick mouthed the words aloud as he slowly read,

> *Scott Addis McClure*
> *To my honored father with heartfelt*
> *love from his grateful son*
> *George John McClure 1877.*

With glistening eyes, Rick choked out his approval, "A lovely sentiment, isn't it? So like George, I know Father will cherish it."

Hans lifted a matched silver watch from a second leather box and read the inscription to Rick,

> *Richard Erastus McClure*
> *Always my beloved brother*
> *and my best friend*
> *George John McClure 1877.*

After a brief pause, the jeweler added, "George wanted to surprise you. That's why the watches took so long. Your brother was quite sober and serious the other day, yet he left another message for you as a jest. 'Smooth sailing on the voyage home—with the sea and with Julie'."

Brushing a sleeve over his damp eyes, Rick laughed nostalgically, "Ha! Ha! Again just like Georgie. Dad and I will miss him on the ranch. Thank you for the fine engraving and for helping my brother."

"My pleasure, Richard. Give Kurt my regards when next you see him, and bon voyage."

✱ ✱ ✱ ✱ ✱

By noon Rick had completed his shopping errands and returned to his room laden with an armful of packages. It was past time to pick up the palomino mare, so he hailed a cab outside Missus Arbogast's boarding house and treated himself to a tourist's ride to Rediviso Stables in the park. His driver was a fount of local history and geography as Rick plied him with multiple questions along the comfortable twenty-minute drive. Several bridle paths wended through the woods as they neared the stables, Rick paying more attention to the horses than the riders. The carriage made a sharp turnaround and came to an abrupt halt. The driver accepted his fare and a modest tip with a smiling nod as he slapped the reins to put his team into motion.

The air cooled noticeably as he stepped out of the sunlight into the barn's interior, Rick standing still to let his eyes adjust to the dimness.

"Richard McClure, what are you doing in San Francisco? Is Scott with you?'

The young man took but a moment to spot the familiar figure before the office door, recognizing Captain Tichenor, his father's friend from Port Orford. He replied, "No sir. He's at home. I accompanied my brother George here so he can go to school with the Jesuits. Dad asked me to pick up a palomino mare he purchased from Señor Alvarez. Say, isn't he a friend of yours?"

"Yes, he certainly is. I bet that horse in the last stall is Scott's. My daughter Ellen was admiring her earlier, and the Alvarez boy got very nervous. Didn't want anyone near her because the new owner was taking delivery today. Come in the office, and I'll introduce you to Señor Alvarez."

After concluding business with Alvarez, including a cursory inspection of Ariane, he joined William Tichenor in the exercise yard. Ellen was working her horse, also a palomino mare, through a series of gaits, ending up with the horse's prancing right up to the fence before the two men.

Flashing a warm smile, Ellen scrutinized the younger man and guessed correctly, "You must be Ricky McClure. You've got your father's good looks, and you're the right age. I haven't seen you since you were a toddler. Does that mare belong to you?"

Grinning widely at Ellen's amiable surmise, Rick answered, "Yes to both counts, and I do look like my father. We both thank you for the 'good looks' remark. Ellen, you could still pass for the belle of Curry County."

"Ha! Ha! With several McGraw children running around my home, I'm hardly a belle any more, but thanks anyway. Do you have time to share a picnic lunch with Daddy and me?"

And so the three early settlers of Port Orford sat in the barn and relived an earlier age through stories of mutual friends. Ariane and her sibling mare were fed carrots by Rick during a simple lunch. Señor Alvarez joined them with a bottle of red wine to celebrate friendship.

Glass of wine in hand, Rick turned toward his palomino stall with a carrot in his other hand and narrowly avoided a collision with the Madsen family. Julie gave him a cool glance, actually a look of disdain, while her parents nodded pleasantly, and Fred exuberantly asked, "Gee, Rick, is that your horse? Is he...er...she a palomino? Can I pet her?"

Unable to resist Fred's puppy-like overture of friendship and unable to make a favorable impression on his sister, Rick handed the carrot to the lad and let him enter the stall. Ariane was not in the least disturbed by the boy's friendly attention.

Ellen waved good-bye as she and Julie mounted their horses and rode away together. The elder Madsens had accepted wine from Señor Alvarez and were being toasted when Rick crossed to the group. He overheard Tichenor intone, "Here's to a fair voyage north, Mister and Missus Madsen! I'm always glad to welcome new neighbors to Port Orford." He acknowledged the return of his young friend with an added, "For you too, Rick, a safe trip home!"

After sipping his wine, John Madsen addressed the young man, "When are you taking your horse aboard the *Empress Trader*, Mister McClure?"

"This afternoon, sir, and please call me Rick. I'm staying aboard tonight. What about your daughter's dun?" Rick queried.

"In the morning, Rick, and my name's John. I hear we sail at ten o'clock. I hope the two mares get along."

Rick nodded in understanding, offering, "I'll be with Ariane when you come aboard, and if Fred will dress in work clothes, we can manage the horses. Mister O'Keefe told me there will be other livestock in the forward hold. If I can avoid sea-sickness, I'll spend a lot of time below decks."

Thanking Captain Tichenor and Señor Alvarez for their hospitality, Rick led Ariane from her stall and mounted bareback, the simple rope hackamore serving to direct her on their way. The mare was young and spirited but had been well-trained, so their trek across San Francisco to the docks was pleasant. The horse became skittish only when she felt the wooden surface of the wharf, and Rick quickly dismounted to quiet her.

Mister O'Keefe had him wait while ship's stores were being loaded and then ordered two deckhands to bring Ariane aboard. Rick led her calmly into the hold, a single carrot the only in-ducement he needed to hold her attention. He spent an hour walking the mare about the confined space, brushing her coat to a golden sheen during the interim.

Treating her to a handful of oats, he returned to Missus Arbogast's to pack his belongings. He managed to devour a scrumptious supper at her bountiful table before bidding farewell, and heavily laden with packages, made his way to the mate's cabin on the *Empress Trader*.

Rick found the mate and a deckhand in the hold with the palomino and two milk cows, the small space seeming to be filled. Seeing the young man grinning at them, O'Keefe laughed aloud and asked, "Ha! Ha! I'll never be a farmer or a horseman. How will you exercise these poor beasts while we're at sea?"

"Oh, the Madsen boy and I will manage. He's a good hand with animals."

"Well, let me know if you need help. Simon here knows a little about milking cows," and in a teasing voice O'Keefe added, "When you finish here, remember the bottom bunk is mine. I have the early watch, and a wagon of cargo is due at daybreak."

✴ ✴ ✴ ✴ ✴

Rick had spent the morning feeding and exercising the livestock and then cleaning their confined "sea barn". Soon he found that a word or a touch from him was sufficient to calm, and in a sense, control the animals. He came topside into bright sunlight, and a veritable rainbow spanned the dock. Several crewmembers were frolicking in a stream of spray coming from a hand-driven fire pump.

He ran down the gangway and joined the impromptu bathing orgy, aware that his next real bath would be in Oregon. Besides he'd like to smell more human and less bovine when the Madsens came aboard. The sprinkling mist was suddenly extinguished as the horse-drawn engine moved away.

Simon grinned at the disappointed expression on the young passenger's face and explained companionably, "Those firemen are testing some new equipment, Mister McClure. Our free bath was unexpected, but I liked it."

Right you are, my friend, even my clothes smell clean. Mister O'Keefe may tire of my company if I spend much time in that hold," Rick commented in ironic tones.

"Well, sir, I've been assigned to tending those animals and have the same problem. I'll trade you favors. I'll wash our 'barn' clothes in saltwater every day if you'll exercise the beasts. You have the knack, mate."

Rick nodded quickly, offering a handshake on their deal as he said, "Agreed, Simon, between us we'll get the job done."

He heard the clip-clop sound of hooves drumming on the wharf and was hailed by an excited Fred, "Rick...Rick, I rode Smokey all the way from the park. Will you help me take her aboard the ship?"

The dun was very nervous on the unfamiliar planking, like Ariane she tossed her head fractiously while prancing about. Fred seemed oblivious to her panicky behavior, and Rick moved smoothly to horse and rider, talking both to the lad and the mare in a quiet, confident voice, "Hello, Fred. And you too, Smokey. Whoa, girl! Hold her steady, Fred, she's skittish...easy now, old girl."

He grasped the horse's bridle, holding her head firmly to his chest as he suggested, "Dismount slow and easy, Fred."

The boy followed instructions, sliding from the saddle and asking in more sober tones, "What do I do now, Rick?"

"Come take the bridle and talk to Smokey, Fred. You're doing fine. I'll find Mister O'Keefe and ask if we can load her now."

Rick left his young friend rubbing down his horse and Simon feeding the cows, going topside to fetch the saddle. Fred was doing a creditable job of handling Smokey and seemed genuinely interested in his charge. Rick thought he had a natural talent with horses and the makings of a good rancher.

Exuding the odoriferous stench of livestock, Rick emerged into the clear air of San Francisco Bay and all but bumped into the elegantly dressed Julie. Her nose twitched perceptibly as she frowned, and catching his own scent he blushed in embarrassment, covering his distress with a laughing remark, "Ha! Ha! Welcome to our seagoing farm, Miss Madsen."

Surprisingly a smile enlightened her face as she too laughed, "I see I need to change clothes before I check on my horse. Is Fred....down there?"

"Yes, your brother is quite a horseman. He rode Smokey down here and then led her into the hold. She is eating oats out of his hand right now," Rick stated conversationally.

Mister Madsen's voice boomed out, "Good to hear, Rick. Thanks for helping my boy."

"Yes, thank you, Mister McClure. Will you show me the way to the hold after I change clothes?" Julie asked prettily.

Rick nodded quickly, and as she hurried after her folks, he wondered how he could lose a little of his barnyard smell.

The ship was steaming clear of the Golden Gate when the Pacific swells took their tolls, Julie retiring to her cabin and Fred to the ship's rail. The rolling gait of the seagoing steamer caused Rick to feel the motion, too, but he girded himself to ignore his queasy stomach and tend the fidgety animals. He thought, *I suppose you fellas feel about like I do. Besides, you're scared because you can hardly stand—even on four legs.*

Unconsciously muttering aloud to Ariane, his thoughts continued, "Old girl, you'll get used to this rolling boat. In a few days we'll be on solid ground again."

"She's a ship, sir, not a boat. Talking to animals does calm them, doesn't it, mate?" Simon observed, adding empathetically with a knowing grin, "And it helps the cowhand, too. Do you want relief? The galley is serving a midday meal. Ha! Ha!"

"Go ahead and laugh at this would-be sailor, my devilish friend. Keeping busy with the livestock is a good way to avoid a bout of seasickness. I'll stay here until evening mess," Rick vowed to both himself and Simon.

✳ ✳ ✳ ✳ ✳

Despite fair weather along the Pacific coast, three Madsens were indisposed on the initial leg of their voyage. John Madsen substituted for his son in tending Smokey, and Rick found him to be a friendly companion. Their conversations were centered on John's family, the young man's interest in Julie being obvious, and on the Elk River. The businessman's interest was clarified when he divulged ownership of a ranch near the Somers place.

"Hazel's uncle left her his 'donation claim' on the Elk River when he passed away in Placerville this past winter," John explained to the curious young man, continuing after a reminiscing pause. "I owned a general store on the American River near Sacramento and sold it last month. Good riddance in my opinion. I've always hated being a storekeeper and dreamed of building something worthwhile for my family. Are you familiar with the Helger ranch?"

"No, but I expect my father knew your wife's uncle and probably knows where your claim is located. You can ask him when we port. Dad will be meeting my ship," Rick averred with surety.

✳ ✳ ✳ ✳ ✳

On the third day out of San Francisco, Fred joined his father and Rick in the hold, pallor and lethargy overcome by the boy's dogged determination to void his illness. After a day of success, color returned to his cheeks, and he ate sparingly of the galley's offerings. He even escorted his sister on the deck to test her legs, Rick being just one of many men vying to provide comfort to a lady in distress. A deck chair, a glass of water, a soda cracker, and an errand run were all samples of their attention. Rick's heart skipped a beat when he won a wan smile as he escorted her below decks to visit Smokey. Even there he discovered Simon proffering a bag of oats to Julie for her horse. As he found in the next couple of days, he had little time alone with the girl, having to be satisfied with her company in the presence of others.

The Port Orford Heads and Cape Blanco were sighted far too soon for the enchanted young suitor and none too soon for the Madsen women, both eager to stand on terra firma once more.

Rick stood braced at his favorite spot on the bow, peering intently through "Oregon mist" at Port Orford, a stiff breeze blowing from offshore.

John Madsen approached, muttering a wonderful query, "How long can fog sit along the beach when the wind is blowing so?"

Shaking his head but smiling, Rick replied, "Ah! But that's home to me, John. The Myrtlewood Grove is probably bathed in sunlight right now. Your place, too. Port Orford is both windy and a bit foggy a lot of the time."

"My wife doesn't like the wind particularly, nor snow either. Does it snow very often?"

"No, snow is rare, but rain is common enough," Rick retorted, and continuing to study breaks in the thin fog, he shouted, "Look! There's the port, and there are people on the bluff waiting for the ship."

After several minutes he waved and pointed, "See that tall man with the wide-brimmed hat and the slight man standing beside him. Both are waving. That's my father and his friend, Louie Knapp, the proprietor of the hotel—that tall building near Battle Rock. It's good to be home."

Chapter Two

The pair of cows struggled up the sandy bluff, Rick digging in his toes and pulling their lead ropes with firm encouragement. When his charges cleared the dune-like hill and reached a grassy flat beside Brush Creek, he picketed the animals. Hefting his Sharps on his shoulder and chewing on a strip of beef jerky, he surveyed his position from atop a cairn overlooking the stream.

He found himself quite alone, except for his two cows, at the foot of Humbug Mountain and estimated that two or three hours were necessary to traverse the rough country this side of the Mason place. Dad had said they owed the Masons a favor, and Rick was repaying it by delivering the cows from the *Empress Trader* to their ranch.

"Ha! Ha!" Rick reacted to his predicament, startling himself back into silent thought. *Johnny Larsen is sparking Julie in Port Orford, and Dad is riding Ariane over to the Sixes River while I'm stuck on the Humbug. Hmph! It was nice of everyone to meet the ship, ha, ha, but I didn't get much attention. Dad was as bad as George Hermann and Louie Knapp in welcoming the newcomers, and Johnny talked to Julie while Fred and I were stuck with the livestock. Ah well, at least I got a hug from "Aunt" Mary, and Mister O'Keefe had a good visit with Dad.*

Bovine lowing suddenly took on a panicky tone, the cows' fear easily distinguishable as an insistent warning. Rick hurried over to them, scanning the area for the source of their fright. He caught the lead rope of one terrified cow as she tore her picket loose, and seizing both ropes in a clenched left fist, he talked soothingly as his eyes continued to search the forest for some critter that might be a threat to the cows.

The obedient beasts followed him docilely up the creek, trusting him as their protector. Winding along a narrow path, more a game trail than a road, Rick was jerked backwards when the cows reared in fright, their eyes rolling as they snorted in alarm. He tied them securely to a fallen cedar and circled the hillside, always within sight of the animals. An eerie feeling overcame his nonchalant mood as his charges continued to low and shuffle about in distress.

Rick's gaze flickered from tree to rocks to rushing water without spotting anything out of place, knowing full well the cows' other senses were more acute than his own. He stepped around the broad bole of a giant fir and espied a patch of sandy soil before him. As he sighted the spoor of a large cat imprinted in the sand, a primal instinct took over, and he leaped back into the shadow of the fir, feeling a slash of exquisite pain along his shoulder as a gray-gold blur passed beside him.

His rifle barely lifted from his side as it discharged a bullet onto the back of a twisting cougar. Rick reloaded on the run, following the tumbling, wounded cat into the graveled creek bed, stopping it cold with his second shot.

Advancing cautiously with his Sharps ready to fire again, he observed scruffy fur and yellow blunted teeth, these factors plus the huge size of the cat marking him as an oldster. *Probably too old to hunt faster game,* Rick thought as he drove his knife blade into the dead cat's throat, and concluded, *He'll make a good rug to match the cougar Dad and Buzz killed before I was born.*

"Ouch!" He said aloud as he reached out with his left hand, and then looking at his upper arm, he saw a long straight slash from elbow to shoulder, his sleeve parted to show the wound caused by the cougar's slashing leap. Bleeding copiously, it was nevertheless shallow, and Rick was able to wash it in cold creek water and then wrap it in the remnants of his undershirt.

Determined to carry on normally, he quieted the cows and then skinned the cougar, sitting exhausted on the riverbank for several minutes before forcing himself to continue to Mason's ranch. The cows shied at the blood scent on the young man, his own and the cougar's, but followed their tender's voice as he sang an Irish tune Mister O'Keefe had taught him. He arrived at dusk in the Mason yard, and Missus Mason dressed his wound properly while her husband put the cows in the barn and fed them a few oats. The couple had to wait until morning for the cougar tale as Rick fell asleep on the floor beside the fire.

✳   ✳   ✳   ✳   ✳

Appreciative of Missus Mason's ministration to his wound, as well as to his empty stomach, Rick nevertheless put off her further attempts to mother him and headed home. He was carrying the cougar pelt, despite its irritation to his throbbing arm and shoulder, determined that Johnny should see his trophy. Besides, Dad would cure the hide for him to be displayed on his own bedroom wall.

Tired and leg weary by the time he reached the cougar's ambush site, Rick sat on the bank beside Brush Creek, sipping water and chewing jerky. Shaking off a nodding desire to rest, he plodded down to the ocean bluff and slid down its sandy slope to the beach, where his measured stride could cover the remaining distance to Port Orford. A vagrant thought crossed his mind, bushed or not, *I'm going to show Johnny and his folks my prize pelt today. I wonder what Aunt Mary is having for supper?*

Rick's dream of being a braggadocio was thwarted in Port Orford, as Johnny and the Madsens were on Elk River, his father was at their Myrtlewood Grove ranch, and even Billy Tucker was gone—off hunting with his father. The elder Hermanns made a big fuss over his pelt as well as his wound, but somehow their attention fell flat on the young man.

After supper he visited Louie Knapp in the hotel, giving his old friend another yarn to tell travelers, and then passed the evening hours with Harvey Masters after accepting his invitation to spend the night. The oldster always spun intriguing stories of the late Buzz Smith and a young Scott McClure along the Umpqua and later in the Sixes Valley.

With an early morning start, Rick headed for home, forsaking a romantic urge to call on Julie Madsen as he crossed the shallow Elk River. His humor surfaced with a thought, *Dad's expecting me, and I don't know the location of the Helger place except it's upriver. Besides, Johnny's already beating my time, and I couldn't see Julie alone.*

Continuing forward with a nonplussed shrug of his shoulders, Rick was reminded of his wound although its itching was almost pleasurable as a sign of healing.

Repeating an easy crossing at the equally shallow Sixes River, Rick turned upstream into the gap and scrambled over

Slide Ridge—still a difficult trail. He savored the wild beauty of this Oregon frontier country as he strode on toward Cascades Bridge, his hollowed footsteps becoming all but silent as he left its log surface and padded up the grassy knoll.

Hesitating as he topped the small rise, Rick's eyes feasted on the family home, the surface of the acre of pond glistening in the sunlight, with the green garden lying before their log house and barn. Chores obviously completed, his father was playing with Ariane, exercising the palomino in the corral.

As Rick continued down the hillside, the myrtlewoods became visible across the fields, their foliage luxuriant as ever covering gnarled dark boles with a ball of verdant leaves. He marveled at the emotional impact this sight always stirred in his breast, thinking, *I guess I'm bound to this land just like Dad. How could George and Anne ever leave the Myrtlewood Grove?*

"Hello, Son! Admiring the view, are you?" came a shout over the yard.

Rick broke into a grin, answering truthfully, "Of course, just as you do so often, Dad. How's Ariane?"

"Just fine…ho, what's wrong with your arm? And what are you carrying home?" Scott inquired with curiosity and concern equally mixed.

"I tangled with an old cougar on Humbug and brought his hide home for you to cure. Aunt Mary dressed my wound last night. It's no problem. Anything new here?"

Scott replied with a quizzical expression fixed on his face, "Well, as a matter of fact, yes. We had a visitor while I was in Port Orford. There was plenty of sign to show he helped himself to a drink of water and looked the cabin over for awhile. He didn't disturb anything, except the funny thing is that he rested in the barn before going upriver. I figured you and I can track him down anytime. How about tomorrow?"

"Sure, Dad. Can you treat my cougar pelt this afternoon while I get reacquainted with our livestock?" Rick paused for Scott's affirmative nod before continuing, "Good! I'll give New Salem some exercise, too. Maybe I'll ride him over to Elk River and see if the Madsens are settled into the old Helger place."

"Ha! Ha! Or see if the daughter is as pretty in a work bib as she is in a dress. I think we'd better look at that arm of yours first. A new dressing won't hurt it."

✳ ✳ ✳ ✳ ✳

Scott led the way up the trail in the direction of the old lodge where Chief Sixes' family had lived in their aborted attempt to avoid incarceration on a reservation. Rick was disappointed that he hadn't ridden over to Elk River yesterday, but ranch work came first. Today his father was leading the way, tracking the stranger on foot being easier in the thick underbrush.

"Looks like this fellow knows where he is going," Scott muttered over his shoulder, adding as an afterthought, "And he isn't covering his trail at all."

Rick gave a low-voiced reply, "Hmph! He's not on our land, so why should he worry?"

His father had no answer for the question except to push forward. Eventually the smell of smoke thinly spread in the still air confirmed their closeness to a campfire, and Scott waved Rick to his side with a gesture from his Sharps. Together they entered Chief Sixes' old camp, brush cleared and the ramshackle lodge under restoration by a busy young man.

His slight figure was clad in dungarees, a red plaid shirt, and ankle-high boots. Sensing their quiet approach, the stranger turned to greet them, "Hello, Mister McClure. Welcome to my lodge."

Scott was taken aback momentarily, his gaze sweeping the Indian for recognition as Rick spoke, "Howdy, stranger! Is this land yours?"

Smooth brown skin stretched over a somewhat flat Tutuni face broke into a friendly grin as the stranger spoke again to the elder McClure, "Don't you remember me, sir?"

The lad's smiling countenance struck an odd note of recognition in Scott's mind as he ticked off the past years. Chief Sixes and his son had died in a chicken pox epidemic on the reservation, but there had been a grandson about this man's age—twenty-three or twenty-four years. Scott remembered Missy feeding two tykes that night the Indian family had stayed in the barn.

Guessing a solution to his little mystery, Scott replied, "You look a lot like my friend, Chief Sixes. Would you, by chance, be his grandson?"

"Yes, the same boy who rode in your saddle with you on the trail to Fort Umpqua. Sleeping in the barn and that ride are my first real memories. My name is Cha-qua-mi, but the reservation agent called me Jack."

"Pleased to see you again, Cha-qua-mi," the older man said as he offered his hand, shaking white-man style as he introduced his partner, "And my son's name is Richard."

"Glad to meet you, Jack. Just call me Rick. Is it all right for you to be off the reservation? I mean…"

Cha-qua-mi's laughter was genuine as he responded, "Ha! Ha! No one cares if I'm there or not. When my aunt went to live with her daughter's family, the Yakimas, I decided to return to the land of my people. I'm the last man of my family, and I want to be free. I can't own land, but I want to live right here anyway."

Scott nodded in agreement as he affirmed the young Indian's position, "I hear of Tutunis living in the area. No one bothers them, but they don't cause trouble either. We'd be happy to have you for a neighbor, grandson of my old friend."

"Sure, Jack, maybe I can help you fix up the old lodge here," Rick offered and added as a second thought, "We have some old lumber around the Myrtlewood Grove, haven't we, Dad?"

★ ★ ★ ★

On Sunday the McClures rode over to visit the Madsens on Elk Creek, leading a milk cow Rick had offered to loan their new friends. The young man fidgeted at the slow pace necessitated by their bovine companion, truckling obediently behind New Salem.

"Come on, you pokey, no-name milker, we're wasting time," Rick shouted in frustration at the cow.

"Ha! Ha! She's named Zelda as you well know, Son, and her gait isn't too bad. Why don't you ride ahead and call on the Madsen girl?" Scott suggested with a conspiratorial grin.

With a light-hearted expression suddenly radiating from his face, Rick tossed the lead rope to his dad and spurred his horse up the Elk River trail.

Reining New Salem into a light canter as he sighted what had to be the Helger-Madsen ranch, Rick was soon dumbfounded to see Johnny and Billy sitting on the stoop visiting with Julie. The trio waved casually to the latecomer when he neared the house, Johnny's devilish grin intended to irk his best friend.

"Your ears must be burning, Richard McClure. We've been talking about you," Julie said with a welcoming smile, blushing lightly as she added, "No one's seen you since we landed last week. Did you really kill a cougar like Johnny says?"

The girl's friendly greeting and blushing interest pleased Rick, his irritation vanishing as he dismounted, favoring his left arm.

"Hello, Julie. It's good to see you again. Are you and your folks settled in?" Rick's eyes broke from the girl's reluctantly as he greeted his old friends, "Hello, Johnny. I thought you were headed back to Salem to college. Billy, I'm sorry I missed you the other day. How's your family?"

Julie answered as the boys nodded, "Everyone is fine, but tell us about the cougar. Is your arm badly injured?"

Satisfying his friends' curiosity was easy for the would-be hero as he embellished the tale of adventure for the pretty girl, her parents joining the youngsters to listen with rapt attention. Rick concluded his narration as Scott rode Ariane into the yard, the bawling cow following on a taut rope.

✶ ✶ ✶ ✶ ✶

Fred appeared in the meadow by the river, toting a pole and a string of trout as he headed toward the house. Seeing a gathering in the yard and afraid he might miss something, he broke into a loping gait, flopping trout not a hindrance.

"Careful, partner, or you'll lose your fish. And here I thought I would teach you to milk a cow," Rick called out playfully.

Fred dropped his load on the side porch and puffingly replied, "Whew! Is that cow for us? What's her name? Can I milk her now?"

Scott threw him the lead rope, laughing as he enjoined, "Ha! Ha! Take Zelda to the barn, and Rick will be happy to assign you that chore. Why didn't you learn coming north on the ship?"

"Ah, I was sick most of the time. Come on, Sis, you need the lesson, too," the boy remarked as he led Zelda away.

Scott smiled knowingly at his son's increased interest in the project as Julie nodded agreeably and followed her brother. As the three young men moved in unison behind the girl, he conspired in filial support, stating, "Whoa! Johnny, how about cleaning up those trout for Missus Madsen, and Billy, I'd appreciate your help in tending our horses."

Rick winked grateful thanks and hurried into the barn, almost running over Julie in the dim interior.

"Oh, Rick, will you show me first. I have to help Momma prepare dinner. It's fun to have company," she said, batting her eyes flirtatiously. Even in the poor light, Rick could see her smiling face and react to her friendliness.

"Sure, Julie," Rick agreed readily, taking a milk pail from the girl and sitting astride a stool Fred put in place.

Alternating instructions, Rick squeezed two teats in rhythm and admired the girl until raw milk covered the bottom of his pail two inches deep. His attention thus diverted from Zelda, he forgot the cow's feelings, and when he rose with bucket to trade places with Julie, Zelda swished her tail and brushed against the teacher. Rick stumbled backward, tripping over the stool and spilling the pail's contents over his head and shoulders.

Laughter erupted spontaneously from Julie and Fred, Rick's face turning scarlet before he waggled his whitened head, turning his faux pas into a riant mood shared by all three friends. Rick wondered how he could feel so foolish and so happy at the same time.

"Hee! Hee! I'm sorry for laughing at you. Hee! Hee! Should I show you how to do it right?" Julie teased as she righted the stool and took her place beside the cow, stroking Zelda until she was accepted as a friend.

Rick's arms encircled the girl's shoulders as he guided her efforts, Julie not objecting to the almost-embrace. Both participants blushed when Fred snorted in derision, but the lesson continued without change. When he snorted a second time, Rick stepped back and helped the girl to her feet.

"She's all yours, Fred Madsen. Fill the pail," the teacher directed.

Tongue in cheek, the impudent brother remarked, "Aren't you going to show me firsthand how to milk Zelda? I mean close-up, partner."

Rick slapped Fred on the head playfully, equally flippant as he replied, "Your sister has to cook dinner after she shows me around the ranch."

Looking at Julie hopefully, he added, "You do have time for a walk, don't you?"

Julie answered by taking Rick's hand and leading him out the back door, a private visit to her liking as well.

After-dinner conversation centered on the original settlement of Port Orford and the Elk and Sixes Rivers. Scott told a bevy of colorful tales featuring people and events of the past three decades, including the famous story of Battle Rock, the bloody Geisel Massacre, and the U.S. Army's subjugation of the Tutuni tribes.

Fred naively inquired, "Where are all the Indians now? I haven't seen a single Rogue yet."

Scott frowned perceptibly at an unpleasant memory as he explained. "They were ordered to live on the Siletz and Grande Ronde Reservations, far from their tribal lands. Only a few Rogues escaped that fate and remained in this area, and they stay quietly out of sight. Which reminds me, folks, the last surviving grandson of my friend Chief Sixes has returned to their family lodge east of us on the Sixes River. His name is Chaqua-mi, but he answers to the name of Jack or Jack Sixes, if need be. We're friends, and I guess I'm his sponsor if anyone asks."

John interrupted with a nod of acceptance, "Well, Scott, if he's your friend, he's ours. Please tell him so. How can he make a living?"

"Rick and I can use a hand now and again. You know, his granddaddy originally gave me the Myrtlewood Grove. We're going to help him rebuild his lodge tomorrow, and then he plans to copy the white man—prospecting for gold, that is. A lot of gold came out of the Sixes River in the early days. A fellow named Dunbar found a two-thousand-eight-hundred dollar nugget in the '60s, and we had a couple of hundred men in the valley for awhile. I even had a fair claim on Hubbard Creek with my partner, Sam Olson. Sam was one of the first fatalities of the Indian fighting around Port Orford."

"Did anyone strike it rich?" Fred asked eagerly.

"You bet, but not as big as several men did in Jacksonville over on the Rogue River. Even Jake Tichenor and Louie

Knapp tried their hand at prospecting, but their real success was in sticking with Curry County and working hard. When the U.S. Army abandoned Fort Orford, and later when the gold played out, it was citizens like the Knapps, the Tichenors, the Windsors, and the Hughes who prevailed. We have a fine community here, John and Hazel. I hope you'll find happiness as our neighbors."

"Here! Here!" the young men shouted, Fred joining the chorus with youthful enthusiasm.

He declared excitedly, "I want to meet your friend, Jack Sixes, Rick. Can I help with his lodge?"

"Yes, Scott, my son and I can spare a day to help your neighbor," John volunteered with sincerity.

Johnny and Billy quickly endorsed the project, and the men agreed to gather at the McClures for breakfast at daylight. Scott added, "Johnny, can you bring a pound of nails and a dozen eggs from your dad's store? Rick and I have everything else we need for the day."

"Sure, Uncle Scott. I was planning to stay with you a couple of days anyway. I return to college in Salem on Thursday. My classes start next week."

"Are you living with Angie's family again this year?" Scott asked.

"Yes, I couldn't manage the tuition for law school without my sister's help, and Uwe pays me when I work in the warehouse. His brother Johann has offered me a position in his office when I graduate, but I want to practice law in Port Orford." Johnny concluded.

The sun hung well above the skyline of hills east of the Sixes drainage when the troupe of six would-be carpenters led two lumber and venison laden horses up the faint trail. Scott was point for the caravan, but it was Billy who spotted the footprints in a small glade, calling ahead in a soft voice, "Scott! Look at all these signs. Does your friend have company?"

Scott reacted by halting the group with a signal and then carefully walked back to squat beside Billy's discovery.

His young friend pointed accusingly at the roiled earth, imprinted with several boot, shoe, and moccasin marks. He said with a touch of pride, I'm a fair tracker, Uncle Scott. I see at least five different signs, although this moccasin track looks pretty old."

"Yes," the older man agreed, explaining, "It appears to be Jack's. And I think that overlapping boot mark is mine, but I can't account for the other three."

He stood erect and studied the lay of the land, remembering anew his freshman days as a frontiersman on the trail with Buzz Smith. Nodding to himself as he came to a decision, he signaled Rick forward, ordering him in a low voice, "We have just two rifles. Take your Sharps and quietly circle the knoll above Chief Sixes' lodge to cover us when we enter camp."

Without a question or any hesitation, Rick moved ahead, melting silently into the forest. Scott turned to his companions, explaining, "Probably nothing, but better safe than sorry. My son and I will handle trouble. John, you stay behind me, Billy and Fred will lead the horses, and Johnny will watch our back trail."

Scott waved the group forward, eyes and ears keenly attuned to the natural sounds of the valley. He signaled a second time when familiar landmarks marked Chief Sixes' lodge, continuing ahead with his loaded Sharps cradled in his left arm, ready for action.

A voice was raised in alarm, and the sounds of men scurrying about camp could be heard just before he stepped around the massive bole of a large fir. He recognized the spot from an adventure of years ago when Buzz had been positioned on the hill. A hint of a smile crossed his lips as he thought, *I hope my boy is as good a shot as his god-grandfather.*

Three men stood in the clearing, each with rifle in hand, their leader gaining confidence when he saw John and Billy were unarmed. Scott studied each man briefly, and the tough-looking, black-bearded, big fellow in the lodge's shadow became his responsibility. Hidden from Rick and sneeringly sure of himself, he appeared a formidable foe. The beardless and blond youngster looked more scared than menacing, his slight frame quivering as he backed into a tree.

The vaguely familiar looking man before him was shifty-eyed, and his manner seemed treacherous. He held his rifle pointed at the ground, but waving it about as if he were expecting trouble.

"Where is the owner of this lodge? What are you men doing in his camp?" Scott challenged abruptly.

Taken aback for a moment, the trio's leader stuttered in confusion, "Why, we haven't seen any Indian...I mean nobody lives here. We're just upriver to do a little prospecting. My uncle told me this was a good site."

"Who is your uncle? Who are you?' Scott demanded with authority, turning his body and rifle toward the lodge as he ordered loudly, "Don't move, mister. You make me nervous."

The big man froze without any sign of fear, waiting for the leader's response.

"I'm Ray Burton from California, and my uncle prospected here years...."

Scott interrupted curtly, spitting out a name, "Tom Burton?"

Ray Burton nodded, confirming his uncle's identity as understanding dawned on his countenance. He retorted angrily, "You must be that McClure fellow—Uncle Tom's enemy."

Without another word Ray raised his rifle barrel to aim at Scott, who in turn lined his sights on the man in the lodge's shadow. A shot rang out from the knoll, and as Burton fell to the ground, Scott kept his full attention on Blackbeard while a distinctive click of his Sharps action being cocked rang out.

Jack suddenly appeared from the brush behind the third interloper and leaped on his back, disabling any threat from the blond youngster.

With an audible sigh of disgust, Blackbeard dropped his rifle and raised his hands over his head in surrender, Scott waving him over to sit beside Jack's prisoner. Johnny sidled across the clearing, gathering weapons and staying out of Rick's line of fire as well as Scott's.

John Madsen knelt beside Burton to examine his bloody shoulder, pronouncing, "A nasty wound but not serious–no bones broken. Your son is a fine shot, this scoundrel is fortunate to be alive."

Frowning as he studied his Indian friend's bruised and bleeding face and arms, he growled angrily, "This weasel might have suffered a far worse fate if my son had seen Jack before he fired. I have less use for the nephew than I had for his uncle. Both are scoundrels."

Chapter Three

George Hermann showed off his latest acquisition, a red wagon with "Hermann's General Store" painted in gold script across from both sides. He boasted, "This wagon is the finest in Port Orford. I can deliver orders to customers now, and Mary can ride to church in style."

"Right you are, my friend. There are only a dozen wagons in the northern end of the county," Scott teased George, "And about a dozen miles of road, too."

Head bobbing agreeably, the storekeeper retorted good-naturedly, "Sure, but I've been appointed to the Curry County Road Commission. More and better roads for Port Orford is my first priority. Say, what about your political career? I heard the sheriff asked you to be his deputy when he collected Ray Burton and his friends."

Scott shrugged his shoulders laconically, muttering, "Ha! So he did—rubbish!"

"Well, Ricky was all for the idea when he told me the story," George interrupted playfully.

"Hmph! My son is always volunteering me for county service." Scott suddenly grinned at the memory, explaining, "That new young town marshal was standing between Rick and me at the jail when the sheriff offered the job. I turned to them and asked which of them was going to accept the deputy's badge. My son pointed to the marshal and volunteered him. Actually the fellow wanted the job and thanked both of us profusely afterwards."

"Like father, like son. You two McClures are dedicated to the Myrtlewood Grove."

Face split by a broad grin, Scott gave George a friendly slap on his shoulder and walked over to New Salem. As he mounted the horse, he called back, "Speaking of my son, I'd better head for the Madsens' place and collect him and my new palomino. We're working on a simple deal with John to buy some cows from a widow in the Coquille Valley, but this is his third trip to discuss details with our partners. Or is it the fourth?"

"Ha! Ha! I can remember his daddy making excuses to visit our schoolmarm, a fine horse necessary to create the right impression. Julie is a lovely girl, isn't she?" George said approvingly as Scott rode away.

Three would-be cowboys bedded their conglomeration of thirty-two milk cows and steers in the pasture beside the Floras River, bedraggled and tired from herding cows in rainy fall weather these past two days.

Jack unsaddled their horses while Rick haltered two milk cows consigned to William Langlois, his father's old friend. They watched covertly as young Fred Madsen wrangled his dad's bull away from the water, intent on securing the beast to a stout fir nearby. A paroxysm of laughter erupted from both men as the hapless lad was brushed backward into the river, his recalcitrant charge tossing his head and lumbering calmly over to the tree where his evening meal lay—a carrot for good behavior. Even their red-faced partner had to smile at his predicament, crawling out of the slimy mud to stomp over to the now-placid animal and tie him securely to the fir.

"Well, the least you jokers could do would be to stop giggling and start a fire. I'm soaking wet and hungry to boot," Fred complained in exasperation.

"Yes, sir! Anyone who can handle a bull so easily deserves special treatment," Rick teased, adding, "Jack, what tasty meal have you planned for tonight?"

"Hee! Hee!" The Indian giggled further, answering in a rare display of humor, "My specialty as usual, Boss—pemmican or cold beans."

"Oh no," Fred groaned, "None of your Indian trail mix. How can you stand pemmican?"

Jack raised one eyebrow in a knowing gesture and smilingly retorted, "I don't like it, partner, but nobody asked me to be the cook, either."

A voice echoed clearly from the edge of the glade, "Hello, Rick. I brought you and your friends a pot of my wife's lamb stew and some coffee—both hot. Does that solve your dinner problem?"

"You bet, Mister Langlois. Meet my hungry friend from the Elk River, Fred Madsen. And this unpopular cook is Jack Sixes, my neighbor," Rick said, concluding, "Partners, meet our benefactor and local rancher, William Langlois."

Shaking hands cordially with the three young men, Langlois asked in his blunt fashion, "Jack Sixes, would you be the grandson of Scott's friend, Chief Sixes?"

"Yes, sir. I'm living upriver from the Myrtlewood Grove in Grandpa's lodge."

"So I hear, young man, and if Scott McClure vouches for you, that's good enough for me. Finding any color in that old gravel bar?" William asked in friendly tones.

Jack nodded in like manner, answering, "Enough to keep me in supplies. One of these milkers is mine—wages and gold dust combined."

The four men ate hungrily in silence, and when both pots were empty, Langlois asked Rick, "Before I take my cows home, will you tell me the story of killing a cougar on Humbug?"

Jack and Fred groaned loudly in chorus, having heard the tale many times, but the "hero" ignored his friends' ribald taunting and kept them all enthralled with his anecdote.

Blustery winds broke up the gray pall overhead in late afternoon, the sun reflecting off the fleecy white clouds drifting across an iridescent blue sky. As a rainbow formed over the Cape Blanco headland, the three herders cheered loudly in unison.

Startled cows answered in a lowing frenzy, eyes rolling and hooves stomping erratically. The trio sang a lively rendition of "Dixie" to soothe their charges, Rick providing volume in lieu of talent as Jack hummed in tune with Fred's tenor voice. With little prompting, the lad continued a melody of songs unfamiliar to his partners but calming to the plodding heard.

As they entered a small clearing in the forest, Fred's voice stilled abruptly, followed shortly by a shout, "There's your dad, Rick. On the ridge ahead," he paused to point to a pair of mounted men and then concluded, "And Mister Hughes is with him."

"Thanks! I see them now. We're only a mile or so south of the Sixes. Let's divide the herd now. Patrick has sixteen milkers so he'll need help to drive them to his corral," Rick ordered with a glance at Jack.

"All right, I'll give him a hand and catch up with Scott later," the Indian agreed.

"Good, I'll help Dad start our cows up the Sixes and then return here. Can you hold your bull and four cows, Fred?"

The youngster squared his shoulders in pride and retorted, "Of course, Boss. I'm an old cowhand now."

The trio laughed in good humor and was busy separating the cattle by the time Scott and Patrick rode into the clearing. Minutes later the Hughes contingent was moving southwest, and Scott and Rick were driving their herd southeast.

"I can handle these cows, Son. You had better stay close to young Madsen, the Sixes crossing is running high with all this rain," Scott opined.

Rick nodded in agreement and suggested, "I'd better stay overnight with Fred's family. It'll be well after dark when we get there."

"Ha! Ha! Well-planned, my boy," Scott gibed as he dismounted and motioned for his son to follow suit. He slipped a pint bottle of whiskey from his saddlebag and took a swallow of liquor before handing it to Rick.

" 'Prosit', as Kurt would say, Son. And happy birthday! Or have you forgotten that today is the seventeenth? Here," Scott said as he handed Ariane's reins to Rick with a flourish, "Ariane is my gift to you—always was yours."

Father and son came together in a bear hug, the rare display of affection quickly concluded as Rick mumbled, "Thanks, Dad!"

"Well, get on your horse and head for the Madsens. Julie's baked you a birthday cake, and Hazel's cooking a late supper. Hurry along, and we'll celebrate another day," Scott ordered briskly as he took New Salem's reins and mounted, pushing his small herd up the Sixes Valley towards the Myrtlewood Grove.

＊　＊　＊　＊　＊

Fred was leading the herd with the bull, his tether secured to the saddle horn, and Rick was riding drag a couple of hundred feet to the rear. John Madsen's voice suddenly resonated through the darkness, "Fred, is that you I hear coming? Follow my light."

"Hello, Dad! I see your lantern waving, and there's another light behind you. Is that the barn door?"

"Yes, bring the cows in. Where's Rick McClure?"

"I'm here, John, chasing an ornery steer up the trail. Your milkers are a lot more cooperative," Rick answered for himself.

The three men put up the livestock, Rick and Fred rubbing their horses down while John got acquainted with his bull. He asked, "What should I do with the steer? I'd hoped for all the milkers. Hughes offered to buy my extra milk, and I could use a little extra cash."

Rick replied without a second thought, "Sell the steer to George Hermann. He'll give you a fair price and a nice profit. Dad and I have enough feed to keep our steers until winter, and better prices, I hope. I'd suggest you make your own butter and cheese. Usually there's more profit in their sale although we sell Hughes our extra milk, too."

"Thanks for the advice, Rick. Now let's go inside for supper. I'm starved," John offered.

"Me too, Dad. Cowboying is a hungry job and a wet one. Rick and I need to dry out from the river crossing." Fred prattled on with chattering teeth.

Diffused light spread over the stoop as the door opened, Hazel quick to give her son a warm hug as he entered. Julie was placing steaming dishes and bowls of food on the table, a pretty flush on her cheeks as she greeted the men.

"Happy birthday, Rick!" She said as she pointed to the white frosted cake in the middle of the table, adding, "I'm glad my brother and you arrived safely. I bet your trip was exciting, wasn't it?"

"Sure," Fred was quick to reply, "We were real cowboys, weren't we, Rick?"

"Yes, and you did a full share of the work, partner. Ladies, pardon us, while we change to some dry clothes and wash up," and with a happy smile for Julie, thanked her, "That sure is a scrumptious-looking cake. Thanks!"

Rick sidestepped around the table, and Julie stood on her tiptoes to kiss him on the cheek, causing the young man to stumble across the room looking foolish and happy simultaneously. He decided birthday celebrations were great, particularly when the older Madsens' faces showed looks of "almost approval". Fred's giggle earned him a comradely cuff on his shoulder as the pair went into the bedroom to change clothes.

✶ ✶ ✶ ✶ ✶

Weeks passed quickly as the McClures prepared for the usually dreary winter season, Rick's trips to town and the Madsens' place curtailed by the swollen Sixes and Elk Rivers. It was nigh on to December before sun appeared through stormy skies, a welcome respite which Scott insisted they use to repair the barn roof.

Rick thought it a bit of a miracle when the third sunny day broke, their chore completed, and the river returned to normal—all at the same time. Father and son rode over to the Madsens only to find their friends absent, signs indicating they had gone to town earlier. Rick's mood became rambunctious as they followed the trail south, his father chuckling in open amusement.

"Go ahead, Son. I'll meet you at Hermann's store later." Scott's words were barely out of his mouth when the young suitor spurred Ariane into a gallop.

Rick reined his horse down to a more casual canter as the houses of Port Orford came into sight, eyes searching the street before George's store for the Madsen horse. He dismounted before the door, and Fred appeared instantly, chattering with happiness at seeing his buddy.

Throwing a comradely arm over the shoulder of the still talking lad, the erstwhile suitor continued looking about.

"Oh Rick! Julie's not here. She and Mom are visiting Missus Hermann. Come inside, I want to show you a rifle Dad's maybe going to buy me. We can go hunting together."

Smiling at the boy's enthusiasm, Rick agreed with good humor, "Sure, Fred. I could come over next week and help you stock your meat locker. There's always a deer or an elk in that burn upriver from you. Let's go inside, and I'll say hello to George and your dad."

A few moments of greetings and small talk were necessary before Rick could slip away, eager to find Julie. He reached the Hermann barn and led his horse inside, caring for the animal before slipping in the kitchen door.

"Hello, Aunt Mary, what are we having for lunch?" He called out to an empty kitchen as he strolled past the stove.

Mary greeted him at the dining room door with a big hug, laughing as she answered, "Just like your father, Richard Erastus McClure. Always stopping to see me when you're hungry. There will be enough fish and chips for your dad, too. Where is he?"

"Being a slowpoke, but he'll be here," Rick responded, hesitating as he saw the Madsen women and then smiling as he greeted them, "Good morning, Julie, Missus Madsen. Fred told me you were over here."

Mary smiled and inserted, "Why don't you take Julie for a walk along the beach while Hazel and I prepare the food for everyone. There's apple pie for dessert."

Rick looked at Julie with an invitation, "Shall we walk down to Battle Rock, Julie?"

"Yes, thank you, Rick," the girl replied, accepting his assistance in placing a shawl over her shoulders and offering him her hand.

They sauntered down the street in silence, Rick suddenly tongue-tied for any small talk. Waving to Scott and Louie Knapp standing before the hotel, he led Julie along a path down the bluff to the sandy beach.

She sighed with a sound akin to remorse, murmuring her thoughts, "It's a lovely day, but I miss California and my friends in Sacramento. It's awfully lonely on Elk River when it's raining and blowing. Is winter weather always so depressing?"

Rick was taken aback by her question, never having lived anywhere else, but was thoughtful in his answer, "Well, I expect it can be. I love the Oregon coast and don't mind its wild nature, but my sister Anne sometimes used to get quite contrary. You know, she would get blue and kind of cranky— not like her normal self. She writes that she is happy in the big city of Salem. Of course, she's in love and living in married bliss. Still, I can see your point about Port Orford."

"Oh, I'm not unhappy, but the rest of my family is so...settled on our ranch. Fred is becoming a real farmer while I feel sorry for myself," Julie paused, a wee smile crossing her lips as she changed the subject, "Enough of that. Can you show me where your dad found his gold?"

"Sure, but not on foot. We'll ride out on Hubbard Creek after dinner. Maybe some day we can visit Jack Sixes and watch him pan for gold."

Julie nodded approvingly and squeezed his fingers, her affectionate gesture stirring the young man's emotions considerably.

★ ★ ★ ★ ★

George arrived late for dinner, walking around the table delivering bedraggled letters to his guests. Apologetically he addressed their condition, "Sorry about the mottled condition of your letters. The postmaster was complaining that he's losing money this fall because of the rain. You know, he has to pay a fine when wet mail is delivered, and two riders floundered in swollen streams this fall."

"Gee, Uncle George, Dad and I got a letter from my brother last month and it was dry," Rick observed.

"Several mail pouches arrived normally, but obviously this bunch of letters came in a river-soaked bag. My store bills are in the same condition as your letters. What do you hear from Anne, Scott?" George wondered aloud.

"My daughter and her husband are expecting a baby in early spring. Why, she's so young—just eighteen last month. Anne says all is well, and Albert is thrilled." Scott grinned broadly with inspiration and turned to Rick with the announcement, "Son, you'll have to take care of the Myrtlewood Grove by yourself for a few weeks. I'm catching the next ship to Portland."

Mary gestured with a fluttering hand, asking plaintively, "Oh, Scott, can I go with you? Angie is having a difficult time with her pregnancy. I'm sure she needs help with the children."

Scott nodded immediately, and George endorsed the idea, "Good! I feel more comfortable with your escorting my wife on such an arduous journey. It's a decent trip in summer, but you two will probably have a rough voyage with winter here."

"When's the next ship? What about that steamer in the harbor?" Scott queried.

George shook his head in denial, thinking for a moment before answering, "She's outbound for San Francisco, but I expect a northbound ship with a load of supplies in the next couple of days. You have time to go home and pack a bag."

John and Hazel had been whispering aside, their faces becoming more and more gloomy, the woman finally breaking into a quiet sob as she leaned on her husband's shoulder for support.

Julie rushed to her mother's side to help John comfort her, asking, "What is it, Father? What's happened?"

"Aunt Jane is very ill in her Portland home, and a neighbor has added a postscript to Jane's letter. From your aunt's erratic script and incohesive writing, I can believe her friend's doubt of Jane's competency. She needs help." John's voice stumbled emotionally to a close.

Hazel sobbed out an explanation, "My sister has been strange ever since she lost her husband. I guess she's overwhelmed by grief and by facing the world alone."

Gulping back her tears as she looked at her husband and said, "But Darling, I can't leave you, our family, and our farm. Our whole life is tied up in its success, and we have so much work to do."

"I'll go, Momma. I'm Aunt Jane's favorite, and I can handle her," Julie volunteered, and at her father's relieved expression, she turned to Scott with a plea, "Will you and Mary escort me to Portland?"

"Of course, Julie. Rick and I will leave for home now. George, you arrange passage on that ship, and my son can pick up our supplies when he delivers me here day after tomorrow."

* * * * *

The next afternoon found father and son leading a balky cow into Hughes' corral, Patrick meeting them as they opened the gate. "That animal looks okay to me. Has she been giving milk?"

Scott nodded, "Yes, but she hasn't been eating properly, and Rick can't doctor her while I'm in Salem. We have a couple of cans of milk for you with more to come. You can pay my son whenever it's convenient."

"Sure neighbor, and I'll pay you full value for this cow when she's healthy. Have a good trip to Salem, and give my regards to Anne," Patrick replied as he ministered the ailing milker.

Scott mounted and rode towards Cape Blanco, Rick following quietly with the understanding that his dad wanted to stand behind the lighthouse in reflection. He too considered it a beautiful and pristine spot to commune with Mother Nature.

Rick held the horses as his father traipsed about the crown of the massive headland, both men reveling in the freshet of moist air striking their faces, advent of an incoming storm. The steamer they had seen yesterday stood in the gathering seas, passing an inbound ship before altering course to the south.

Scott turned back and called out, "Looks like my ship is arriving on schedule. Let's quit daydreaming and get busy. I've still got to pack a bag before bedtime. We'll need an early start tomorrow."

Of like minds, father and son rode home and finished a handful of chores, working side by side until everything was in apple-pie order. Scott packed while Rick fried steak and potatoes, carnivorous appetites sated before any conversation occurred.

Rick asked diffidently, "How long will you stay in Salem, Dad?"

"I don't know. Depends on Mary, I suppose. I'll spend Christmas with Anne for sure, but I can't return until Mary is ready. Did Julie tell you how long she would be staying in Portland?"

"She thinks until summer at least. I'm already feeling sorry for myself. I'll miss you both, living all alone at the Myrtlewood Grove," Rick smiled without conviction.

Scott's attention focused on the sound of rain on the roof, commenting, "That storm is here. I'll have to leave at first light or that ship will leave without me. Goodnight, Son."

✶　✶　✶　✶　✶

Rick stood in the pouring rain on the sandy beach long after the Madsens and George had retired to the Knapp Hotel. A burst of wind buffeted the young man as the steamship was skewered on its anchor line, his father gripping a guy line firmly as he followed Mary and Julie aboard. Soon the sound of the anchor chain being raised reached his ears, and the vessel moved out of the harbor into the teeth of the oncoming storm.

Unable to distinguish figures on the ship's deck, Rick waved good-bye with a futile gesture of his hand and turned to climb the bluff. George met him on the street and hurried with him toward the store, puffing as he spoke, "Hazel invited us to Christmas dinner. Why don't you come in the evening before? I'll treat you to one of Grandma Knapp's delicious suppers, and Louie offered to buy us a round of drinks. Harvey and Marshal Ashton will be there—maybe a few others."

Nodding agreeably as he opened the door for the limping George, Rick responded, "Thanks. I'll be here. Now I'd better help Harvey pack those gunnysacks. Is that flour in the can?"

At George's nod, Rick walked over to the old man, passing the time of day as he stowed supplies and then tied the two sacks together. He bade farewell to his friends cheerily and strode out the door, straddling New Salem's saddle with the sacks and tying their rope to the horn. He'd have to hurry home or the well-wrapped perishables would be spoiled.

Heading up the trail at a time-consuming gallop, he passed the Madsens, Hazel astride their horse with John and Fred afoot. Rick shouted, "Thanks, I'll see you at Christmas!" and continued unabated toward the Myrtlewood Grove.

Chapter Four

As the mass of gray clouds edged eastward, Jack called out from behind a muddied plow, "Your horse is through for the day, and that's rain coming upriver. Field is already sloppy."

"Ho! Is it New Salem or Cha-qua-mi who's tuckered out? All right, I'll finish pruning these apple trees while you clean up," Rick responded good-naturedly. He was happy to have accomplished a few spring tasks during the short break in the weather.

A yell came from atop the knoll, Fred's voice recognizable as he announced, "Mail call! Hello, Rick and Jack."

The three friends met at the door of the cabin, New Salem waiting patiently as Jack opened a letter from Scott and perused it slowly, mouthing the words as he read it word by word. His friends offered no assistance, aware of his pride at having attended the reservation school for two years and learning his three R's.

Rick read his father's letter hastily, nevertheless noting the news contained on its pages. Anne was healthy and due very soon, Angie had lost her baby girl in a miscarriage and was recovering slowly, and Mary was being a wonderful grandmother. She was needed, so they wouldn't return home for a few weeks. Scott was earning his keep by working for Kurt and Uwe.

Julie's letter was just as newsy, although not as exciting. Her Aunt Jane was improving daily, but still dependent on her niece, and the girl wrote that she was spending the summer in Portland. She mentioned that Roger was a big help, though she missed her family and Rick.

Who's Roger? Was the jealous man's first thought, Rick retiring to the rocker beside the fireplace to contemplate the situation.

As Jack disappeared with the horse, Fred announced, "Dad's driving your milker up the trail. All three of our cows are carrying calves. Julie has a boyfriend in Portland. Mom said to come..."

"Oh well, just a fellow who works in the bank. He's old—almost thirty. That's all I know, really." Fred grinned as he backed out the door, adding, "I have to help Dad. You haven't noticed my rifle. It's a Sharps like yours."

"Well, I saw it at Christmas. Oh, we were going hunting, weren't we?" Rick remembered aloud as Fred trotted across the yard. Rereading Julie's letter again improved neither his melancholy nor his jealous state of mind. He was meditating when a rifle shot sounded from downriver, a second crack of a Sharps echoing as he and Jack met at the cabin door.

"Saddle both horses and follow me. The Madsens must be in trouble," Rick ordered as he grabbed his Sharps and a coil of rope from inside the house. He ran down the trail in a mile-eating lope, seeing no sign of his friends until Slide Ridge was in full view.

John Madsen was astride a deadhead at the river's edge, having crossed half of the narrow trail. Fred held the horse's reins and adjusted a rope looped over the saddle-horn, its other end wrapped about the cow's neck. The milker was submerged in the rolling stream, its hooves thrashing for purchase on the gravelly slope.

As Rick watched in apprehension the cow kicked the deadhead a hardy blow, the anchor-like root system pulling free of the loose gravel. Three actions occurred simultaneously, John flipped over backward into the swift waters, the cow slipped free of its tether and was struck by a free-flowing log, and the hillside fell from under Fred's feet, tons of earth and gravel swooshing twenty-five feet down the slope.

Rick ran forward, calling out, "Hang onto the reins, Fred. Your horse is on solid ground."

In short order Fred was leading the horse away from danger and voicing his near-panic as he cried, "Where's Dad? I can't see him."

Shaking his head with no answer for his friend, Rick searched the river's course intently, breathing an audible sigh of relief when he spotted a waving hand far downstream. John was visible holding onto an alder sapling in the middle of the cut below Slide Ridge.

"Leave your horse and follow me—careful now," Rick yelled as he ran across the foot-wide path, all that was left of the wagon trail after the washout.

Glancing over his shoulder, Rick observed the boy following him too closely and saw Jack arriving on the scene. As he entered the cut, he heard John's thin voice calling, "Help! Over here!"

Tying one end of his rope to a fir stump and the other end around his waist, Rick explained, "Fred, I'm going to jump into the river above John and swim over to him. It's about thirty feet, so I should be able to make it. I'll grab your dad, and we'll drift aslant of the current toward shore. You and Jack can pull us ashore if need be."

Rick hesitated as a fir bough floated by, and then drawing a deep breath, cast himself feet first from the high bank, striking the muddy water at an angle, surprised to feel his feet touch bottom as he submerged. Surfacing quickly, he struck out for the hidden gravel bar with the protruding alder, which John was holding. He missed his target by several feet but found gravel under his boots and enough traction to reach the elder Madsen. "Give me a bear hug and don't let go," Rick shouted in John's ear, both men tumbling in the rolling water as soon as they were entwined in each other's grasp. When the rope tautened, they drifted toward the north bank, rescue completed when Fred and Jack hoisted them onto a grassy patch of the low bank.

Spewing river water from his lungs and stomach, John sputtered spasmodically, "Where's the cow? ... cough...cough...can't lose her."

Rick continued pounding the older man's back with his open palm, answering matter-of-factly, "We'll look for the cow after you spit up the rest of the Sixes water, my friend. First thing's first is a good motto."

Madsen coughed up phlegm laboriously for almost a full minute before rising to his knees and brushing Rick's helping hand aside. He looked downstream toward his son, who quickly shouted, "I can't see her, Dad. Are you strong enough to ride?"

"Yes…cough…I'm ready…cough," John said with determination, standing beside his horse and accepting Jack's boost into the saddle.

Fred ran far ahead of the faster horses, all four searchers coming together at the Sixes crossing, all eyes scanning the water's surface unsuccessfully. Fred moved on through a patch of blackberries to the next bend of the river, the horses necessarily circumventing the brambles.

The lad's triumphant shout was easily discerned as a discovery, "There she is, Dad, entangled in a log jam—right here."

Rick urged Ariane into a canter, rope in hand as he dismounted while his horse was sliding to a halt. Observing the struggling animal in the midst of several logs, he handed Fred one end of his rope and ordered, "Tie it to the saddle-horn and hold Ariane's reins."

Scrambling hastily down the muddy slope, Rick turned cautious as he scampered across a dozen bobbing logs. He saw the cow's badly broken leg wedged between two logs and quickly slipped a noose over the half-drowned cow's head. Carefully backing away from the dazed but fractious animal as well as the rolling logs, he signaled Fred to pick up the slack. Suddenly, two legs broke free from the jam, the cow upended underwater until the rope tautened.

Rick waddled along the sucking mud of the river bank while Jack ran forward to reach the now still beast first. The Indian threw up his hands in disgust, bemoaning the loss, "All that work for nothing. The cow broke her fool neck."

"Not for nothing, Jack. She had a broken leg and would have to have been butchered anyway," Rick commented.

John sighed nervously as he offered to compensate the McClures, "I owe you folks a milk cow, Rick."

"Nah, we can butcher this carcass here and now. We'll send the meat to George, and you can buy us all a beer at Jack's Saloon. Dad's old friend moved back to town during the winter and set up business in that shack near the ruins of Fort Orford."

His sigh changed to one of relief as he agreed readily to Rick's solution, "That's a done deal, my friend. And you're invited to supper on the way home. Hazel's beef stew is a real treat."

★   ★   ★   ★   ★

Apple blossoms were long gone, and new green shoots of life were everywhere as Rick sat on his chopping block in contemplative thought. *Sunshine feels good for a change, but it makes me feel a mite lazy. Maybe I should go fishing before the sun disappears. Or better yet, I'll just lean back against this woodpile and rest my eyes.*

Acting on the latter idea, Rick's chin soon sagged to his chest, and his daydreaming turned fanciful. He could see Julie dancing with Johnny in Knapp's parlor, but when he approached the ethereal figures, both of them became faceless strangers.

Startling half-awake, Rick smiled at himself and his all but forgotten dream, a chiding thought came to his semi-conscious mind, *I'll think of Mother and her chickens—exasperating in their infernal clucking. Hmn! I can hear them now. They've wandered up the knoll.*

Awareness flooded the young man's consciousness as he realized the sounds were real. Complemented by the clopping of hooves on the bridge a moment before, he knew someone was coming to the ranch. Yawning volubly and stretching his extended arms skyward, Rick rose to his feet and turned toward the knoll.

A familiar voice called out teasingly, "Here I've been telling everyone what a hard-working son I have, and I catch you napping in the middle of the afternoon."

Scott laughed as he continued, "I bet you've wondered if I was ever coming home."

Rick studied the apparition in the yard, his father leading the Hermanns' horse laden with gear. Straddling the saddle were two chicken coops, along with his dad's old traveling bag and a gunny sack bulging with "mysteries".

"Welcome home, Dad! I was just following one of Buzz's old sayings. You know, the one about resting while you can, more work will always show up. See, here are chickens to tend."

Father and son met in a crushing bear hug, Rick brushing aside the brief moment of sentimentality to ask, "How is Anne? And her baby? And Angie?"

"Whoa, Uncle Rick! Anne's proud and pleased with Albert Junior. He's a robust boy with a great pair of lungs and a healthy appetite—always hungry and vocal about it," Scott's own grandfatherly pride showing as he described the newest member of the family.

Changing tones, he answered his son's last question, "Angie lost her baby, but she's fully recovered and strong enough to deal with her loss. Mary was a big help to her, so we stayed in Salem until the women were ready to part company."

Scott paused before admitting, "I was more worried about mother than daughter. I told Angie before we left that the Gerbrunn family should visit Port Orford next year. I don't think that Mary is up to the trip north."

"How's Johnny doing at Willamette? Is he coming home for the summer?"

Grinning at a more pleasant memory, Scott recalled, "We managed a few hunting and fishing trips. He said to say hello. Johnny is such a good student that Albert has him reading law for the partners this summer. I doubt he will be home. Here, let's unload, and I'll pass along the news. One of the letters in my bag is from Johnny."

Late that evening, long after his weary father had retired, Rick reread his letter from Julie. Anne's baby announcement and John's hasty note were trivialized by the girl's message. Julie was remaining with her aunt in Portland for an undetermined time. She described her seventeenth birthday party, thanking him for the silver necklace her father had delivered to her and mentioning a savings account Aunt Jane had started for her in Roger's bank.

Hmph! Roger again, what's going on? he thought in perplexity. *Maybe I should visit Portland this summer. Nah, I guess not. I promised Patrick Hughes that Jack and I would trail his cows down here from Myrtlewood Point. He's depending on me, and besides I get my choice of two milkers—at half cost to boot. And Johnny wants Billy and me to take over that Mason job up on Humbug Mountain.*

Still, working all the time is pretty dull. Maybe I'll ride up to Bandon and visit Charlie Spackle's daughter. She's not bad looking for a town girl. What is her name? Irene or Isabel?

Ah, I guess not, all she could talk about last month at the dance was her dad's business and money.

Then there's the Hankins girl from Langlois that Billy and I met at the dance. She isn't half as pretty, but she's a lot nicer. But then, Billy has been up there a half a dozen times on some excuse or other.

Laughing at his thoughts, his mind roamed on, *Ha, ha, and then there's Abigail, the shotgun girl. Homely as a mud fence and willing, with her father primed for a shotgun wedding.*

Of course, there's fourteen-year old Alice Hughes or twenty-six year old Widow Barnes. Ugh! I hope Julie decides to come home soon.

The three herders arrived home from Myrtle Point just in time for the twenty-seventh anniversary of Battle Rock. Scott joined the trio in delivering chickens to Hazel—Fred's wages for herding cows. Jack Sixes received the only cash payment from Hughes for the delivery of his small herd.

Over coffee and sugar cookies, Scott mentioned Battle Rock's history and was subsequently encouraged to tell its story.

He recalled, "When Kirkpatrick told me about Captain Tichenor's plan to settle this area, I was interested. I might have been at Battle Rock with those nine adventurers if my friend Sam Olson hadn't hated Kirkpatrick, but that's another story."

Gathering his thoughts he continued, "The party left Portland poorly armed. As I recall, they had only seven firearms, mostly muskets and a few knives. Oh yes, one man had a sword. Well, the *Sea Gull* sighted Cape Blanco on June 9, 1851, and sailed into the harbor in short order. Captain Tichenor saw a few whales and a couple of Indians and confidently loaded the supplies and men into boats. When Kirkpatrick was approaching the sandy beach near the island rock we now call Battle Rock, Indians appeared out of the forest to threaten his boat, their antagonistic gestures obviously a warning not to land."

"Well now, Kirkpatrick did not lack courage, but he wasn't foolhardy either. He ordered the sailors to row back to the ship, and to Captain Tichenor's chagrin, refused to land with his poorly armed men. Which man suggested taking the ship's cannon ashore is debatable. I've only heard the Captain's side of that argument. But with the cannon, the landing party regained confidence and landed on Battle Rock, despite the harrowing tactics of the Indians. They set up camp atop the island and built barricades across the only trail to their position. Athwart the ridge they placed the cannon and manned defensive spots overlooking the tidal approach. More and more Indians arrived to line the bluff opposite Battle Rock—right about where Knapp's Hotel sits today."

Downing a swig of coffee to moisten his throat, Scott renewed his tale, "Those nine men had little sleep that night, the Indians' presence being noisy and foreboding. The next morning Red Shirt arrived by canoe from the south with more men. He was a Tutuni war chief and a ferocious warrior, immediately rallying his tribesman in the attack across the sand and up the ridge trail. A couple of settlers were wounded by musket fire, and the defenders were forced to fire the cannon into the charging horde—now over a hundred men strong."

Nodding at the unasked question in his audience's eyes, he added, "Yes, many Tutuni died on that ridge. Stories vary from eight to twenty-five dead Indians, and one body positively identified was that of Red Shirt. A truce was called to palaver, the Tutuni spokesman being a white man known as Russki. He's said to have been the survivor of a Russian shipwreck, and at the battle he was considered a great warrior. Kirkpatrick met Russki on the beach and talked—probably in sign language. Kirkpatrick promised to leave in fourteen days when the *Sea Gull* returned to Battle Rock and allowed the Indians to retrieve their fallen comrades. When Russki bent over Red Shirt's corpse, he stripped his shirt ignominiously from the body, kicking it in contempt before he left it in the swirling surf below the tidal rock."

"On the fifteenth day the war party came again, too numerous to count now, and demanded the white men leave their land. The *Sea Gull* had failed to appear on time, and the second attack was inevitable. Hundreds of Tutuni moved forward, led by a new Red Shirt. Some say he was Russki himself and others say not. Anyway, this new Red Shirt was killed in the first volley, and the Indians retreated to elect another war chief. Once again the red shirt was stripped from the fallen warrior, and his body left behind to wash away with the tide."

"Kirkpatrick had had enough, and during the night led his party off the rock and up the coast trail to the Umpqua River. All of the men survived their wounds and their flight through the wilderness."

John asked curiously, "What happened to the *Sea Gull?*"

"Captain Tichenor had financial problems in San Francisco and sailed three or four days late. When he reached Battle Rock, he saw canoes racing south, nobody in sight alive or dead, and a wrecked campsite. He assumed everyone had been killed and continued onward to report a massacre. I met him in Portland and signed up for his second expedition, but that's another story, folks. Let's go into town and help celebrate the anniversary."

With a chorus of enthusiasm, the gathering agreed and was soon on the way down the trail.

Entering the town traversing the full length of the north-south street, John Madsen looked about for people to little avail. Port Orford was very quiet on its birthday, raising his inevitable question, "Scott, didn't you say the twenty-fourth was a special day? Where's everybody?"

"Yes, I did. Louie told me there would be a festival. Maybe he meant the twenty-fifth—the last day of the battle. It wasn't the ninth, I know. Let's go to the hotel and ask Louie about it."

As they approached the familiar structure, Louie Knapp opened the door and called out, "Sorry, Scott, our celebration didn't work out. But come on in, Lew Ashton and the Hermanns are having a toast to Battle Rock with Mom and me. Maybe someday we'll get people interested in a holiday for the occasion."

Leading his entourage through the doorway, Scott greeted the marshal, "Hello, Lew, your job is an easy one today."

"Yes, unfortunately so, I was looking forward to a party, and we're the only folks to show up," Ashton demurred with a hand gesture toward the Hermanns.

Scott grinned as he replied, "Not quite, my friend. I led this group astray," and turning to the Hermanns, he ventured, "Greetings, all! What's new?"

George spoke up, a welcome smile on his lips, "Mail's in, Missus Knapp is preparing a meal for us, the beer's sudsy, and the view of Battle Rock is inspiring."

✳   ✳   ✳   ✳   ✳

Rick sat at the dinner table reading his latest letter from Julie for the third time and mulling over a covert wish to visit Portland. *That damned Roger again,* was his woeful thought. *And she's staying with Aunt Jane until Christmas at least.*

With a perplexed sigh, he rose from the cluttered table, remnants of a festive meal lying about as the diners lined the hotel's windows, watching the arrival of the *Vallejo Pacifico.* Maybe I should talk to Father about going up to Portland. That schooner may be headed north, or I could ride Ariane to Salem. While he turned his thoughts over in his mind, Louie announced that the ship was anchoring off Hubbard Creek for a load of Port Orford cedar from the Gould Mill.

Scott had been especially attentive to the schooner's arrival, and as her sails were furled he suddenly declared, "She must be headed for San Francisco. I'm going to book passage and visit Georgie. He sounds kind of lonesome in this letter I received today. I'll make sure he hasn't changed his mind about being a priest."

Damn! Rick cursed to himself, *Dad beat me to it. Now I'll have to stay home and tend the Myrtlewood Grove.*

He smiled wanly as he clapped his father on the shoulder, lending his support in a mild voice, "George will love to see you, Dad, but he won't change his mind. I know my brother."

"I know, Ricky, but I need to see that all is well and that George is happy in his choice. He writes that he will take his final vows next year," Scott paused as he apologized, "I'm sorry to leave you alone at the ranch again. You can take the next trip out."

"That's a deal, Dad. Why don't you go home and pack while I buy your ticket? Look, the lighters have started to load the schooner already. She'll be sailing tomorrow."

George concurred with a gruff nodd, "Rick is right, Scott. Why don't you stay over with us and board her before the morning tide?"

Turning to the young man, he stated, "Don't look so gloomy, Rick, your father will be home by harvest time."

Rick nodded in agreement, but his thoughts were more secretive. *Nobody knows I want to go to Portland, and there's no use crying about it. Dad and George need to see each other. I hope Roger's only a friend.*

✱ ✱ ✱ ✱ ✱

Leaving two quarters of venison and a huge rack of horns in Madsens' meat shed, Rick and Fred walked their heavily laden horses toward town. The excitable lad jabbered all the way south, describing his hunting adventure as if his friend had not been present.

"Three elk! Will George Hermann be able to sell all this venison? Gee, Rick, I shot my bull through the heart over a hundred yards away. I did just like you told me to, held my breath, looked right down the barrel, lined up my sights, and squeezed the trigger. I was as calm as could be, wasn't I?"

Rick smiled at Fred's exuberance, the term "buck fever" coming to mind, and continued nodding in response to his buddy's monologue. He did a double take when the lad repeated his last question, "Isn't that your dad up ahead?"

Sure enough, he saw the elder McClure waiting at the edge of town, shouting as he waved a greeting, "It's good to see you boys. George sends his brotherly love."

As the caravan closed the distance, Scott continued in a normal voice, "That load of venison is sizable, and I see you saved a rack for Harvey. He told me you were paying off our supply bill with venison. Come along, we'll hang these quarters of meat in the store's meat locker for Harvey. He's all alone since George is attending a country roads meeting."

Working steadily for over twenty minutes, no conversation was necessary. When John Madsen stuck his head in the doorway, Fred picked up where he had left off the trail, and the McClures departed for home happy in the quiet of nature. They rode fast, anxious to reach home and complete ranch chores. They had plenty of talking to do at supper.

Standing before a hot stove with skillet sizzling near his hand, Rick turned over the browned onion rings, swirling another dab of butter in the pan before adding cuts of elk liver. He commented, "Dad, these onions and the potatoes I ate the other day have emptied our root cellar. I guess I'll thin out the onion field one of these days. Green onions will taste good in a few weeks."

Scott nodded agreeably, noting his observations upon arrival home, "You've kept the ranch in fine shape, Son. The potatoes are doing great, and the hay is ready to be cut again. Reckon Jack will help with the harvest."

"Yes, and the Madsens, too. John says he and Fred will trade labor for potatoes and apples. Fred has hinted that his folks are short of cash this year."

Scott guffawed lightly, "Ha! Ha! Who isn't? My gallivanting has cost a pretty penny. We'll have to put some harvest money aside for the winter ourselves. Maybe we should pan the Sixes for gold. Jack seems to be doing all right."

Rick chuckled in response. "If you mean eleven dollars in dust since early spring is any kind of wage, you could be right. Jack and Fred are coming over tomorrow to help us with haying. Maybe I'll go back to Jack's lodge with him after we're done—try my hand at panning gold."

"The Sixes is pretty well prospected out although a little dust can still be found in its gravel," Scott commented wryly, adding in more serious tones, "But you've earned a break. Let's walk over the Myrtlewood Grove after supper and plan our harvest, then I can tend to chores while you play prospector."

* * * * *

Handing over a dozen flecks of gold dust to his host, Rick bemoaned his success—or lack of it, "What the devil, Jack. That gravel bed is really dry—of water and gold. I haven't panned a dollar's worth of dust all week."

With a carefree smile, his friend replied, "Me too, Rick, but I'm enjoying your company. Maybe we should go hunting tomorrow."

"No, I'm going to try something Dad told me once about his old partner, Sam. It seems Sam always found more gold than my father because he didn't mind getting wet. He was always knee-deep in the river looking for a pocket of dust and nuggets. I'm going to test the bottom of that fishing hole of yours, the one right below our stingy gravel bar."

Now grinning broadly, Jack volunteered, "I'll help, but you can stand in the water. It's damn cold, Rick, and six feet deep just beyond the gravel."

Nodding jerkily in thought, Rick ventured, "The sun's still high in the sky, and I'm rarin' to go. Let's try it now."

Promptly striding toward the fishing hole, Rick stripped to his breeches and woolen socks, and with bucket in hand, stepped gingerly into the chilling waters. Glancing to and fro as he edged into deeper water, he called out, "Here I go, Jack. Stand by for a bucket of gold."

He dunked the bucket underwater and then sank to his knees, finding himself submerged in four feet of water. Holding his breath as he scooped a conglomerate of sand, gravel, and muck from the bottom, he rose to gasp air and troddle over to his waiting partner.

While Jack worked the batch in his pan, Rick repeated the procedure with a second bucket, continuing his experiment without respite for an hour. A sharp pain on the bottom of his left foot halted his operation. His digging in the riverbed and his unshod foot had found a relic of the mining boom—the remnants of a broken whiskey bottle. He crawled ashore with a bloody instep from a cut and with bluish skin from the cold stream, only to find Jack with nary a touch of color in his pan.

Not easily dissuaded, Rick handed his partner the last bucket with a warning, "Be careful of the glass shards. It's obvious someone was here before us, my friend."

As he was cleansing his small wound, he shuddered from a clap on his back, startled further by Jack's shout in his ear, "Wow! Look at this nugget. Your hunch was right, Rick."

Suddenly hopeful, Rick scanned the contents of the extended pan, a sizable gold nugget enmeshed in the sandy residue. He picked it up eagerly, examining the object with a progressively dreary look on his face.

Observing his partner's change of mood, Jack queried, "What's the matter? It's gold, and you found it in this fishing hole. We're a success, right?"

With a self-derisive grimace, Rick announced, "This nugget has a hole in it, and I think this piece of wire probably went through it. Some prospector's necklace or bracelet, I suspect. So much for my idea. Well, it'll make a good present for Julie."

Jack spent the next two days digging sand out of the fishing hole while Rick searched bucket after bucket for a trace of gold. They concluded Rick's project was a failure, and with a dispirited chuckle, Rick observed, "My father is a wise man, Jack. Farming is certainly more fruitful than prospecting. I reckon I'd better get home and prepare for harvest."

Rick leaned back in a rickety chair situated on Harvey's stoop, his gaze fixed on the soaring gulls over Battle Rock. His eyes followed their graceful flight with unseeing intensity. In his lax fingers fluttered a single page of a newsless letter from Julie—nothing personal included.

Hah! Rick thought morosely, *So Aunt Jane is ill again. Fred says she gets sick every fall—doesn't like rainy weather. Julie could at least write about herself or ask about me. Well, at least there is no Roger in this letter. Hmph! I wonder, is that good news or bad? I wish I'd found a little gold dust in the Sixes before harvest so I could sail up to Portland for a visit.*

"Isn't the view grand, Ricky?" Harvey asked from the doorway, continuing pensively, "And imagine such a warm afternoon sun this late in October. My Alma loved to sit right where you are and watch the coastline."

Rick stirred, looking up at the old-timer as he muttered querulously, "Women, huh! How did you meet Alma? How long did it take you to get married?"

"Whoa, my young friend. What did Julie have to say in that letter?" Harvey asked in rhetorical tones, pausing with an understanding smile to recollect his own youth.

"Well, Alma was so pretty and spirited that I fell in love the first time I saw her. It was a church picnic one Sunday afternoon. I skipped services as usual and showed up for the social afterward. Alma was visiting her cousin, a real religious girl who thought me a wastrel," Harvey shook his head and with a grimace, apologized, "I've just never cared for church—took after my father, I guess."

He sat down on the top step, facing about toward Rick to voice an opinion, "I figure a man ought to be good to his fellow man naturally. I'm not sure preaching about sin and the devil's doings changes many people. Why, the worst sinner in my mother's church was a rich banker, and of course he was a deacon as well. Never could abide hypocrites."

"Was Alma religious, Harvey? How did you win her heart?"

"Heh! Heh! No, but I thought so and played the absolute fool in taking her to church meetings trying to impress her. I fell in love, and became a terrible hypocrite, and almost lost my sweetheart. Her last Sunday in town she refused to attend church with me—just said no when I asked. I was so dumfounded I blurted out an invitation to go fishing at my favorite hole on the river. She smiled and kissed me on the cheek and went with me. Hee! Hee! We fished and kissed all day. On the way home she informed me that she was extending her visit another week. Well, she never went home. We were married that summer."

A reflective silence fell as the old-timer concluded his tale, a thoughtful Rick complimenting his friend, "That's a wonderful story, Harvey. I wish Julie could hear it."

"No, I don't think so, my boy. She would have been more thrilled with Alma's version, which was much more romantic. You know, you're the only person who can convince Julie to be your wife. Instead of pining over her absence, go to Portland and tell her how you feel," Harvey advised professionally. Genuine rib-shaking laughter accompanying his final remark, "Ha! Ha! Now I sound like a preacher. Good luck, Ricky."

Chapter Five

Rick was awakened by the howling moan of a southwester, pounding surf and pelting rain adding to the storm's symphonic voice. Lying snug between warm blankets, he belatedly realized he was in a strange bed. His confusion abated quickly as he remembered accepting Harvey's invitation to spend the night. The two of them had eaten the old-timer's specialty of goulash and then walked over to Jack's tavern for a beer.

Come to think of it, Rick recalled silently, *the sunshine disappeared before supper, and a drizzle fell on our way home from the bar. Hmph! Typical Port Orford weather—clear one day and stormy the next.*

"You awake, Rick?" Harvey whispered from across the bedroom.

"Yes, and ready for breakfast. I see a little gray at the window. Be daylight by the time I fix flapjacks for us," Rick responded.

Rustling bedclothes stilled as the host lay back down, murmuring, "Good, I'll catch twenty winks while you fix breakfast. Did you hear those voices in the storm awhile ago?"

"No, the wind just woke me."

Listening for a moment, Rick continued in a teasing manner, "Either your ears or your imagination is in great shape, Harvey. Go to sleep. I'll have breakfast ready in half an hour."

Rick was mopping up sugar syrup with his last piece of pancake when Harvey suddenly exclaimed, "There are those voices again. Do you hear them?"

"Yes, it sounds like men yelling," Rick agreed as he hurried to the front door and opened it, a blast of damp air and a plethora of sounds caroming briefly off his face, quickly lost as the wind shifted back to the east.

Holding the doorframe with one hand as he braced himself, he shook his head in wonder at the sight before him, explaining over his shoulder to the slower-moving old-timer, "By God, that coastal steamer that anchored yesterday has run aground east of Battle Rock. I think a salvage crew is working her cargo. Yes, there's a lighter on her lee side coming to shore. We must hear them when the wind shifts."

Harvey watched over Rick's shoulder, muttering in exasperation, "Damned eyesight! There's enough light, but I can't make out her name."

"Ha! Ha! Neither can I in this misty rain, but I saw her clearly last evening before dark. She's the *Santa Clarita* out of San Francisco. I'd better get dressed for the weather and lend a hand," the young man decided.

Moments later he was walking down the trail to Battle Rock and up the beach, spotting George Hermann as he neared a pile of cargo nestled in the sand. The merchant was dickering with the steamer's mate, hands gesticulating as he argued his point.

As Rick came to halt beside the pair, the mate woefully accepted a sheaf of bills and a signed receipt. Seeing help at hand, George cried into the wind, "This cargo is mine, but I need help toting it to my store, and the tide's coming in. Want to earn a commission?"

"No problem, George. You stay here, and I'll fetch Ariane and a couple of strong backs. In fact, there's Billy Tucker with Harvey in front of the hotel. Stay here and watch your goods. Is that a case of wine I see?" the young man asked rhetorically as he strode away.

Signaling Harvey as he topped the bluff, he shouted, "Go to the store and open the back door. George has a pile of salvage goods to fill his shelves."

Billy asked helpfully, "What can I do?"

"George offered a commission on the sale of his salvage goods. You go down and start hauling the smaller bundles to Harvey. I'll bring Ariane to tote those gunny sacks of beans and that big crate."

Two hours later the four men gathered around the heap of damaged salvage items in George's storeroom, the merchant's words vibrating with excitement as he eyed his treasure horde, "Harvey, open up while I fix a sign declaring today's salvage sale. Rick, you and Billy bring the perishables up front as soon as you unpack them. Wait! Bring the wine first and save a bottle."

Two sacks of beans in dilapidated condition were carried up front along with several bolts of sodden cloth, where George arranged them on the counter and affixed prices quickly. Rick set aside one bag of beans, which appeared undamaged, repeating the procedure with flour and salt, sorting out the hardware as the pile was depleted.

He was opening cases of canned fruit, some with labels identifying them as peaches and some as pears, and many without any markings whatsoever. George bustled up to him with a gleeful smile at his good fortune and gathering a handful of tins, ordered, "Rick, take all the labels off. I'll sell the lot as 'unknown preserves'. People love a mystery. Hurry! We're selling everything as fast as we can put it on the counter."

By mid-afternoon the Hermann sale was over, and a lightened *Santa Clarita* rode at anchor in the harbor, having been pulled off the beach during high tide.

Harvey voiced the enterprising salvagers' thoughts as he lamented, "I hate to profit from another man's problems."

His comrades silently agreed, although without feeling particularly guilty. In fact, their manner mellowed to humorous when the ship's mate showed up with a "lost" consignment of supplies for George.

"Well, sir! I see you've sold those salvaged supplies already. Saves a trip to Gardiner. Your lot here was stored in the aft hold and came out high and dry, I'm happy to say."

Signing the cargo manifest with a flourish, George queried, "And how is your ship, mate?"

"The old *Santa Clarita* has survived her share of mishaps and will be as good as new after a bit of repair work in San Francisco. A couple of buckled plates shouldn't stop us from reaching home port. See you next voyage north, gents," the mate said in bidding them a cheery farewell.

✷ ✷ ✷ ✷ ✷

Gray mist filled with drops of rain swirled around the soaked and shivering young man as he rode Ariane across the knoll and down into the yard. Rick hastily dismounted and led his horse into the warm barn, animal smells, sounds, and body heat a welcome relief from the stormy weather. He took the time to rub his horse down after unsaddling the palomino, his faithful companion in crossing the swollen Elk and Sixes Rivers just as weary as he was.

His father was waiting at the door with a cup of hot coffee, the aromatic brew a double treat for Rick's senses.

"Thanks, Dad! Just what I need. Is that venison stew heating on the stove?"

Scott laughed with relief and then suggested, "You need dry clothes and a fire to warm your backside on. You'll catch pneumonia if you're not careful. I didn't come looking for you today because the river was so high. What kept you?"

After stripping to the skin, Rick donned a clean set of longjohns. Wrapping himself in a blanket, he settled into the rocker next to the stove, all the while relating the story of the *Santa Clarita*'s grounding and George's salvage sale. He paused when Scott handed him a bowl of stew, continuing between mouthfuls to describe the day's events.

He chuckled at the memory of the arrival of the Hermann freight, explaining, "Ha! Ha! Here we were feeling bad about the beached ship when the mate casually informed us that the salvaged goods had been bound for the Gardiner store. Harvey broke into laughter, reminding us over and over again that he had owned that store, and he reckoned the cargo got to the right person if not the right place."

Scott's head bobbed in understanding, a pleased expression crossing his face as he said, "I'm glad Harvey was so amused, he's too somber these days—and forgetful. His age is showing, I guess."

"I know what you mean, Dad. He remembers details of events years ago, but he loses things around the house. Yesterday he put his skillet in the wrong cupboard and couldn't find it at suppertime. But don't worry, George and Mary look after him, and he enjoys clerking in the store."

Taking the empty bowl from his son, Scott commented, "Yes, and George teasingly claims that Harvey will outlive all of us. Was there any mail at the post office?"

"Just a short note from Julie. Her aunt's taken a turn for the worse. I don't know when she'll be coming home," Rick concluded glumly.

Suddenly the blanket-shrouded figure gasped out, "Achoo!" Rick's shivering form exposed as he covered his face with both hands. "Achoo!" resounded again, only slightly muffled as he moaned, "A damn cold is coming on."

Scott shrugged good-naturedly, noting, "There goes your usual two loud sneezes. Georgie always sneezes three little achoos. Well, it's time for a hot toddy and a warm bed. We'll knock that cold out of you in no time."

The subject of Julie in Portland was forgotten for the moment.

Following days with a runny nose and fits of coughing, Rick replaced his father doing chores as the elder McClure came down with a fever and sore throat. Scott's sense of humor was still present as he crawled into bed, muttering with a tinge of sarcasm, "Sharing is a virtue, Son, but not with this ailment. Well, it's your turn to tend the stock and the chickens."

Remembering the latter order, Rick cooked a thick chicken and potato soup. The concoction comprised Scott's next three meals and drove him to the supper table the next evening. He ate a full plate of mashed potatoes and gravy plus a few bites of venison.

"I'm glad to see you eating regular food again, Dad. It's already December, and I've been thinking that it's time I saw Julie. What do you think?"

Scott smiled wanly as he remembered his own courtship of Melissa and replied agreeably, "I've been wondering when you'd go to Portland. Every time Billy Tucker stops by after calling on the Hankins girl, you become 'Mister Gloomy'. It's time you saw how Julie is doing. Take our nest egg and sail to Portland. Our credit is good, and I can always butcher a steer if I need cash. When do you plan to leave?"

Rick stood beside the ship's mate as the schooner cleared the Orford Heads, sails blossoming in full glory as the *Coral Bay* fairly flew to the northwest before a stiff breeze. The weather was wintry, but not inhospitable, clouds of rain scattered about the predominantly gray sky, an occasional patch of blue or ray of sunshine presenting itself to the sailors. The young farmer's stomach remained calm as the ship rolled and sea spray touched his face.

Well, I'm not seasick, he thought silently as the mate left him alone at the rail. *Am I a better sailor, or is the sea smoother than the last time I was on a sailing ship? I hope this weather holds along the Oregon coast until we reach the Columbia River.*

Rick heeded the mess call promptly, settling on the bench beside the mate, platters of pan-fried cod and sliced potatoes already on the table. The cook called from the galley, "Mate Olson caught the cod this morning, and Mister McClure brought the potatoes from his farm. You men owe them a vote of thanks."

Crew members mumbled thanks as they wolfed the delicious meal down, Rick acknowledging their remarks with a mouthful of food. "You're welcome...gulp...but give Mate Olson the credit. I had to bribe him with fresh vegetables to get aboard. I understand the *Coral Bay* seldom carries passengers."

"Aye, lad," the mate responded, "We've no passenger quarters on this schooner, but if you don't mind sharing my cabin, you're welcome aboard her. Right, men?" The crew members once again agreed as they dug into second helpings.

Rick curbed his healthy appetite, standing up while still hungry. The mate smiled in approval, commenting sagely, "Light meals and fresh air will put sea legs under you. You'll be a true sailor by the time we reach Portland, my boy. Come up on deck, and I'll show you how we set our course for the night. Maybe we'll see a colorful sunset."

Sure enough, the western sky was alight with a vivid display set in the red spectrum, orange through magenta blossoming between stripes of faded blue sky and slate gray clouds.

With a pleased expression covering his visage, the mate intoned,

> "Red skies at night
> Sailors' delight.
> Red skies in the morning,
> Sailors take warning."

He added, as Rick quietly looked askance, "The poem is an ancient mariner's rhyme that's a damn fine weather forecaster. Fair weather tonight means we can keep plenty of canvas aloft and make good time."

* * * * *

Maritime life seemed a boring routine to the young farmer, sleeping long hours only a partial solution to his ennui. Rick had volunteered to help on a couple of occasions but found he only got in the crew's way. Walking the schooner's deck to stretch his legs was fine in daylight, but aside from keeping the mate company at the helm, there was little for him to do at night.

No wonder I'm up so early this morning, he thought. *Between the mate's rolling out of his bunk to stand watch and the ship's banging around, I can't sleep. I may as well take a turn on deck before mess call. Maybe land will be in sight at daybreak. We are supposed to cross the Columbia River bar later today.*

A white-capped swell burst over the bow as Rick stepped on deck, a shower of salty droplets spraying his face. Grasping a line amidships and bracing himself against the ship's roll, he watched the rail crash in and lift out of the turbulent sea. Overflowing scuppers drained the intrusive waters all too slowly as the schooner struggled forward at a slackening pace.

Dawn was at hand, and Rick was impressed with the rapidly burgeoning colors at the eastern skyline. A vague outline of land became visible before the red skies, as the mate's called out, "A pretty sight, lad, but a storm warning nevertheless. Remember the mariner's rhyme."

Rick was about to ask about the land when his bunkmate shouted to the quartermaster, "Bring her ten points to port, Ole," and then turned to the passenger with an explanation, "That's Tillamook Head astern. With rough water and heavy wind we'll have to stand out to sea and approach the bar carefully. It'll take most of the day to come around to the Columbia's entrance. Say, you'd better not eat too much this morning. Strong winds are quartering our course, and I expect very rough seas all day."

The mate's words certainly were prophetic, Rick thought as he paced the rolling deck on still seaworthy legs. *My stomach is queasy, but I'm holding my own despite these rough seas. I may become a sailor yet, but not like those men aloft. Why are they furling canvas?*

"Ahoy there, Mister McClure! Brace yourself against the bulkhead and grab a line; we're coming about in a moment. I expect the seas will get nasty for my old girl here," the captain shouted down from the helm.

"Yes, sir! When do we cross the Columbia bar?" Rick rejoined.

"Around four bells if all goes well—that's two o'clock farmer's time," the skipper grinned in jest, then ordered the helmsman, "Bring her slowly starboard to a northeasterly heading."

Rick quickly lost interest in further questions as the ship yawed first one way, then another, the massive swells tossing her about, sailors clinging precariously to their perches in the rigging. The schooner was being pushed awkwardly on her new course with only a pair of sails controlling her progress, the skipper's face grim as he barked headings, "Bring her ten points to starboard...steady as she goes...five points to starboard...damn! Hold her steady...Ole! Get up here and give a hand with the wheel."

Rick felt a hand on his rigid arm and heard the mate's voice from beside him, "Come below and have a mug of hot coffee with me. You look frozen, lad."

Following his friend below decks, Rick's teeth chattered as he replied, "Thanks, I need to warm up, but where is land anyway?"

"Dead ahead, Rick, but we're at least ten miles out, and the rain is heavy. You'll see it when the captain calls all hands on deck. All of us hold our breath in tricky seas, and the skipper will be tested again today. He wants to cross the bar in mid-channel on a high tide—not as easy as it sounds," the mate explained with the cook's observant approval.

The toothless old-timer nodded readily, chortling his opinion, "Been sailing with the old man for years and trust him completely, but I still get the willies when there's a storm over the Columbia River bar."

"How deep is the water over the bar?" Rick asked naively.

"Plenty deep on a wave's crest, but awfully shallow in the trough. Besides, all the sand shifts daily, so we can never be sure of the depth or the breadth of the channel. It's a tough enough crossing on a sunlit day, but today we'll all earn our wages," the mate responded, and a half-dozen arriving seamen chorused with "Right, mate."

The group of men continued the discussion of storms and sailing ships for some time, Rick listening more than talking. He could tell the men were concerned but confident, each sailor knowing his job aboard the ship. The farmer admired their self- assurance and the teamwork they needed to master such a task as crossing the bar. He finally excused himself and went to his cabin to change his stockings. All parts of his body were warm except his toes, and dry socks seemed to be a reasonable solution.

Perched comfortably on the mate's footlocker with recovering toes, Rick drifted into a reverie, anticipating his arrival at Julie's door. Faint voices and muffled footsteps interrupted his shut-eye, the would-be sailor realizing he'd been dozing while all hands were called on deck. Stretching his arms widely and stomping his feet, he buttoned his gear securely and made his way topside to that comfortable spot before the helm.

Rick looked about with interest once he held a line in his fist, the deck's contortions caused by its proximity to the raging ocean swells crashing over the Columbia bar. Less than two miles aport was a headland, which he took to be Cape Disappointment, a long line of turbulent seas reaching south to a distant blur of land—Oregon. The *Coral Bay* was adding sail as she attempted to parallel the bar, striving to reach the elusive channel entrance which the skipper had overshot in making landfall.

The stout schooner fought for leeway, quartering a persistent wind, which continued to push her toward the breakers. Unable to turn back and dangerously close to the bar, minutes seemed eternities to Rick as the skipper strove to find a point fixed only in his mind.

Even the inexperienced farmer could feel the pull of the breakers on her hull before the captain shouted, "Hard aport!

Set the bowsprit due east...all hands hold position...steady as she goes."

The ship reeled as she struck the confluence of fresh and saltwater, rising high on an undulating wave and sliding down the far side as froth covered the deck.

Suddenly the schooner rose on a mammoth swell to a crest high enough for Rick to see the relatively calm waters of the Columbia River just ahead, seemingly without an obstacle before them. A surging force of air drove the vessel down a smooth slope until only sky was still in Rick's view.

A moment later the ship jerked with the grinding sound of a collision with the sand bar, skewing sideways as the breaker crashed over the distressed schooner. Wind and water fought to disable the reeling vessel as a man was shaken loose from the rigging, luckily striking the flooded deck at Rick's feet. The seawater cushioned his fall, and the passenger's steely grip bound him to safety.

But the *Coral Bay* was a stout ship, rising from beneath the surface to float clear of the tempestuous seas. Her foremast was sprung and sails shredded, still she could make headway across the bay to Astoria, a bit the worse for wear but still seaworthy.

A brief glint of late afternoon sun struck the topsails and the mainsail of the sparsely rigged schooner, cantankerous weather seeming to have left the Lower Columbia region. Rick was surprised by the number of isles and sloughs cluttering the well-traveled waterway of the great river. He remembered that Captain Tichenor had been granted one of the first pilot's licenses in the Oregon Territory.

Smiling at his fickle memory, he searched upriver in vain for Fort Vancouver. Where had Dad said it was located? Across the Columbia from Portland?

"Hmph! Is this another island coming up?" he muttered under his breath.

"No, lad, we're about to enter the Willamette River channel. We'll be docking with the hour," the mate informed him.

"All right, but where's Fort Vancouver?" Rick queried in complaint.

His friend shrugged with a sailor's lack of interest in landmarks not significant to the sea, answering dutifully, "I understand the old fort is about five miles up the Columbia that way—never been there myself. If you want to see it, you'll have to follow a wagon road out of Portland and ferry across the Columbia. I suppose your father visited the fort in the old days."

"Yes, I remember sitting on his knee as a youngster and hearing about the Hudson's Bay Company, wild Indians, and Portland City," Rick replied.

"Well, Portland is a mighty fine city for this wild frontier of yours, if you can stand the rain. Watch for outlying farms as we round this bend ahead. We're getting close. Are you all packed?" the mate joshed, having heard Julie's name often enough to understand the young man's eagerness to reach port.

Grinning his reply and nodding in good humor, Rick declared, "I'm ready. Guess I'd better bring my gear on deck."

Duffel bag slung casually over his shoulder and trailing his Sharps lazily in his right hand, Rick entered Mickey's Tonsorial Parlor as a lone customer left. He halted with a stutter-step as he beheld his multi-reflected image in the mirrored interior. *Why, I bet Dad looked about like this scruffy character when he first arrived in Portland.* Gawking at his likeness for an extended moment, he finally chuckled in self-humor.

The proprietor interrupted, "Welcome to Portland, stranger. I'm Mickey. I catch a lot of men admiring themselves in my fancy mirrors. Shave and haircut?"

Blushing lightly at his egotistic daydreaming, he nevertheless grinned at the humorous situation as he introduced himself, "And a bath, Mickey. I'm Rick McClure from Port Orford. Just off ship and a might scraggly. Can you tell me where Madronna Street is?"

Silent as he wrapped a barber's apron over his customer's shoulders, he pondered half-aloud, "Hmm! Must be in a respectable neighborhood, Rick. Probably on the hill south of here, but I'm not sure. You know, wandering along Dock Street alone at this time of day is not a good idea. You can't tell the roustabouts from the thieves—might be one and the same. Even that Sharps isn't much against a gang. Times remind me of San Francisco in the fifties. Portland's a friendly city but still a bit wild, like most frontier towns."

Waiting for a moment for the straight razor to be lifted from his throat, Rick held his position, eyes almost nodding in reply, "I appreciate the advice, my friend. Maybe I should find Avery's Boarding House before exploring Portland."

"Reuben's place? It's near my house on Mill Street. I'll walk over with you, if you'd like. In fact, you can take a bath over there. How do you know the Averys?"

"My dad has stayed with them a couple of times when he's been in Portland," Rick said quickly, holding still as Mickey finished shaving him.

A few minutes with comb and scissors were all the time the barber needed to shear Rick's mop of hair. Quietly the older man doused his oil lamps, donned his coat, adding Rick's payment to the cash drawer's contents before shoving the lot in his trouser pocket. He blew the third light, following his customer out the door and locking it. Neither man paid any attention to the three shadowy figures scurrying ahead of them, briefly visible in the lights of the corner.

Strolling up the plank sidewalk, Mickey chattered easily, "There's two saloons up ahead where Dock and Mill Streets meet—only real light around. Avery's Boarding House is just a dozen houses up the hill, and my home is a block further. Reuben will know where Madronna Street is located in town. He's an old-timer and kind of a snoop. Keeps tabs on everybody in the neighborhood, and checks out every new business downtown. Claims he's shopping for bargains, but I think he's keeping out of his missus' hair. Heh, Heh! She's the boss in their home. Of course, she does most of the work, too. Their place is neat and tidy, and her meals are tasty. Sh! I'd better stop talking about my neighbors, or they'll overhear us."

Mickey stopped before a large two-story house, soft lights glowing within, and announced, "Here we are, Rick," pausing to raise his voice a notch as the door squeaked open narrowly, and concluding with a smiling voice, "The Averys keep the best boarding house in Portland, Rick. Have a good stay."

Mickey broke away and strode up the hill as the door opened wide, lamplight spreading dimly over the stoop. As Rick stepped forward with his Sharps plainly visible, a stooped old man scurried past him, asking, "Is that Mickey? I'm Reuben Avery. Come on, we need to catch up to him, I saw three shifty characters skulking by just a moment ago."

Choking back a laugh and wondering if Reuben was eccentric, Rick nevertheless dropped his duffel and hurried after the shuffling figure, which was shouting "Mickey" to no avail. Grunts and thuds could be heard a few yards ahead as Rick stepped around the shouting old-timer and discharged his rifle into the air.

He ran toward a muffled, "Here!" swinging the butt of his rifle at an oncoming shape, striking a man's chest solidly.

The young man shouted with all the lung power he could muster, "Come on, men! We've got a gang of thieves here."

He swung at a second figure and missed as the culprit sprinted down the street, followed by a third man. The thief at his feet crawled away on all fours, and as he rose to his feet, Rick planted a boot in his rearmost anatomy to speed him along.

The huddled shape on the ground slowly unfolded with a series of groans, muttering at last, "Did those blackguards get away, lad?"

Happy to hear the sound of Mickey's voice, Rick helped him to his feet with a sigh of relief and uttered a concerned reply, "Yes, Reuben and I chased them away. Are you all right?"

As the barber grunted affirmative response, Reuben Avery interrupted in teasing tones, "Hello, Mickey, I knew they couldn't dent an Irishman's thick skull. This lad is a quick thinker, calling on his 'men' to clean out the gang. You and I weren't going to be much help if they called his bluff."

"Aye, friends, thanks for saving my money as well as my head. Will you walk me home, gents?"

A dram of Irish whiskey encouraged the young traveler to answer Missus O'Rourke's questions while she cleaned her husband's cuts and abrasions. Afterward he followed Reuben home and repeated his answers, and more, to satisfy an inquisitive Missus Avery. She fed him a late supper along with her many questions, drawing him a bath to keep him talking.

And so passed Rick's first evening in Portland. Tomorrow he would search out Aunt Jane's house and visit with Julie.

Chapter Six

Smiling inwardly at the glances cast his way, Rick McClure gripped the single red rose in his fisted hand and strode along the busy street. Missus Avery had tendered the fresh bud to the young lover at breakfast, a token for Julie from her garden in the enclosed sun porch. Passersby seemed to know his mission on this wet but sun-streaked morning.

Oh yes, this corner ahead must be where Madronna Street goes up the hill, he thought as he searched for a street sign. Failing to discover one of Portland's civilized markings, he pondered his next move for a moment. *Let's see, I'm four blocks up from the bank building, and according to that delivery wagon driver, I'm at Madronna. Where are all the people when I have a question? Guess I'll have to knock on the door and ask for help. Hmn, it's a nice neighborhood. I wonder if I'll get a courteous reception?*

Proceeding toward the nearby gabled house, he halted at arm's length from the windowed door, and with two fingers pinched the wrought iron knocker, tapping firmly three times.

Moments later the ruffled curtains fluttered and the door swung open, a pleasant and matronly women eyeing his face and the red rose with equal approval.

Rick doffed his hat, and respectfully greeted the lady, "Good morning, ma'am. I'm sorry to disturb you, but I'm a bit lost. I'm looking for the Rigney house on Madronna Street."

"Good day to you, young man. You must be a friend of Julie's—with a rose yet. She's a dear girl, caring for her dying aunt like she is. They live in that yellow house with brown shutters across the street," the lady said pointing up the lane three houses.

"Thank you, ma'am," Rick replied as he nodded courteously and backed away, hurrying as he angled across the road. Looking over his shoulder, he saw her still standing in the doorway. He gave a quick wave of thanks as he turned up an overgrown sidewalk to the square single-story house, not as fancy as its neighbors', but still comfortable looking.

Hesitating briefly as he steeled his nerves for the highly anticipated reunion, he finally rapped on the solid door with fisted knuckles. He brushed air on his third knock, as a well-groomed man in his thirties filled the doorway.

A condescending smirk and a petulant, "Yes," affronted Rick as he thought, *This has to be Roger. He's handsome enough and seems to know it—a real snob, I bet.*

He held his feelings in check, maintaining a calm demeanor as he queried, "Is Julie Madsen at home?"

The man shrugged muscular shoulders as he stepped forward, all but closing the door behind himself, still treating Rick like a peddler as he announced, "She's tending her sick aunt and can't be disturbed. Perhaps you can return another time."

Rick caught a movement behind the big man as the door opened wide, Julie's face bobbing into view, her happy cry reward enough for the journey.

"Oh, Rick, it's so good to see you again," she bubbled as she brushed past the dumbfounded man, throwing her arms around Rick's neck and kissing his cheek before remembering her manners.

"Julie, you're still the prettiest girl in all of Oregon—just like this red rose," Rick uttered with a foolish grin, extending the stemmed flower when she stepped back.

"Oh, Rick, thank you, it's lovely. Where did...?"

The overbearing man cut off her gay voice quite rudely, Rick thought in anger, when he admonished her, "Really, Julie, your aunt shouldn't be disturbed. Can't this fellow come back later?"

Julie frowned in annoyance as she retorted sharply, "Richard McClure is my dear friend from Port Orford, Roger. You came to see Aunt Jane, so you can visit with her for an hour. I'm going for a walk with Rick."

Unceremoniously reaching behind Roger, the girl grabbed her wrap and her handbag and stomped past the befuddled banker, Rick smiling openly at her spirit as he offered his arm.

The pair strode hastily across the lane, Rick cheerfully waving to Julie's neighbor watching from her corner window.

Julie giggled and followed suit, whispering conspiratorially, "Missus Evans doesn't like Roger.   She actually withdrew her savings and put the money in another bank last summer and then called him a 'pompous ass' when I asked why.   Her husband's Aunt Jane's doctor and feels the same about Roger, but let's change the subject.   How is my family?   Is Fred growing as fast as Mother says?   He seldom writes about himself, but he does praise you.   You're his best friend."

"You're brother is a fine young man and a real help to your folks.   He's learning the ranch business through hard work.   Your dad studies books and talks to neighbors about farming, but Fred just does it until he gets it right.   Actually, they make a good pair, like Dad and me," Rick concluded.

"Is Mother well?   And how about your father?   And the Hermanns?"   Julie prattled in rapid-fire fashion, her excitement barely suppressed as she sought news of family and friends in Port Orford.

"Everyone's fine.   Hazel sent this letter for me to deliver. I'd almost forgotten," he admitted as he dug the envelope from his pocket and gave it to Julie.

They stopped before the bank building while she read her mother's single page of writing, and looking up with happy tears in her eyes, she announced, "Let's go in the bank.   I'm going to withdraw half of my savings, fifty dollars and send it to my mother.   She says my family is selling eggs to Mister Hermann for credit on their supply bill.   I should have helped when Aunt Jane started my savings account."

Rick moved hastily in her wake as the excited Julie rushed into the bank, listening to her conversation with the gray-haired teller.

"I'm Julie Madsen.   I'd like to withdraw fifty dollars from my savings account."

The polite old man was deferential as he requested identification, "What is your account number, Miss Madsen?   And do you have some way to identify yourself?"

Julie retrieved a bank deposit slip and a city tax receipt with her name on it from her purse, handing them to the teller and asking, "Will these do?"

"Thank you, Miss Madsen. Let me check your account," he said, stepping over to the record file and thumbing through cards.

A frown distorted his lips upon his return to the cage window, and he advised, "I'm sorry, Miss Madsen, but this account is listed jointly in the names of Missus Jane Rigney and Miss Julie Madsen. Mister Townsend has left instructions that he must approve any withdrawals. He should return to this office at any moment. Would you care to wait?"

Julie's eyes flashed in anger, but she remained outwardly calm and ladylike in answering, "No, thank you, sir. I'll see Mister Roger Townsend when I have time. Good day."

She whirled about, and once again Rick found himself hurrying after her as she exited the establishment, her indignation bursting forth once they were outside, "That officious scoundrel! How dare he? Aunt Jane gave him explicit orders to deposit that money in my personal account. I wonder what other liberties Roger has taken with Aunt Jane's property?"

"Why would he want to control your account? I thought he was your friend," Rick pondered aloud.

Shaking her head in negation, she retorted, "He'd like to be more than a friend," and seeing her visitor's jaw tighten, Julie quickly added, "But I turned down his proposal of marriage. I believe he's a fortune hunter. Aunt Jane has money, and I'm her sole heir—some of Roger's manipulation. He talked her into changing her will last summer and replacing my parents with me. I thought he was looking after our welfare, but neither of us knows what he's doing. I'm a minor, and Aunt Jane is too ill to care. What should I do?"

"No wonder he didn't want me calling on you. I might figure out he's a charlatan. You know, I don't know a bank crook when I see one. I think you need a lawyer. Let me ask my brother-in-law in Salem what he can do. I'll need a letter from you and your aunt authorizing Albert S. Lee to represent you," Rick paused as he looked askance at Julie concerning a letter.

"Of course, I'll prepare two copies for Aunt Jane to sign and give you one to carry to Salem. You need to meet Aunt

Jane and witness her signature. Ha! Ha! She wants to meet my beau from Port Orford anyway."

The two strollers had increased their pace as they conspired to challenge Roger's management of the Rigney estate, and they were soon abreast of the Evans house.

"Hello, Julie dear! Did you enjoy your walk?" came the lady's dulcet voice from the doorway.

"Yes, thank you, Missus Evans. I'd like you to meet Richard McClure, a friend from…?

"Port Orford! Oh, I know, dear. We met earlier, didn't we Mister McClure? I thought your red rose was a lovely thought. I wish my husband were as romantic," Missus Evans paused as a memory caused her expression to change. Between pursed lips she exclaimed, "I suppose that's why that pompous ass Roger left in such a huff shortly after you turned the corner. Should he have left Jane alone?"

"Where did he go, Missus Evans? We didn't see him at the bank," Julie inquired.

"Oh my no! He rushed off the other way. Up to no good I bet. Wait a moment, and I'll go with you to Jane's house. It's time I visited her," Missus Evans declared, stepping inside briefly to return with a shawl over her shoulders.

The three wasted no words as they strode over to the square yellow house. Julie found the door locked and took a moment to insert her key and enter, rushing to the rear bedroom to check her aunt.

Rick overheard Julie's voice for several moments, another woman's weak response confirming that all was well. Soon after exchanging relieved glances with Missus Evans, he heard Aunt Jane call out not so feebly, "Richard McClure, you come in here. I want a word with you."

Walking into the bedroom, he faced an aged woman propped up by three pillows, her wrinkled and weary face split grotesquely by a welcoming smile. Frail hands, not much more than skin and bones, reached out to him.

Accepting her birdlike fingers lightly in his powerful hands, the young man intuitively leaned forward and bussed Aunt Jane's brow. His face was creased by the famous McClure smile as he straightened to greet her, "I'm glad to meet you, Aunt Jane. Hazel sends her love. So do John and Fred."

Searching his countenance with care as Julie left the room, Jane fairly cackled in joshing him, "Hee! Hee! What took you long, young man? I was afraid my niece was sweet on a willy-nilly boy. But you'll do, Richard McClure. Here, sit beside me and tell me about my sister and her family."

Julie returned with Missus Evans, holding two papers in her hand patiently as Rick finished relating news of the Madsens.

"Well, Niece, don't just stand there. I trust your judgment. Missus Evans can bear witness to my lucidity. You think Roger Townsend is up to no good, and you want to investigate him and his bank. Where do I sign?"

Julie placed a tray before her on the bed, two all-but-identical documents displayed. She dipped a quill pen into the inkwell and gave it to her aunt. Jane slowly and deliberately scrawled her signature on each copy, whereupon Julie signed, and Missus Evans and Rick followed suit as witnesses.

The girl handed Rick one copy and put the other in the desk drawer, announcing, "Rick will hire his brother-in-law, Albert S. Lee of Salem, to represent us, Aunt Jane."

"Good! Good! Now I'd better rest. You take care of everything, Julie dear."

Pondering a related concern for Julie's safety, Rick queried hesitantly, "Roger worries me. I have to go to Salem. How do we keep him away?"

Missus Evans volunteered, "I'll send my husband over this afternoon. He will order no visitors, but doesn't Roger have a key?"

"Yes, and he uses it as he pleases. Rick do you remember the locksmith shop around the corner from the bank? Could you ask him to change the locks?"

Grinning with wholehearted approval at Julie's plan, Rick agreed, "Sure, I'll get him here. Hmn! Drag him over here if need be. Missus Evans, could you stay here until I return?"

✶ ✶ ✶ ✶ ✶

An hour later, Julie paid the grumpy locksmith and sent him on his way; Missus Evans chuckled quietly as she bid good-bye.

Shaking her head in consternation, Julie asked, "Is it true, Rick? Did you really drag that poor man up the hill?"

"Well, I didn't give him much choice when he talked about tomorrow or the day after. I said right now, and he soon understood that I meant it. Of course, I couldn't let him out of my sight until he finished the job," Rick replied with a straight face.

Smiling still, Julie motioned him toward the kitchen, offering, "I cooked a pot of potato soup for Aunt Jane—her favorite. There's plenty for us, too, and there's a piece of day-old apple pie for you. Let's eat while Aunt Jane's sleeping."

"Thanks, Julie, I've worked up an appetite today."

Rick went to the sink to wash his hands and then settled into the chair Julie pointed out. She served him a large steaming bowl of thick soup. Before she could join him at the table, a metallic scratching sound came from the door, followed by thumping and a muffled curse.

Julie smiled nervously and mouthed, "I'll handle it."

She walked to the door as a loud rapping sounded, opening it partially to a red-faced Roger.

"What's going on? Why doesn't my key fit, Julie?" The angry man blustered as he attempted to enter the house, actually bumping into the girl as she stood her ground.

She squeaked indignantly but held her position steadfastly, both antagonists glaring at each other and unaware that Rick was a step away.

Roger put his hands on the girl's shoulders, pushing her gently aside in his attempt to gain entry and dominate the situation. She reacted immediately, uttering coldly, "Take your hands off me Roger Townsend. You are not welcome in this house."

Roger persisted in an insolent tone, "You can't keep…"

Rick swung the door wide and slipped alongside Julie, seizing Roger's right wrist in both hands as he propelled him off the porch. The big man swung a fist, and though it bounced off Rick's head in a glancing blow, the younger man held on firmly. Shifting his feet on solid ground, he twisted Roger over his hip, sending him sprawling into the yard.

Red-faced and crazed with anger, Roger charged on all fours for Rick's legs. Dancing nimbly aside, the younger man struck Roger's upturned face a sharp blow with his clenched fist, blood suddenly trickling from a flattened nose.

The larger man rose quickly, lashing out with a foot, and Rick turned his body to absorb the kick on his thigh, thinking this fight was not going to be pretty.

Several neighbors appeared on their porches, watching the brawl, both with interest and disapproval. Roger was momentarily taken aback by the thought of his unseemly behavior before bank customers. Shrugging his shoulders at this unexpected opportunity, Rick lunged forward on his aching leg and drove a solid fist into the banker's unprotected stomach.

Spectators now forgotten, the two men punched, elbowed, kicked, and kneed each other for several minutes, neither battler giving an inch. Slowly, Roger seemed to lose momentum, breath short as a result of a soft living and Rick's lucky punch.

Gasping hoarsely and taking a deep breath, the big bruiser charged forward, his roundhouse right striking Rick's shoulders with enough force to topple him over. The younger man rolled over and shuffled away as he rose to his feet. Roger charged a second time, but Rick glided deftly aside, tripping his oncoming foe and then pouncing on his prone form. All niceties long forgotten, he pummeled Roger into semi-consciousness. Weary and breathless, the defeated man conceded, "Enough! Enough!"

Julie and a stranger pulled Rick to his feet, and when Roger's tattered form crawled out of the way, released his arms. Soon the two men faced each other across half a lane, the vanquished battler bowing his head but still cursing Rick.

"Save your breath, Townsend. You're never to come near my girl again, and you're not welcome in the Rigney home. Now get out of here!" Rick spewed out the order with a threatening gesture.

Startled by the venom in the tone of his voice, Roger backed away, silently trudging down the hill as he tried unsuccessfully to straighten his aching body with what little dignity he had left.

In the meantime, Rick swayed defiantly on braced legs until his adversary had turned the corner and then shuffled over to Julie and her friend.

"Mister McClure, let me help you. I'm Doctor Evans, Julie's neighbor. Here, put your arm over my shoulder, and let's go inside," the stranger directed.

Julie stood at the door wide-eyed, obviously shocked at the debacle. Rick remembered her unsettling frown in San Francisco when he and George had settled a score with those two sailors and now worried contritely at the thought of her disapproval.

"I'm sorry, Julie. I didn't mean to embarrass you before your friends with such violence. Roger's putting his hands on you was the last straw," Rick mumbled apologetically.

"Oh, Rick, look at you, all bruised and barely able to stand. Go into the kitchen with the doctor and his wife so they can patch you up. I'll talk to Aunt Jane; she's no doubt eager to hear this story. Her late husband ran a logging crew and used his fists regularly," Julie prattled, hesitating for a moment as she added, "Did you...I mean...am I really your girl?"

Aunt Jane's cackle came from the next room, "Hee! Hee! That's right, Julie. Pin him down and then come in here and tell me about the fight."

Warm rain pelted the weary horse and rider, adding woes to their fatiguing trek along the muddy road to Salem. Despite his aches and pains, Rick had ridden away from the livery stable at dawn, determined to reach his destination before dusk.

He pulled the rented mare aside to allow a northbound wagon passage, a casual wave exchanged with the truculent teamster whose frown seemed a permanent fixture under the soggy hat brim. A gust of wind shook the Douglas fir above them, Rick shivering as globules of water cascaded from its boughs. His horse shied again in an irritating habit, and he reined her in firmly as he muttered, "Whoa! Quit that Daisy!"

Rolling her eyes until all whites showed, the mare nevertheless seemed calmed by his voice, so he continued, "I know it's a wet day, old girl. No getting around it, we can both stand a dry place to spend the night. Come on, Daisy, we've only got three miles or so to go."

He fell silent as the mare plodded forward, dreams of a warm fire and a hot meal persisting. *The rain is bad enough*, he thought to himself, *but the mud holes and swollen streams are worse. That ferryman claimed this air is warm enough to*

*melt snow in the mountains. He expects flooding on the valley.
Brr! Boy, I could use a hot toddy.*

"Well, Daisy, you're pretty good at crossing streams even if
you are a skittish female. Come on, old girl, I see houses up
ahead. We're almost to that dry barn."

Reining the mare aside as he approached the brick building
in mid-block, Rick was pleased to see the old fisherman's di-
rections were accurate. Lamplight profiled a block letter sign
on the nearer window, announcing the offices of Lee,
Gerbrunn, and Lee.

The weary traveler tied his horse to a corner post and
hurried forward, hoping Albert would be in his office this late
in the afternoon. Gray rain clouds made dusk seem earlier
today, but actually it was well before the supper hour. Rick
stepped inside to see Albert, Johnny Larson, and Johann
Gerbrunn in conference around a desk.

The elderly clerk behind an intervening rail had barely risen
to ask his business when Johnny shouted gleefully, "Rick!
What are you doing in Salem?" His friend reached forward
eagerly to shake hands and pull their drenched visitor to the
rear of the office.

Albert's smile of recognition was delayed, but enthusiastic,
and he quickly seconded Johnny's greeting, "Yes, welcome to
Salem, Rick. How's Scott? And George?"

A likely smile creased Johann's somber countenance as he
belatedly recognized a McClure, and with a hearty hello and a
clap on the shoulder, added, "How's everyone in Port Orford?"

"Everyone's fine, and they send their love. Sorry, Johnny,
Mary sent a box of cookies, but I shared them with my
shipmates..."

"You rascal," Johnny laughed in high humor, "You always
managed to garner a lion's share of Mom's baking—and
Melissa's, too. Only Anne could match your crafty ways
around the cookie jar."

Laughing quietly at Johnny's exuberant humor, Albert and
Johann were nevertheless aware their visitor had a problem—
his bruises a dead giveaway. Johnny was less perceptive but
still as observant as he blurted out, "Who have you been
fighting with?"

Rick grinned as he glanced fleetingly at Albert and responded to their mutual curiosity, "There's a banker in Portland

who's trying to swindle Julie's aunt, and I threw him out of their house."

Johnny fought to keep a straight face as he quipped in jest, "Roger? Julie's 'friend'?"

"That's not funny, Johnny Larson," Rick rejoined with a forgiving grin, continuing, "Besides, she's my girl."

He returned his glance to Albert and confessed, "My visit isn't all pleasure, brother-in-law of mine. I need help. I want Lee, Gerbrunn, and Lee to represent Julie and her aunt. Here's a letter of authorization to you, Albert," Rick concluded as the lawyer accepted the oilskin-wrapped parcel.

"Of course, Rick. Anything you need. Let me read this document and then you can tell us your story." Albert said as he unwrapped the letter.

Johann arranged chairs around the conference table, motioning everyone to be seated as he released the old clerk, "John, you can go home for the day. Lock the door on the way out. We'll close up after we've discussed Mister McClure's problem."

The four men settled about the table, Rick explaining the situation and Albert asking pointed questions. Within a quarter of an hour Johann stood up, announcing, "Rick, my partner has accepted your case, and he has a good grasp of your concerns. I certainly support him, and I recommend that Johnny work with him in Portland. Since you'll be leaving early in the morning, I'll tell Anne you're here for the night. Dad, Uwe and Angela and I will prepare a supper celebration this evening at seven sharp. Why don't I ride your horse home and you gentlemen take my carriage?"

Seeing the nod of agreement from the others, Johann donned a heavy coat and walked to the door. Rick hastily spoke, "Thanks, Johann. We'll be along shortly."

✷ ✷ ✷ ✷ ✷

Holding seven-month old Junior on his lap with a tentative, yet sure grip was instructional and invigorating, but Rick was more than just relieved when Anne repossessed her son for a diaper change. Angie shooed her three children into Cousin Kurt's bedroom to play, leaving the men to discuss business. Rick could report to his father and the Hermanns that all was well in Salem, Anne and her baby healthy, Angie fully re-covered from her miscarriage, and the Gerbrunn patriarch, Kurt, aged but as active as always.

An almost unearthly quiet fell over the large room in the absence of children's voices until Uwe broke the silence, "Rick, will you tell my in-laws that Angie and I will bring the children to Port Orford for a visit next summer? Our youngsters are anxious to see their mother's 'home'—and Grandpa and Grandma Hermann, of course."

"Sure, Uwe. We expect you at Myrtlewood Grove, too. Uncle Scott will take them upriver to pan for gold."

Kurt recalled Scott's recent visit to Salem and a promise made, "You must take your nephew Kurt, Uwe. Scott offered all the children a chance to dig gold and to hunt deer. I wish I could go along, but someone has to mind the business."

Pausing but briefly the old man inquired in his brusque Germanic manner, "Now stop being civilized lawyers and tell me about this bank fellow."

The men laughed at the patriarchal demand, Rick and Albert nodding in unison as the lawyer deferred to his brother-in-law.

Rick joshed, "And here I thought I would hear more about Johnny's lady friend," pausing to begin his tale of Julie and Aunt Jane versus the terrible Roger Townsend. Everyone smiled at the young man's prejudicial treatment of the 'villain', and the beautiful damsel in distress, but he was uninterrupted throughout his narrative.

✴   ✴   ✴   ✴   ✴

Three drenched horsemen rode the trail paralleling the Willamette River, a light rain still prevalent in the valley this dreary afternoon. Scattered about their route were modest houses marking the outskirts of the city, and they proceeded along a well-defined road into Portland proper. Rick signaled with his free hand, pointing to a prominent brick building fronting a business corner. His voice cracked hoarsely from disuse and the shivering clime as he announced, "That's the bank."

He led his partners up the hill to Madronna Street, shifting reins to his left hand and pulling his Sharps free of its scabbard when he sighted a carriage before the Rigney house. Two men were standing on the stoop and a third left the cab to stand on the walk before the oncoming cavalcade, a silvery badge exposed on his blue uniform coat.

Albert muttered aside, "Put that rifle away, Rick, and let me do the talking." He dismounted with a flourish, and handing his reins to Johnny, advanced to face the officer.

"Good day to you, sir! I'm Albert Lee, legal counsel for Missus Rigney and Miss Julie Madsen. What seems to be the problem?" he demanded officiously in a clear and carrying tone.

Looking beyond the stoic blocker of his path, he saw a young woman holding the doorway against two men. Surmising correctly that she was Julie, he lifted his voice as he decried, "Julie, is Aunt Jane all right?"

As Rick moved to his side, Albert slipped by the distracted officer and deliberately brushed the larger man aside, his bruised face identifying him as Roger Townsend. He grasped the puzzled but relieved Julie by her shoulders and leaned forward to kiss her cheek, whispering conspiratorially for her ears only, "Get inside and lock the door!"

As quickly as she did so, the lawyer spun to face a short gray-haired man who not only wore a badge on his breast but exhibited sergeant's stripes on his dark sleeve. Speaking before the officer could object, Albert explained, "My name is Albert Lee, partner in Lee, Gerbrunn, and Lee of Salem. My firm represents the ladies of this household in the matter of mismanagement of funds by a banker named Roger Townsend. Are you perchance acquainted with him, Sergeant?"

A sputtering sound erupted behind him as the policeman stymied a grin and spoke solemnly, "As a matter of fact, yes, Mister Townsend is standing behind you, Mister Lee. He claims a Mister Richard McClure attacked him on these premises two days ago."

"He did! He did! He jumped me without provocation. That's the McClure fellow over there. Arrest him, Sergeant," Roger demanded, his finger shakily pointing to a silent and peaceful Rick.

"Well now, sir, Mister McClure isn't running anywhere. He seems to be as bruised as you are, so I expect you two men did have an argument. What do you know about this affair, Mister Lee?"

Albert shrugged his shoulders eloquently, stating simply, "Since everyone in the neighborhood saw Mister Townsend crawling in the mire, it's no secret that Mister McClure threw him there when he refused to leave the property. The scoundrel offended the young lady and then tried to force his way through the doorway."

"Lies! Lies! Sergeant, are you going to arrest Mister McClure or not?" Townsend railed, visibly shaking by the confrontation.

"I think not, Mister Townsend. Perhaps you'd like to accompany me to City Hall and speak to the magistrate. He might issue a warrant after hearing both sides of this matter."

"No! No! I've heard enough of your bungling efforts. I wash my hands of the lot of you!" Roger bellowed in frustration, glaring at Rick as he left the scene in full stride.

A grin played fleetingly on the officer's lips before he somberly asked, "Now, I'd like a few words with the ladies, Mister Lee."

"Of course, Sergeant," Albert agreed readily and tapped on the door. It sprang open to show a smiling and untroubled Julie.

"Come in out of the rain, gentlemen. Aunt Jane and I are eager to talk with you," the poised young lady uttered as she led them to her aunt's bedroom.

✳   ✳   ✳   ✳   ✳

No wonder he is such a good lawyer, Rick thought. *That brother-in-law of mine really treated a nosy Missus Avery like a lady, talking all evening without saying anything. For a fact, Albert answered every question with a question, and my landlady never realized he hadn't answered at all. She was so proud to have real lawyers boarding overnight that she fed us a veritable feast. Why, she placed another piece of apple pie before Albert every time he took breath—four pieces before he said no.*

I reckon a gift of gab and a bit of tact are a useful combination for a lawyer. I wish I could have listened to him in court, but he told me to have breakfast with Julie and Aunt Jane. Hmph! I bet those two friends of mine just wanted to eat all of Missus Avery's grand offering.

Breaking his stride as he reached the closed bank, he scanned the dim interior for a sign of life. As expected at this early hour, there was no activity. Rick turned the corner and hurried up the hill, suddenly eager to see Julie again.

He was doubly gratified when she opened the door as he approached the house, obviously happy in awaiting him. He took her hand and held it awkwardly for a moment as they stared dreamily into each other's eyes. Throwing caution to the wind, he pulled her gently forward and leaned down to kiss her expectant lips.

They were entwined in each other's arms when Aunt Jane interrupted their rapture, calling in a teasing voice, "Richard McClure, stop kissing my niece and close the door. I'm ready for my breakfast and news from our lawyers."

Rick filled the wood box, chopped enough kindling for several weeks, repaired the back fence, and cleaned up the yard before Julie signaled all clear through the kitchen window. He hurried inside, almost on tiptoes, in hopes that he and his girl could be alone for a visit.

Julie was of like mind, motioning him toward the table where two steaming mugs of coffee rested. She brought a plate of sugar snaps with her as she sat beside him, speaking in lowered tones, "Aunt Jane should sleep for an hour or so. Tell me about your sister and her baby. Did you hold little Albert?"

"Ha! Ha! Of course I did, just as my nephew wet his diaper. I guess I looked like a typical bachelor in my confusion. Everyone had a good laugh, anyway. You know, Anne's face shone all the time Johnny and I played with her son. She's obviously happy with her family life. I always knew she would be a good wife and mother."

Rick paused as he reminisced, choosing a sentimental memory of the family swimming hole, "I wasn't afraid of the water or how cold it was. Probably I wouldn't be here today if Buzz and 'Uncle' Ivan hadn't watched me like hawks. I just sank naturally to the bottom of the pool and walked or paddled around. I swam underwater pretty good before Buzz could teach me properly."

"Anyway, Johnny and I always tried to best one another in everything we did, and I admit that he usually won. However, we were mortified when an uninvited Anne joined in our swimming contest and swam circles around both of us. She was good at everything she did, including putting up with her two brothers and Johnny. She reminds me a lot of our mother who could…"

Rick was interrupted by sounds of footsteps on the porch, accompanied by an abrupt knock on the door. He stood quickly and stepped into the hallway, facing the front and listening.

A voice called out, "Rick, open up. It's Albert."

As Rick walked forward to admit the attorney, Aunt Jane's drowsy voice could be heard, "Julie, bring our friend back here. I want to hear the news."

Moments later the men settled in their chairs, and Julie was perched on the bed beside her aunt. Albert cleared his throat hesitantly, describing his morning's activities. "Johnny and I visited the judge and obtained an order for the bank to open its books to me, and our friendly sergeant came along to confront Mister Townsend in his office."

Shaking his head in consternation, he continued, "We found the bank teller, he remembered talking to Julie, in conversation with a gentleman who identified himself as the owner. They were in a tether because their smooth-talking manager has absconded with an unknown amount of the bank's funds. I suspect he has been embezzling your money, too, Aunt Jane, but we won't know until later. I left Johnny to monitor their audit until I return."

A look at the dismay slowly crossed Jane's thin and haggard face as she cried, "Oh, what will we do now, Julie dear?"

"Don't worry, Auntie. Albert will handle the problem," Julie comforted her, looking to the lawyer for support, "You can help us, can't you?"

"I hope so, ladies. The bank owner promised to stand behind his depositors, so I'm optimistic. In the meantime, I'd like Rick to accompany the sergeant in tracking down Townsend. Julie, would you be willing to cook a meal for us if I send Johnny up here with fish and potatoes? I expect we'll all be hungry by supper time."

* * * * *

Rick hung on to the armrest with a firm grip, the uncommunicative sergeant racing the team through crowded streets, intent on avoiding people but determined to reach his goal. As the carriage approached the docks, he reined the sweating horses back to a walk and finally shared his thoughts with his passenger, "If I had a satchel of money and needed to disappear, I'd catch me an outbound ship. Townsend is smart enough to stay out of the Willamette Valley, or go to Columbia for that matter. He might try for Steilacoom on the Puget Sound, but I bet he's sailing to San Francisco."

They stopped before the ships' chandlery, and both men dismounted, Rick following in the officer's footsteps as they entered the building.

"Good day, Captain Smithers," the sergeant addressed an old man, no doubt a retired sea captain, tersely stating his business, "I'm looking for a thief who might have sailed in the last twenty-four hours. A scoundrel named Roger Townsend, who looks like a well-to-do gentleman."

"That banker fellow? Why I saw him board a steamer this morning, just as she was casting off her lines, Hmn, let's see," the old mariner muttered as he checked the ledger on his desk, "She the *Pacific Tern*, outbound for San Francisco. Her captain was in yesterday afternoon and told me he planned to cross the Columbia bar before dusk and steam straight to her port of call. I think your crook escaped, Sergeant."

"So it would seem, Captain. Thanks for your help."

As they stepped outside, Rick asked, "What now? Is the old man's story sound?"

"He's honest, and his eyesight is still good. Yes, I believe him, but I'll check around and report to the station. We'll notify San Francisco authorities, but I doubt we'll ever catch up with the money. Do you still want to trail along with me?"

Rick smiled his appreciation to the sergeant but demurred, "No thanks, I have a few errands to run on my way back to the bank. Thanks for your help."

Studying the two women during Albert's recital of the facts, Rick's feeling of empathy was augmented by admiration for their courage. Julie was somber throughout the detailed explanation but more concerned about her aunt's reaction to the theft than the actual loss of the six thousand dollars. Even Aunt Jane displayed mild concern about the crime, seeming to be embarrassed that she had trusted a scoundrel.

Her comment when Albert concluded his report was self-incriminating, "And to think, Julie might have married Roger because I trusted him."

Julie patted her aunt's bowed shoulder and comforted her, "There, there, Aunt Jane. I was fooled, too, but we discovered the truth soon enough."

"But your inheritance is gone, child," Jane bemoaned.

Julie glanced at Rick with a recognizable plea as she replied with more optimism than she felt, "He didn't get the hundred dollars in my account, and that will pay Albert's fee and your property taxes. Rick says he can help. He found a job in the Griggs sawmill..."

"And Missus Avery cut my room and board in half because I'll eat supper here, and I'll keep her larder filled with venison and salmon. Johnny will partner with me on a hunt next month," Rick was quick to add.

A slow smile spread over Jane's face at the earnest concern expressed by the young people, and with improved spirits she offered, "We'll sell my Swiss music box and those trinkets I keep inside it. That jeweler on Dock Street always wanted my late husband's diamond ring and that box."

"Good, Missus Rigney, you're thinking positive," Albert praised her attitude, adding, "The bank owner promised to make restitution when they catch Townsend. You'll do just fine."

"Oh, pshaw, Albert! They'll never find a dollar of that stolen money. Roger's too crafty," Jane scoffed at the notion in good humor, followed by a gentle demand, "Now help me to the table, Richard. Julie's fixed a delicious supper for us all."

Chapter Seven

Rick watched their quarry lift his antlered head high, testing the air with his quivering nostrils. Standing stock still amid an open burn, the observer's casual attention seemed at odds with his intent. The deer returned to browsing but a split second before a shot rang out, and the luckless beast dropped in his tracks, a testimony to Johnny's marksmanship.

As echoes rolled across the verdant hills, Rick flexed his tense shoulder muscles and drew a deep breath. He returned a congratulatory wave to his expectant partner, backing up the heavily laden pack teetering atop a charred cedar stump. His arms slipped through the padded leather straps, and he clinched them over his chest. Without further ado, he rose in a fluid motion, the hundred pounds of butchered venison riding his shoulders and back with enough impact to slow the husky man's stride downhill.

Hunting had been good today, as Rick bagged a deer before noon, with Johnny now matching his success. Even the weather was cooperating as they anticipated a dry camp tonight. Reuben Avery had found a butcher who would buy all their venison tomorrow. With dusk settling over the small glen where Johnny had dropped the stag, Rick figured they could enjoy a relaxed camp tonight.

Matching wits with wild animals now concluded and only his strong back involved in the expedition, Rick daydreamed about Julie as they plodded through the forest. Memories of a quiet Yuletide spent together in Aunt Jane's parlor brought a serene smile to his lips, disappearing gradually as less cheerful thoughts entered his mind.

Well, I guess Griggs had to close his mill, lumber stacked in his yard the way it is. Several small outfits are shut down until spring. Eight days' wages barely paid the Averys for my room last month, and this load of game should cover my January bill. Might be a few dollars left for Julie and Aunt Jane. Maybe I should take Kurt up on his offer and be a teamster. I could see Julie every trip north and keep her larder filled.

"Damn Townsend anyway!" he blurted aloud, Johnny raising his head from the butchering task at the angry sound of his voice.

"Talking to yourself won't get camp set up, Rick," his partner called out in loud but teasing tones.

Laughing in good humor, Rick crossed the clearing in long strides and unceremoniously dumped his bundle on the ground, muttering, "Whew! That's a load to pack...how many miles do you reckon we are out, Johnny?"

Still in his joshing mood, his carefree partner responded, "You're the taskmaster who insisted on two deer and full pack for that butcher fellow. Oh, I'd say we are five miles are so from Julie. Heh! Heh! We'll take that many hours to trail home through the forest with these loads to carry."

Laden with duffel bag and Sharps, Rick approached the now-familiar yellow and brown house, his grim expression softening as he saw the flutter of curtains in the front window. Julie flung the door open and rushed forward to embrace him, crying softly, "Oh, Rick, can't you stay over? Aunt Jane had a bad night, and Doctor Evans is with her now."

Kissing her upturned lips, the newly employed Gerbrunn teamster answered gently, "I wish I could, Darling, just as I wish we could get married soon. But I have to pay the bills, and you have to care for Aunt Jane. Anyway, Uwe is waiting on the Willamette Road to teach me the ropes. I'll see you once a week."

When she gazed into his eyes with love and understanding, he concluded, "Now I'd better say good-bye to Aunt Jane, or I'll have to walk to Salem."

Placing his burden on the hallway floor, Rick put his arm around Julie, and with an affectionate hug he called out, "Are you up to a visitor, Aunt Jane?"

"Of course, Richard," a weak fluttering voice replied from the bedroom, followed by a faint cough.

Being a frequent visitor to her home blunted the shock of Jane's haggard condition this morning, but her vibrant smile showed a buoyant spirit and will to live. Rick's expectations for Aunt Jane's recovery were nil, an opinion shared with no one.

Hope is eternal, he thought as he leaned over the bed to kiss his friend's brow, *but Aunt Jane is all skin and bones. She can't improve without putting some flesh on her body. Every setback seems to result in the opposite.*

"Well, Rick, your visit is doing more good than mine," Doctor Evans declared cheerfully, adding in concerned tones, "Jane needs her rest, so bid her farewell quickly."

Julie accompanied the doctor out of the room, and the tired patient took Rick's hand and murmured, "Go spend your time with Julie, young man. I overheard your conversation in the hall. You're both wonderful family, and I thank you."

Her hand squeezed his fingers gently, and he responded in kind, grinning broadly as he left her to rest.

Doctor Evans and Julie were awaiting for him near the front door, the doctor leading them outside before telling them the news, "The corner bank changed hands yesterday. I understand from the old teller that the former owner was broke but salvaged enough from the sale to join a brother in Monterrey. Jane won't recover any of her savings unless Townsend is caught. I'm sorry to be the bearer of bad news."

"Thanks, Doctor Evans, I hadn't heard the banker was quitting, but it was no real surprise to us. I hope you can continue to wait for payment. I'll have a little money each week I come through town," Rick replied.

"No problem, my friends. Missus Evans and I are glad to help, and under these circumstances, payment is not necessary."

Julie blurted out an insensitive denial, "Oh no, Doctor Evans, we can't take charity." Blushing profusely at her prideful gaffe, she quickly corrected the intent of her answer, "I mean, thank you for extending our credit, and Aunt Jane and I appreciate the meat pie your wife brought over yesterday. You're good friends and neighbors, but you have to make a living, too. Rick and I insist on paying you when we can."

She bestowed a kiss on the doctor's cheek, eliciting the expected response, a cheerful grin and a generous offer, "As you say, Julie, but I am Jane's doctor, with or without fees." He turned his head and headed for his home.

Rick and Julie shared a brief embrace before the young man gathered his gear and set off for his rendezvous with Uwe. The banker's news caused him more concern than he admitted before Julie. Money had never been a worry for the single man living on the Myrtlewood Grove, but providing for an almost-family of three in Portland was a marked departure from his casual lifestyle.

✳   ✳   ✳   ✳   ✳

Rick wheeled the empty wagon into the Gerbrunn yard, reining the sweating horses toward the side of the loading dock near the great barn. He waved to Kurt, standing in his office door and began removing harnesses from the tired horses.

Young Kurt burst out of the house, running awkwardly in the mire as he shouted, "Can I help, Rick?"

"Sure, Kurt. Throw a half-dozen handfuls of oats into a couple of buckets and let's treat our hard-working horses. They've had a long day." Rick accepted his offer with a grin, aware that the boy's grandfather was pleased as punch with the lad. The old man doted on Johann's son, vying with his father for the boy's vocational interest—business versus law.

Rick freed one horse and led the mare into the barn and her stall, oats and a rubdown gratefully accepted by the animal. Unshackling her partner and repeating the routine, he found young Kurt busily tending his charge.

Working side by side, Rick wondered aloud, "How come you're not in school, my young friend? Playing hooky?"

"Naw...well, maybe a little. I did get excused early today. I finished sums without an error and told Miss Alcot that I had chores to do before dark," Kurt said with pride in his expression.

His grandfather joined them, cleaning and straightening the harness as he teased, "Why didn't you come and help me with the books?"

"Oh, Grandpa! I don't know anything about your books, but I'm a big help with the horses, aren't I, Rick?"

Going over the mare with a meticulous inspection and then comparing the two horses, Rick clucked and fussed until the lad's look became tentative.

"Ha! Ha! You bet, Kurt. You're a born teamster," he chuckled, his teasing manner turning serious as he continued, "Your work is much appreciated by the horse and by me. Now, I reckon I have time for a real bath before supper. Johnny's bringing his girl over for dinner."

"Ja, me too! Maybe Kurt will feed the rest of the animals while I close the office," the grandfather said in high humor.

✳ ✳ ✳ ✳ ✳

Tinkling laughter emanated from the pretty blond girl as Kurt told her one of his flamboyant stories of Wuerzburg in the "old country". Johnny's expression of adoration made Rick wonder if he looked at Julie like that.

His friend looked up and caught Rick's eyes, cocking his head with a look that said, *See, she's charming as well as beautiful.* Rick returned a nod of affirmation and continued his surveillance.

Sarah Barton is as pretty as Julie, I suppose, although she seems awfully young. Blond hair, blue eyes, red lips, and rosy cream complexion. All suggest good German stock. No wonder Kurt is charmed also. And Sarah is much more sociable than our staid Johnny—a good match.

Glancing again at his best friend, he mused silently, *Johnny is smarter and better looking than most of us—me included, but he is a brooder. He takes after his mother, Sally, his coppery complexion and stubborn streak come from her Calapooya heritage. Actually Johnny's blond hair and blue eyes are his dominant features, but he's quick to acknowledge his Indian blood. He can be downright moody when he meets more prejudice, particularly the term "half-breed".*

Rick's contemplative silence was interrupted when Johnny and Sarah rose from the table, the young man apologizing, "I'm sorry we can't stay longer, but I promised Missus Barton that I'd have Sarah home before Mister Barton returns from his lodge meeting. Thank you for the delicious supper."

Sarah chimed in with a charming smile, "Oh yes, thank you all, and I love your stories, Mister Gerbrunn."

"Ho! Ho! You're welcome, child. Bring Sarah again, John, I have many more good German tales," Kurt chortled with a wink to his family.

Johann showed the young couple out while Uwe and Angela bundled their children in warm coats for the short walk home. Young Kurt looked at his grandfather hopefully, but a shake of the gray-haired head sent the lad to his room.

Kurt waited until the bedroom door was closed before commenting dryly, "Sarah is a beautiful girl, but so young and spoiled. Johnny is smitten, and the young lady obviously likes him, but her pious, righteous father does not. Barton is a successful merchant, an elder in his church and potentate of his lodge, but... well...he's a snob. He'd never admit it, of course, but he doesn't like Johnny because he's part Indian—a snob, like I said."

"Father, for once I agree with you. In fact, I was surprised when Barton let his daughter come to supper with Johnny," Johann pondered aloud in question-like tones.

Morning fog was dissipating slowly over the Gerbrunn Freight Yard, glimpses of blue sky promising fair weather for his trip north. As Rick completed harnessing the team and its yoke, Kurt emerged from his office with a handful of dispatches.

"Richard, will you deliver these letters to the Captain of the *Alma Ross*? That's faster than our regular mail service."

"Sure thing, Boss. Do you have my bill of lading there?" Rick asked as he walked over to Kurt and accepted the proffered documents.

"Yes, and God speed to you. You should make the Portland docks by nightfall. Ach! Last minute jobs are more...."

"Rick! Rick! Can I ride to Portland with you?" an agitated and distraught Johnny burst out as he ran across the muddy yard.

Gulping perceptibly for air, he blurted, "Kurt, is it all right?"

Both men nodded quickly, Rick murmuring, "Glad to have company, Johnny. What's your hurry?"

"Sarah left for Portland early this morning with her father. He's sending her to school in San Francisco, far away from me. He doesn't think I'm good enough for his daughter," Johnny lamented as he waved a slip of lilac-colored paper in the air.

While Johnny climbed onto the wagon seat, Rick glanced quickly at Kurt, whose "I told you so" expression was accompanied by a hand signal to get going. Rick clambered aboard, seized the reins in his fist, released the brake, and in a single practiced motion had the wagon on its way.

His usual taciturn friend jabbered all the way through town, mainly commenting on the weather and the town. None of his words related to his personal dilemma, so Rick said little during the couple of hours on the road.

After leaving the ferry landing and several minutes of silence by his friend, Rick asked, "What did Sarah say in her letter?"

Johnny blinked a tear out of his eye and spoke in muted, somehow resentful tones, "Sarah said she loved me last night on her porch. We kissed, and everything was wonderful." With that non-answer, he handed over the note, a tinge of lilac odor reaching his nostrils. Seeing a clear road ahead, Rick opened the fold to read silently,

> *Dear John,*
>> *My father forbids me to see you again. He thinks*
> *We're too young to be serious with each other.*
>> *He is driving me to Portland today to take passage*
> *On the Alma Ross for San Francisco, where I will*
> *attend a finishing school near my cousin's home.*
>> *God bless you and keep you well.*
>>> *Your friend,*
>>> *Sarah*

Rick pondered to himself the impersonal quality of the message, finally attributing it to the father's censorship. Aloud he volunteered, "My load is consigned to the *Alma Ross*."

"Good! Then I can see Sarah and talk to her. I love her. I want to marry her, Rick."

A good deal of fretting by Johnny and little conversation between the two friends marked the remainder of the journey.

Unfortunately, the sun set before they reached Portland, darkness obscuring the road ahead until the moon appeared. It was well after midnight when the wagon reached the docks and the *Alma Ross*.

The mate was on deck to meet them and turned out the watch to help Rick unload the wagon. His straight-forward response to Johnny's inevitable question was easily given. There were no passengers aboard overnight.

After the wagon's load was safely stored in the ship's hold, the teamsters were invited to the galley for leftover coffee, rolls and roast beef. Johnny reiterated his question on passengers, the mate humoring the young man by leaving for a moment to check the ship's manifest. He returned with the news that there were two Barton women sailing with the ship in the morning.

Rick left Johnny in conversation with the mate to stable his team, feeling guilty that the two horses had been overwhelmed and neglected. The night hostler was sleepy and cross, not at all helpful when Rick began rubbing the animals down. He was thorough in tending his charges, dawn almost upon him as he walked back to the waterfront.

The first rays of sunlight touched the hilltops west of town as Rick rounded the corner and headed down Dock Street. He heard strident voices raised in anger before he saw his friend arguing with Mister Barton.

"My daughter is not going to marry any half-breed lawyer, friend of Gerbrunns or not," shouted the well-dressed but red-faced gentleman beside the carriage with two women seated side by side.

Rick moved quickly to Johnny's side and laid a restraining hand on his friend's taut arm, afraid he might strike the older man.

In the ensuing moment of tense stillness, a meek, but unforced utterance came from the carriage, "I don't want to marry you, John. I'm going to San Francisco to attend the best finishing school on the coast. Please don't fight with my father."

Johnny went limp in Rick's grasp and turned away, disheartened and at a loss for any further argument. Sarah had done the unthinkable, siding with her father and rejecting his proposal. He was silent and morose all the way to the Averys and said little through breakfast. Missus Avery apologized for having a full house, with no beds for her two friends. Rick just smiled as he paid for the meal and said they'd catch a wink at Aunt Jane's.

Johnny followed docilely behind Rick, shocked into disappointment. As they approached the Madronna Street house he muttered bitterly, "I'm going to be a bachelor. To hell with women."

The visit with Julie and her very ill aunt was short and strained, neither man sleepy at all. After a bowl of chicken soup and an explanatory aside to Julie, the two friends bid adieu and proceeded to the warehouse where their return load was waiting for them. They could sleep in the wagon tonight and breakfast at that quaint little inn near Canby.

It was the Ides of March before Rick enjoyed another haul to Portland in sunshine, solar rays actually warming the nape of his neck as he sat hunched in his wagon seat on the Malolla ferry. Feeling a nudge on his left knee, he glanced up to find a shaggy gray-bearded old-timer in a beaver cap holding forth a pint bottle half-filled with amber liquid.

"Cah fuh a shoh, fellah?" the toothless octogenarian offered, quickly adding, "Gooh fuh thuh...hic...". Leaving the sentence hanging, he leaned on the wagon bed and raised the pint higher.

Rick accepted the bottle and sniffed its contents, the fragrant aroma of maple syrup and alcohol tempting his taste buds. He took a small sip and swallowed, the swizzle blazing a path down his throat to his stomach. He wheezed visibly, face flushing a bright pink in the sunlight.

"Hee! Hee! Gooh, huh?" the venerable old frontiersman said with pride.

"Rick, you be careful with Curly's elixir. He brews a powerful batch of white lightning," came late advice from the ferryman.

"Whew! But it's amber in color," Rick corrected as his breath returned.

"Mapuh sugah, fellah," Curly explained in his slurred dialect.

The ferryman pondered, "Didn't you say your daddy lived here in the fifties, Rick? Maybe he knew old Curly Lambeau, one of the original trappers in the territory."

"Could be. Dad and Buzz Smith partnered in those days. Did you ever meet Scott McClure, Curly?"

"Suh, thahs ith, yuh look lyh yuh poopah. Huh ish Scoh?" the old man mouthed.

And so Rick had an interesting drive to Portland, listening to tales of the old Oregon Territory, replete with the fanciful doings of Buzz Smith and his father. Curly even remembered Jedidiah Smith and his ill-fated expedition up the rugged California-Oregon coast although he had forgotten that Grandfather McClure had perished in the Umpqua Massacre. Curly left him at the Vancouver junction, the bedraggled old "landmark" plodding toward McLaughlin's fort.

Orange hues had faded into deep purple as twilight embraced the warehouse, a crew unloading the wagon as Rick tended his horses. It was dark when he slipped away, hastening in long strides down the streets on the familiar route to Aunt Jane's. In his haste he stumbled in a few chuckholes but soon found his steps were carrying him to the square-framed shadow of his destination, discovering the home was dark.

Figuring it was too early for Julie to be abed, he knocked on the door, thinking she would be in Aunt Jane's room. He repeated his knock without a light appearing, so he peeked through the front window, finally becoming worried. *Where were the women? Had something happened to them?*

Looking about the neighborhood, he espied several lighted windows in the Evans house and hurried across the street to knock on the door. Doctor Evans opened the portal wide, seeming to expect Rick as he stepped aside and motioned the young man inside.

The doctor announced loudly, "Rick is here, Julie. Let Mama finish the dishes."

Turning to the confused young man, he explained, "Aunt Jane passed away night before last, and Julie didn't want to stay in her house alone. Now that you're here, we'll hold services tomorrow. How long can…?"

Julie burst forth from the kitchen, tears of relief large in her eyes and a wan smile on her lips, content to rush into his arms and be held.

Doctor Evans repeated his query, "How long can you stay? Of course, Julie is welcome to..."

"I don't want to impose, Doctor Evans. You folks have done so much for me already," Julie interrupted in a voice muted by Rick's coat.

He concurred quickly as he answered Doctor Evans' question, "I'm supposed to return tomorrow, but Kurt will understand if I am a day late. Julie can stay with my sister Anne while Albert comes up to handle the Rigney estate."

Giving his beloved a squeeze, he asked emphatically, "I hope Aunt Jane's passing was peaceful. She was so strong in the face of pain and failing health."

"Yes, she went quietly in her sleep. You know she wasn't eating much these past weeks, and her death was not unexpected," Julie explained, sorrow evident but with her grief in control.

★ ★ ★ ★ ★

Sitting astride the whitewashed corral fence and studying the two mares with the attitude of a serious buyer, Rick's concentration was broken by the feel of a hand on his outboard knee. He twisted toward his benefactor and asked, "Which is 'Main' and which is 'Rhine'?"

"No, no, Main is pronounced mine, it rhymes with Rhine. I guess I will never be able to teach you good German, my young friend," Kurt replied in mock dismay, artfully dodging the question.

Rick chuckled at his duplicity, "Ha! Ha! All right, tell me which is Main."

Kurt giggled at his own humor, "Hee! Hee! The younger mare...the one looking at you as you spoke her name. See, she has a patch of white under her left eye, and her coat across her withers has more dark hair."

Rick shook his head ruefully, responding in kind, "I knew that...I just didn't know which was which. Are they sisters?"

"No, cousins. Your Salem has some of the same blood. Have you decided which horse you will buy?"

"Both of them, if Albert returns from Portland with some of Julie's money...part of the house sale. Is my credit good if my brother-in-law fails to pry her estate away from the court?" Rick asked, the answer known before Kurt nodded agreeably.

The old man shuffled away as a freight wagon entered the yard, Rick noting the stumbling steps Kurt made when in a hurry. He thought, *Kurt Gerbrunn is getting old, although he refuses to slow down. As much as Uwe plots to ease his workload, the old man stays busy. I suppose I'd better help unload that wagon, or Kurt will do it. So much for my day off.*

✶ ✶ ✶ ✶ ✶

The Lee house seemed crowded with wedding guests, only the bride and groom unseen this fair April day. Sunlight streamed through parlor windows, lighting the space where Reverend MacDougal stood waiting patiently. At Anne's nod, Johnny stepped out a side door briefly, reappearing with a nervous and flushed Rick in tow to stand before the minister.

Soon the remainder of the wedding party walked into the room, Albert escorting Anne and Uwe escorting Angela. Finally the bride came down the stairs on the arm of Doctor Evans, who was giving her away in the absence of her father. Julie was beautiful in her simple dress, her eyes finding those of her betrothed as she walked slowly forward. Neither bride nor groom was concerned at their absence of finery, both eschewing the expense of wedding garb, although Julie wore Anne's veil and carried her bridal bouquet.

The good Reverend understood the meaning of simplicity in their home ceremony and kept his sermon in consonance, the ring exchange and marriage kiss concluding the services. "Mister and Missus McClure" sounded good to the two lovers as they accepted the congratulations of friends.

"When will we leave, Wife?" was Rick's question to the bride as he drew her aside.

"We still have to cut the wedding cake, Husband. Don't be so impatient, I'm having fun," Julie answered, and seeing his sorrowful look, quickly added, "I'll tell Anne to bring out the cake."

He and Johnny followed the women into the kitchen, carrying the wedding cake, table and all, into the parlor. Johnny nodded in response to his whispered aside to saddle their horses after he ate his piece of cake.

When all their friends were ensconced in their chairs with cake and coffee or brandy, the newlyweds slipped out the back door and mounted the waiting horses. But as they rode around the house they were greeted with cheers for a happy life and a shower of rice. Undeterred by their loss of secrecy, the couple trotted out of the yard with but a casual wave to their well-wishers.

"Will we reach the Albany Inn before dark? How far is it? Why did you want to honeymoon there?" Julie asked inquisitively, never having traveled the Willamette Valley before.

Rick explained, "I delivered a load of furniture to the Barkley's last month and liked the quiet setting. We'll have the upstairs to ourselves for the weekend. Then we have a long ride home. Dad's told me of a couple of inns south of the Albany, or maybe we can stop over in Elkton—that's where Mom and Dad first met."

He reined the horse next to hers and leaned over to kiss her, their jostling lips only putting more ardor in his eyes. It would be a long trip to the Myrtlewood Grove.

Chapter Eight

The two riders breasted the notched crest of the forested ridge, sky-lined for a few minutes as they rested their horses. Both figures were bundled in layered clothing to fend off the air of the Calapooya Pass, but long brown tresses marked the trailing rider as a woman.

"It's a beautiful panorama, Rick, but where's Elkton? I'm getting tired...and so is Main," Julie announced in a tone bordering on both wonder and complaint.

Rick pointed down the river valley winding toward the southwest and replied, "Well, Honey, if you were an eagle, you could see the town beyond that far hill, maybe five miles that way."

He kicked Rhine gently forward, riding to a swale on the south side of the notch. Handing his reins to his wife, he pulled his Sharps free of its scabbard and slid off the far side of the horse, voicing a terse, "Wait here while I scout our back trail."

Rick trotted up the gentle slope, dropping to all fours as he crow-hopped to the crest of the pass, sliding behind a towering fir beside the trail. He studied the northern approach, thinking silently. *Sure enough. There they are. Those three roughnecks from the stagecoach station have been trailing us all day. I didn't like the looks they gave us all day—particularly Julie.*

Scooting backward in a crab-like manner, Rick soon rose to his full height and ran to his wife, explaining, "I think those three men from the station are following us. That stage driver said there were thieves in the hills. A couple of robberies of miners in gold camps along the Rogue and another on the stage road near Winchester were committed by two or three masked men. The look he gave those toughies told me the whole story. He didn't trust them, and neither do I, so let's ride fast. Follow me, Honey."

Rick seized his reins, mounted smoothly, and holding his rifle at ready, urged his mare forward, trotting down the steep slope on a switchback trail. Glancing over his shoulder to affirm that his wife was close behind, he spurred Rhine into a mile-eating gallop as soon as the slope leveled off and he could see a straight path before him.

After a quarter of an hour, he slowed the lathered animal into a mile-eating trot. Upon entering a dense copse of firs, Rick signaled Julie to stop, and he repeated his scouting technique. Seeing no movement to his rear, he remounted and sheathed his Sharps, riding steadily down the trail until they sighted the outskirts of Elkton. Glancing back one last time, he escorted his wife to the center of the bustling village in search of an inn for the night.

The newlyweds were the center of attention during supper as they sat around a large table in the common room with the other guests. Most questions were discreetly directed to Julie by their hostess and a middle-aged farmer's wife, but the men hung on every word the bride uttered, Rick feeling a pang of jealousy as her natural beauty was enhanced by her conversation and her smiles—looks of admiration abounding.

No one left the circle until Julie excused herself to retire to their upstairs room, telling her husband, "Stay and enjoy your drink, Rick."

"I'll be up in half an hour, Dear," Rick replied, bidding goodnight to the farmer and his wife, followed by the three traveling salesmen.

Burt, the innkeeper, was a likeable young man of thirty or so, who had bought the hostel two years before. Although he was too young to know about Elkton's early days, Rick figured he was in a position to hear all the latest news along the Umpqua.

The old-timer who had been sparse with words all evening might remember his father or Buzz. His gray beard and hair marked him as the right age, although his piercing brown eyes didn't seem to miss a trick, and his slouched buckskin-clad figure was deceiving. *He's fit as a fiddle*, Rick thought as he observed out of the corner of his eye, *but I bet he's even older than he looks.*

Wondering how to ask about robbers on the road west, Rick offered, "Drinks are on me, gents."

Burt brought three foaming mugs to the table, joining his two guests in their silence, asking conversationally, "Your wife said you're headed for Port Orford. Do you live down there, Mister McClure?"

"Yes, my wife's family has a place on the Elk River, and my dad and I are located on the Sixes River. Maybe you've heard of my father, Scott McClure. He and Buzz Smith lived in Elkton thirty years ago. Dad stayed with Doctor Wells and his wife when he had pneumonia. That's where he met my mother."

"Doctor Wells, eh? Heard of him. He's been dead for years. Horse accident if I heard right," Burt chattered affably, continuing, "Folks west of here named a creek for him. He had a place out there called Green Acres or something like that. Not many of the trappers left around here. You know, the Hudson's Bay Company operated a trading post over there—Fort Umpqua."

Rick nodded in understanding, smiling at his recent meeting with Curly Lambeau and relating the story to the two men, concluding with, "Dad was acquainted with a lot of people, but Buzz Smith knew everybody in those days. He was my godfather. That's how I got the middle name of Erastus."

The old-timer finally spoke, "Not many people knew Buzz's real first name, young fellow. And thanks for the news of Curly, I haven't seen him in ten years."

Studying Rick's face for a moment, he bobbed his head in confirmation and stated, "Yup, you're Scott's boy—look like him, by golly. Careful like him, too. I saw that today."

Rick raised his eyebrow in a question as Burt asked right out, "What? Careful? What do you mean, Augie?"

The old-timer spoke to Rick in deliberate tones, explaining, "I saw you looking over your back trail at twilight, and so did those three varmints who followed you and your missus into Elkton. They're camping in the ruins of the old fort across Elk Creek."

Rick wagged his head in agreement, "I thought as much, but I couldn't find them. Thanks for the tip, Augie. I'm beholden to you."

As he paused over his plans for the morning, Burt exclaimed in excitement, "Do you think those fellas might be the robbers working the stage road? What do they look like?"

Augie smiled broadly for a moment, his lack of teeth making him seem much older, but he was obviously young at heart, suggesting, "Why don't we travel to Scottsburg together. Those three toughies won't bother a party with two rifles carried in plain sight."

★ ★ ★ ★ ★

Augie was waiting west of the old fort as pale sunlight rose over the eastern hills, mounted horseback astride a scruffy gray mule seemingly planted in the muddy roadbed. Doffing his floppy-brimmed hat to Julie, but speaking to Rick, "Well, young fella, those three varmints broke camp at daybreak and headed west at a gallop."

Julie smiled with relief as she opined optimistically, "See, Dear, they are just in a hurry to reach the coast."

Shaking his head laconically, the old-timer corrected her gently, "No, ma'am! I trailed them apiece. They holed up in a copse of giant firs a couple of miles down the Umpqua Road—likely spot for a robbery."

Augie kneed his mule forward, shrugging a slung musket from his shoulder and offering it to Julie. She accepted the antique with a hesitant and quizzical expression as the old-timer muttered, "It's not for shooting ma'am, but three guns look fiercer than two. Maybe those varmints will leave us alone."

Grinning a toothless smile of encouragement, their benefactor kicked his cantankerous-looking mount into a trot, Julie following him and Rick bringing up the rear, all three riders carrying their weapons in plain sight. As Augie approached an open glade straddling the road, he slowed his mule to a walk and covertly signaled toward a stand of virgin timber a quarter-mile ahead.

The cavalcade crossed the meadow and entered into the dark forest, Julie copying the old-timer by carrying her musket in her left hand, barrel pointing uphill. Rick covered the downhill side with a casually moving muzzle, hoping the sight was sufficiently threatening, but confident he could hit what he aimed at.

Rhine's nostrils twitched and snorted abruptly, an answering neigh echoing from uphill. Rick swung his Sharps toward the sound and spurred his horse forward past Julie, who reacted alertly in staying close behind him. Augie now brought up the rear as the trio galloped away.

Rick drove his horse forward until he saw the road disappear behind a rocky formation at the foot of a steep, forested slope. Reining in behind the cairn, he waved Julie and Augie on. He dismounted and tied his reins to a fir stump, before climbing a dozen feet to the top of the rock pile. Laying his Sharps across a flat boulder, he cocked and waited.

A long minute passed before he heard oncoming hoofbeats, and moments later the three would-be robbers rode into view. His Sharps echoed as Rick laid a bullet into the shale beside the road. He heard a faint buzz overhead as he slid down the cairn, the bullet's accompanying crack heard a split second later.

Standing behind a notch in the boulders, he observed his pursuers, one rider holding the reins of the milling horse as a second shot struck granite atop the pile. With a gunfight in progress, Rick felt but a twinge of regret as he lined his sights on the horse with a rider and squeezed off a round. He was stepping clear of the notch as the horse collapsed, and a bullet struck the granite near his head.

With a methodical dispatch he untied the reins and mounted Rhine, leaning low over the saddle as he trotted west. A mile down the road he passed Augie standing behind a huge fir, setting a similar barricade to the robbers' pursuit. Around the shoulder of the slope, Julie was astride Main, and the old gray mule was foraging on clumps of grass.

Reining her horse alongside her husband's, she looked him over carefully and asked, "Are you all right? I heard shots."

Rick gave her a quick nod of assurance, waving toward yet another bend in the road and announcing, "Let's ride over there and wait for Augie. Enough of…"

The clear sound of a shot came from nearby as the pair raced away, three muted return shots marking their adversaries' position up the road.

Ensconced behind a small rise, Rick completed his earlier thought, "As I was saying, Dear, enough fooling around with warnings. If they follow Augie, I'll shoot the riders instead of the horses."

He waited tensely for a few moments before relaxing perceptibly as Augie and his mule trotted into view. Rising to stand in plain view so his friend could see him, Rick pointed to a deadfall on the far side of the road and then settled back into his own niche. Julie leaned back against a stout fir, out of the prospective line of fire.

After a half-hour of fretful waiting, Augie led his mule across the road and ordered, "You folks go ahead. I'll watch our backtrail although I reckon those varmints finally got smart and quit."

★　★　★　★　★

Julie muttered an irritable, "Damn!" as she shifted positions in the saddle for the hundredth time since leaving their cozy inn. "We should have accepted the Langlois' offer. They seemed to be nice people. Ugh! I'm sore all over. How far is it to the Sixes?"

"It's this side of the ridge ahead. We'll be home in an hour, Honey," Rick consoled the weary rider.

Thank God Augie knew everyone in Scottsburg, Rick pondered silently. *Julie and I had to confirm his story of the robbers and ride on to Coos Bay. We got there before dark, to boot. Now, I'm eager to reach home. I've missed the Myrtlewood Grove—and Dad. Gee, is it May already? Time has sure flown since Aunt Jane died.*

"Oh! I see where we are. That's the trail up to your…our home over there," Julie uttered in surprised tones, her finger pointing to the easily recognized cut in the hills. She grew animated and a lilt touched her voice as she concluded, "We can visit all evening with Scott and then ride over to see my folks tomorrow."

"What? You want to ride some more?" Rick teased his wife, reaching across the void to squeeze her fingers affectionately.

She answered her husband in kind with a snippy expression, kicking Main into a trot and leading Rick through the defile and across Slide Ridge. They were going home.

Soon their horses' hooves reverberated across the log bridge over Cascade Creek, and they reined their horses to walk down the knoll, coming into the yard as shadows fell over the ranch. Scott left his casual stance in the doorway with a rush, giving Rick a "Hello, Son," as he moved to Julie's stirrups and gallantly lifted her out of the saddle. She threw her arms around his shoulders for support as she stood on feeble legs and planted a daughterly kiss on his cheek.

In a rare display of affection, Scott returned her hug and kiss, holding her in his left arm as his right encircled his son.

"Congratulations, Mister and Missus McClure! Fred brought your letter over last Friday, and your folks are as pleased as I am. Come inside and rest, Julie. You can put your things in the bedroom; I'm living in Buzz's cabin. Your brother helped me fix it up this week."

"Oh, Scott, we don't want to drive you out of your home. Rick thought you could bunk in his old room," Julie replied in consternation, her flushed face turning pinker as her father-in-law just laughed.

When Rick joined in the laughter with a teasing, "Two's company, three's...", Julie was forced to accept his offer.

"Thanks, Dad, but you'll live here with us during the day. Besides, I have to practice my cooking on you as well as your son."

★ ★ ★ ★ ★

Rick came awake with a start, an unknown sound reaching him at dawn. Before he was fully alert, he heard it again, recognizing the sounds of their cast iron range in use. A faint smell of wood smoke drifted into the bedroom, and he settled back into their warm cocoon of a bed. Evidently his father had started a fire to warm the house.

Not unexpectedly he heard the muffled cracking of eggshells and their accompanying sizzle in the fry pan as Scott became less stealthy with his wake-up breakfast.

"Hmn, that smells good. Is Dad treating us to breakfast? I smell bacon and eggs," Julie murmured sleepily.

Slipping out of bed and dressing quickly, Rick answered affirmatively and then called out, "Julie wants bacon with those eggs, Dad."

"Ha! Ha! How about fried trout instead? Been out of bacon all month," Scott replied with humor in his tone.

Minutes later the three sat about the table eating the cook's bounty with voracious appetites, Scott bringing the newlyweds up-to-date on their neighbors.

"The Hughes family is healthy, and Patrick is still buying land. Do you think we should purchase the hillside above us? Anyway, I was selling him milk regularly, so I just sold him three of our milkers. We're a little short of cash, but our credit is good."

Julie offered as he paused, "Albert is handling Aunt Jane's estate, and we'll get some money this summer. We could use some of it to buy that land."

Scott smiled broadly as he accepted, "Thank you, Julie. I can see you are taking our partnership seriously."

He hesitated a couple of times before admitting, "I didn't tell you last night that your folks are in debt. John lost a steer in the rain-swollen Elk River, and times have been tough along the coast."

She nodded as she replied, "I suspected as much from family letters."

Turning to Rick, she suggested, "We can share Aunt Jane's estate with Mother, can't we, Dear?"

"Of course, Hazel deserves more than a few trinkets left in Aunt Jane's jewelry box," Rick responded readily, asking Scott, "What about Jack?"

"Well, Jack Sixes comes by now and then. Does a little work for me and takes his pay in food supplies. He's been a regular hermit this winter. Looks around for you, and when I tell him you're still in Salem, he heads home again. The other Jack, our friendly bartender, pulled up stakes during the winter and sailed to California. Let's see, we talked about everyone else last night. I can't think of any other news," Scott's voice trailed off as his gossip was gone.

He stood to gather up dishes, motioning Julie to remain seated as he demurred, "No, young lady, you go see your family and friends. I'll clean up. Enjoy yourself today because Rick's turn to do chores starts tomorrow."

✷ ✷ ✷ ✷ ✷

Rick and Julie were almost to the front door before Fred burst out of the barn, yelling loudly, "Julie, Rick, when did you get back? Gee, it's good to see you, Sis. Oh congratulations, I think...."

The door swung wide, and Hazel rushed forward to clasp her daughter in a tight embrace, tears of joy running down her cheeks as she muttered, "Julie, darling."

Rick shook his brother-in-law's hand and threw his arm over his shoulders in a comradely fashion, both men smiling happily at the reunion.

Hazel finally released her daughter, turning to Rick and holding out her arms for his bear hug, kissing his cheek as she accepted him into the family, "Welcome to the Madsens, Richard. And thank you for being a friend to my sister."

Smiling nostalgically and nodding, he agreed, "We were buddies. Aunt Jane told me a thousand stories of your childhood shenanigans. I'll share them with you one day. Maybe I can jar your memory. Where's John?"

Fred stopped chattering at his sister to respond, "He went into the Hermann store to buy supplies. Said he would be gone for most of the day. Can you stay for supper?"

Julie shook her head, "No, we have much to do in the house. Scott moved into the cabin you helped him repair, Fred, and I need to do a spring cleaning. Why don't you come over Sunday for a chicken dinner?"

"Of course, Dear, but come inside and visit for awhile anyway," her mother urged.

"Go ahead, Julie, I'll help Fred with his chores. Besides, he's eager to give Rhine a turn around the yard."

★ ★ ★ ★ ★

Riding south along the wide street toward Hermann's store, Captain Tichenor, taking his morning stroll, hailed the couple.

"Hello, Rick, Julie. Is it Mister and Missus McClure now?" Smiling at their happy nod, he continued, "Congratulations! Mary Hermann shared your news with Elizabeth and me. Julie, my wife would love to have you for tea when her health is better, but she's abed with a cold today."

Julie responded sympathetically, "Oh, Captain Tichenor, do give her our regards. I hope she feels better soon. I'll stop by your home on my next visit to Port Orford."

Tichenor tipped his hat and walked on, Rick and Julie riding to the hitch rack before the store. The dun Smokey neighed and stomped excitedly as soon as the girl called his name, recognizing the sound and smell of his mistress.

John Madsen burst forth to grasp his daughter in a great hug as she dismounted, no words necessary in their emotional meeting. Rick was momentarily forgotten until his father-in-law greeted him, "Welcome home, Richard, and congratulations. You married the prettiest girl in the country—and the sweetest."

Grinning unabashedly in agreement, Rick quipped, "Yes sir, you're absolutely right."

"And I'll vote for Julie, too" George sailed for the open door, as he added, "Congratulations, my young friends. Was your wedding as grand as Angie wrote it would be?"

"Yes, Mister Hermann, and your daughter and Rick's sister were entirely responsible. We all became good friends while I stayed with Anne," Julie answered.

Stepping around her father and husband, she reached out to George, placing her hands on his shoulders as she kissed his cheek, saying, "That's from Angie—and me."

The aging merchant fairly beamed as he blushed and stuttered "Th..Than..thank you. John, why don't you take these newlyweds to see Mary while I take care of your order?"

Rick held forth a list of his own, suggesting, "How about filling my order, too. Can you join us for a visit?"

"Sure, leave your horses, and I'll have my clerk load the supplies on them," George acquiesced readily, adding in worried tones, "Harvey hasn't been able to work much this past spring. He's a might frail these days."

Rick's expression showed concern as he volunteered, "We'll drop by his home before we leave town."

George nodded in concurrence, passing another message to the couple, "Grandma Knapp asked about you just yesterday. You're to stop by for tea when you get home. Oh yes, Rick, Louie mentioned brandy for you."

The McClure men were harvesting their second hay crop of the summer when Bill Tucker rode through the myrtlewoods, around the grazing cattle and mounded haystacks toward them.

A love-struck grin creased his face as he proclaimed, "We're getting married! Beth Hankins said yes, and her parents agreed. Her mother insists on waiting until September for a nice wedding in Langlois. Will you be my best man, Rick?"

"Of course, Bill, it would be an honor. I wish you and Beth the best. You're a lucky man, buddy!"

Scott shook the exuberant suitor's hand and asked, "Best wishes, Billy. What does your dad think of your plans?"

"He says that he approves, but he's sorry Mama isn't with us any longer. She could tell us men how to behave properly," Bill responded nostalgically, suddenly remembering, "Oh yes, I brought Julie your mail, and she wants to see you both right away. Something about her inheritance."

Bill rode away with undue haste, urging his horse to a trot as he headed for the Hankins place for supper. Julie waved as he passed the house, waiting eagerly in the sunlit yard to share her news with Rick and Scott.

"That Portland court finally released my money," she fairly shouted across the corral, Rick's grin matching his wife's.

"Well, was there enough for Albert to buy the land north of us?" he asked.

"Yes, we received the deed from him, plus a bank draft for five hundred eleven dollars. That's enough to pay all the McClure and Madsen bills. I wish there were more money to help my family," Julie moaned as she waxed from exuberant to morose in a changeable mood.

"Dad and I have been talking. We can spare a yearling and one of our horses, which should make it easier on John and Hazel. New Salem is old enough to turn out to pasture, and we each have a Gerbrunn mare to ride. Dad thought John would like to own Ariane, but you'll have to figure out how to make him accept the idea as something Jane left her sister. He's a might stiff-backed about charity, so get a good story ready."

Supplies draped over New Salem's saddle, Rick walked the faint trail upriver to Jack's, the Tutuni loner an infrequent visitor to the Myrtlewood Grove since his marriage. Shaking his head at his friend's thinking process, he recalled Jack's visit to Julie's eighteenth birthday party. *Gee, he seemed happy, and my wife has always been friendly to him. Why is he so stand-offish this summer? He didn't even show up for the Battle Rock celebration. Ha! Ha! A gala event, which fizzled out again. Well, Harvey enjoyed himself anyway, and Louie was a good host to the Madsens and McClures.*

A voice at his elbow startled him out of his melancholy, "Boo! Ha! Ha! It's a good thing, Rick, that I'm a friendly Indian."

Rick grinned sheepishly, retorting, "You got me, Jack! But I don't know about 'friendly', you never come to see me. Don't you get lonely up here?"

"Yes, but I don't want to disturb you newlyweds. Besides, I'm jealous," the young hermit avowed.

"Jealous? Why?"

"I'm old enough to have a wife, but there is no woman around here for Cha-qua-mi," Jack using the third person in his pessimism.

"Well, your plumb wrong, my Tutuni friend. Chief Te Cum Tom told me there are several families returning to their ancestral land, their moves not unlike yours," Rick replied.

"Old John from Hubbard Creek told you our people are returning? Where are they?"

Rick smiled as he responded, "Julie and I ran across a family with two boys near Floras Creek, and Old John says his cousin is living on Euchre Creek. No doubt there are more Tutuni about, but keeping out of people's way."

Slowly a grin creased Jack's cheeks, and emotion akin to excitement sparkled in his brown eyes. His idea formed into words as he stated, "I will talk to the Quah-to-mah Chief, Old John, and search out the families. Perhaps I will find a girl of the age for marriage. I will do this right after I help you harvest your crop. Will you help me get ownership of my land? You know, white man's paper."

An entourage of clan members debarked a steamer in late September, Angie and her family filling the Hermanns' home to the joyful greeting of grandparents. Anne and her two

Alberts rode out to the Myrtlewood Grove while Johnny Larson and Johann's son, Kurt, moved in with Harvey Masters.

Harvest was quickly completed with extra hands available, and sunny weather prompted a holiday picnic in the myrtlewoods near the river. Jack and Johnny were successful in bagging a small deer for the barbecue while Rick showed Albert the knack of catching salmon.

"Father will be sorry he missed one of your famous barbecues, Scott. He's just too old to travel these days," Uwe said as they tended the spit.

"Maybe I'll sail up to Portland in the spring. Rick and Julie need a little privacy now and then. Tell Kurt his favorite teamster will visit him next year."

Rick and Albert approached the fire pit with armloads of wood, breathing sighs of relief as Rick complained, "Women! We've been running errands for our wives all day. Maybe we can hide over here with you. Dad, where do you suppose Johnny is with that keg of beer? We've got a hundred thirsty guests."

"He's bringing Harvey with him, and I think I hear them crossing the Cascade Creek bridge now."

As soon as the keg was astraddle a pair of sawhorses, the men gathered around it in conversation. The harvest, the steamer's voyage, and Port Orford news were soon supplanted by politics.

Albert didn't like President Hayes, describing the 1876 election as a Republican fraud. He quoted the Oregon Elector freely, pride and prejudice equally mixed as he spoke of his acquaintance with the man who connived to be the 185th vote, for Hayes-Tilden received 184 votes.

Next fall's election was an ensuing topic, and a conservative George supported Hayes, stating heatedly, "Rutherford Hayes has done a fine job. What more can we ask of a man? Tilden was no man for the job. He's such a cold fish, and a bachelor to boot."

Albert retorted with equal fervor, "Have you read Henry George's book *Progress and Poverty*? He ties government and taxes together quite nicely. His ideas are better than anything Hayes, Arthur, and Garfield have to offer—Tilden and Hancock, too. But I expect neither party to endorse them. Maybe George will form a third party."

Scott chuckled at the all too serious tone of politics and changed the subject, "Ha! Ha! This discussion needs a topic more interesting to Oregon. When is Villard's Northern Pacific going to reach Portland?"

Uwe reacted with a grinning, "Bah! Humbug! Dad's worried that the railroad will take over our business, but I see it as more business for us. We'll just have to change with the times."

"They call our times the 'Industrial Revolution' back East, but it'll be a long time reaching Oregon, I hope," Johnny chimed in just before Julie banged two pans together. The food was ready.

A week later Jack Sixes showed up at supper time, accepting Julie's offer of a meal and Scott's extra bunk. He was leaving the Sixes for awhile on his quest to find a "proper Tutuni wife". The McClures discovered that Johnny accepted the Indian's case for claiming his land, and his cash horde of fourteen dollars, at their barbecue picnic.

Scott loaned his friend two silver dollars against ranch work in the spring. He explained to a puzzled Julie, "I doubt that Johnny can create a miracle on fourteen dollars. I'll write him that we'll help with the court costs. Might have to sell a steer or two this winter."

Rick rode Rhine around the house, leading Main, and announced, "I decided to ride with Jack to Old John's place. I have Julie's grocery list, and we are due some mail. Maybe I'll have time to visit Harvey."

"Oh, wait Dear! You can take a batch of cookies over to my folks when you deliver that dress material I put on your list," Julie conspired as she hurried into the house, emerging with a package wrapped in butcher paper and tied with old twine.

Scott was equally demanding, "Bring back a bottle of brandy or whatever else George has on hand. You'd be smart to return in daylight. Our river crossing can be treacherous after a couple days of rain."

★ ★ ★ ★ ★

The drum of horses' hooves on the log bridge brought Scott running from behind the corral, his son waving a letter over his head as he crossed the yard.

"Dad! You have a letter from George," he shouted exuberantly, dismounting before the house and saying in normal tones, "I didn't open it since he usually addresses it to both of us. Here, what's he say?"

Scott grinned at his son's eagerness, realizing his own fingers were shaking as he ripped open the envelope. He read the short note to himself, and looking up with consternation across his features, he announced, "George is taking his orders in November and will join a mission going to China at the first of the year. I think he wants to see me although he doesn't actually say so. I'm going!"

Taking the flimsy note from his trembling hand, Rick shared it with Julie, endorsing Scott's visit to San Francisco, "Of course, you should go. Julie and I are sorry we can't see him again, but give him our love."

"I will. I suppose it'll be the last time I'll ever see Georgie. Most of those missionaries spend lots of years over there. We'll have to sell my mare and a couple of steers to pay for the trip. What little cash we have will barely last you the winter," Scott conjectured, accepting Rick's nod as agreement.

Julie offered her help, "Rick will just have to sell more eggs and do more hunting. George always sells all the venison you men offer him. And I can make some more of your clothes, at least work shirts and knitted stockings. We'll get by just fine."

"Thanks, both of you. I'll ride in to Hermanns in the morning. Were any ships in port today?"

Rick answered thoughtfully, "Yes, but the steamer left while I was visiting Harvey. A lumber schooner was loading off Hubbard Creek. You should have plenty of time to book passage tomorrow, although sailing ships can be a bit slow."

That evening Scott wrote letters to his daughter about George, to Johnny about Jack's land, and to his friend Kurt about Johnny's legal work for the young Tutuni. Then he and his son planned his trip and the winter's ranch work. By the time they were finished, Julie had washed and ironed Scott's "town outfit".

"Thank you, Daughter, but these clothes will be all wrinkled as soon as I pack my duffel bag," Scott repeated his objection made before supper.

"It'll be simple for you to find a Chinese laundry and have them pressed before visiting George. And remember to get a proper haircut, Dad. My scissors aren't good enough for your son's graduation or whatever the Catholic church calls it," Julie chattered anxiously.

Rick's lips smiled readily at the thought of his father seeing George again, but his eyes wore the haunted look of farewell to his altruistic brother, happy and sad being conflicting feelings for the young man.

Chapter Nine

A chorus of yipping echoed through the deep purple twilight enveloping the cairn where his father and Buzz had killed the cougar years ago. Rick patted Fred's taut shoulder, comforting the lad as he murmured, "Relax, Fred, that's only the coyotes talking to each other."

Rick was silently amused by his young friend's jumpiness as the evening came alive with the sounds of the forest's denizens. As Fred's form eased back to a slumbering position, Rick's thoughts recalled their long hike upward through decade-old firs and bleached snags. He had led his hunting partner along a trail faint with use, the verdant forest blossoming in all its glory these past few years. The scar left by the great fire of 1868 had been healed by nature, and only a few surviving behemoth firs and a multitude of rotting snags were visible along their path.

Sign of game was still scarce in many areas of the forest, and as in previous hunts, they had seen none today. Rick smiled as his stomach grumbled. Full of Julie's biscuits and fried chicken and facing the fire separating their recumbent bodies from the darkness, he closed his eyes and relaxed.

I'm glad Dad wrote a note describing Georgie's becoming a priest and their daily visits while he prepared for his mission's departure to China. I guess he's on his way now, and Dad will be coming home as soon as he earns enough money for passage from San Francisco. He promised to be home for Christmas.

Ha! Ha! Julie and I are just as bad off. I'll be hunting all winter to pay off our supply bills. Julie's cache of egg money makes an awfully tiny sound when she shakes that can. Maybe enough for presents but not much else. Times along the Oregon Coast aren't too bad, but cash is scarce.

Hmn! Maybe I should follow Langlois' advice and get a job with that black sand mining outfit. Gold digging makes sense when wages are paid. I'll talk to Dad when he gets back, and with his final thought he drowsed off.

* ★ ✭ ✭ ✶

Leaving their shallow cave behind, the hunters nibbled on day-old biscuits and smoked salmon, washing them down with sips of water from their single canteen. Rick led the way across the high ridge into the rising sun, stopping to scrutinize game trails traversing their route. Two hours later Rick was rewarded with fresh sign; Fred quickly spotting a deer's spoor on the north slope.

With a hand signal from Rick, Fred set a brisk pace after their prey, disregarding noise on the likely assumption the animal was far ahead of them—probably at the Sixes water hole. When the lad reached a spur jutting out into a rugged gully, his demeanor changed abruptly. Silence was now golden as he crept forward, the deer's deep hoof marks continuing down the slope. The hunters pressed forward swiftly, yet quietly, Rick taking the point as the glint of rippling waters came into sight through the dense forest. The Sixes was a few hundred feet away, and their game trail led to it.

A small gesture quickly sent Fred gliding to their right toward a mound of rocky soil while Rick light-footed it downhill to stand behind a fractured stump with a clear view of the Sixes. He spotted their antlered stag browsing in the brush across the river just as a shot rang out. Fred's bullet knocked the deer off its feet, its stunned body rolling over a five-foot bank onto the gravelly river bottom.

Fred sprang to his feet and rushed forward, Rick following suit as they slipped down the embankment into waist deep and ice cold water. The lad's energy was running high as he knelt beside his prey and began butchering the carcass. Rick discerned a widespread rack of horns as he approached, five or six points indicating a heavy old buck.

As he hunkered down beside his young partner, Fred asked with pride in his voice, "Do you think he'll dress out at two hundred pounds, Rick?"

"Pretty close, buddy. You made a fine shot from...hmn...maybe three hundred feet. I wish Jack were around to help pack out the meat. His lodge isn't far away," Rick commented and then suggested, "Save some liver for our midday meal. I'll start a cooking fire large enough to dry our clothing. Hauling that venison to Port Orford will take the rest of the day, and I plan to be as comfortable as possible."

With clothes hanging on improvised racks before the crackling fire, the nude butchers set to work on the carcass, soon having their two packs full, plus two haunches to carry over their shoulders. The pair frolicked in water, quipping that their Saturday night baths were completed as they donned dry clothes. Their holiday aura was concluded as they doused the fire, buckled on their packs, and felt the first drop of rain. Winter was on the way.

Father and son stood before the Cape Blanco Lighthouse, their postures denying the near gale wind blowing out of the southwest. *The Pacific was not living up to its name*, he thought, as he watched giant breakers savage the shoreline. Behind him the Hughes' apple trees quivered with the violence as white blossoms flew through the air. Pondering the vagrancies of life and death was new to the younger McClure, yet events of the winter had left bitter memories in its frigid wake.

Rick remembered a good start in successful hunting forays, his father's return from San Francisco, and the grand Christmas dinner, which Julie had prepared for their two families and the Hermanns. Even Johnny Larson and Harvey Masters had joined the festivities, the young lawyer having returned to Port Orford to set up shop in a corner of the store. He had been reasonably busy preparing a dozen wills, probating one such document in court, and was working on several land acquisitions, frequenting Ellensburg and Coos Bay courtrooms on behalf of his clients. The world had seemed rosy.

Change had come all too swiftly on New Year's Day, Harvey dying in his sleep during the night. His demise was not unexpected, frail health and age claiming a victim, but it was disturbing to his friend, nevertheless. Johnny moved his practice into the former Masters house, which he had inherited, but few new clients showed up.

A bout of influenza claimed the life of Billy Tucker's father and kept Elizabeth Tichenor, George Hermann, and one of the Hughes children abed for many days. A month later George heard that one of Chief Te Cum Tom's cousins had died, and Jack Sixes was ill with the disease somewhere along the Rogue River.

Unknown to Rick and his family, a minor epidemic was spreading over much of western Oregon, including Anne's home in Salem. All three members of the Lee household became deathly ill, Angie tending Anne and Junior while Albert struggled out of bed to make a court appearance. His day outing resulted in a relapse, followed a week later by his death from pneumonia. Junior had recovered and was staying with the Gerbrunns while Anne was still in critical condition.

Rick thought silently, Or so today's letter from Angie says. *Dad is shaken to his core, Georgie gone to China, Anne deathly ill, and his son-in-law dead.*

"Dad, little Albert is healthy, and Anne is a fighter. Angie's letter was written two weeks ago," Rick comforted his father with a hand on his shoulder.

"I know, Son. Brooding won't help solve our problems. I'm going to Salem in the morning—on Rhine, if you'll loan him to me."

"Of course, Dad, and we should stop by the Hughes place. We'll sell Patrick that milker if he wants, it'll pay for your trip north. I can bring her over tomorrow," Rick suggested as he planned their next twenty-four hours. His father was healthy enough, and he knew the route to Salem, but he wasn't thinking straight at the moment.

✱   ✱   ✱   ✱   ✱

At breakfast Julie stowed fresh biscuits in Scott's saddlebags and dug out her cache of egg coins to add to the Hughes cash lying on the table, gratefully seeing a wan smile crease her father-in-law's face.

Rick observed the interplay, silently thanking his wife for her warmth and sensitivity. A fleeting memory of his dark thoughts yesterday brought forth his eternal optimism on the subject of life as he confided, "Dad, Julie's expecting in August. How does the name Scott McClure sound to you?"

Scott brightened visibly at the news, even managing a humorous retort, "Great if my grandchild is a boy, but it's a terrible moniker for a girl."

Laughing riantly at his quip, the couple exchanged glances of relief that he was able to put aside his worries, even fleetingly.

Rick accompanied his father down their dilapidated path to the Sixes crossing, both partners advocating repair work on the roadbed, as well as other improvement projects to their ranch. Such talk easily avoided more painful subjects, so that Scott could wave a casual good-bye, flash his famous McClure smile, and trot away up the coast trail.

Rick continued westerly toward the Hughes barn, his backward glance sighting his father's strong back as he spurred Rhine into a gallop, soon out of sight as the dark verdant forest enshrouded him.

✶ ✶ ✶ ✶ ✶

On Sunday the solar rays penetrated broken clouds with an actual warming effect. The Madsens scheduled to visit so Julie could tell them firsthand of her pregnancy. There was a chicken roasting in the oven for their Easter feast.

Galloping into the yard ahead of his folks, Fred called out to Rick working in the corral, "Let's go fishing. It's sure a nice day here, even if it is cloudy a mile downriver."

"You've got a deal, Fred. Put up your horses while I finish my chores," the rancher agreed, waving hello to the older Madsens who were descending the knoll at a more sedate pace than their energetic son.

As it turned out, Julie's father tagged along, hooking a steelhead and dragging him onto the gravel inexpertly, but effectively. Since Fred had lost two fish with self-proclaimed expertise, his father smothered his smile and presented his trophy to the womenfolk for cooking.

Everyone was admiring the sea-going trout when the clop of horses' hooves echoed over the log bridge. Soon a shout could be heard from the knoll, "Hello, Rick and Julie. Is dinner ready?"

Down the knoll trail and into the yard plodded a scruffy bowlegged piebald horse, Jack Sixes riding her bareback, a grin spread over his face from ear to ear. Nestled on his backside clung a small figure with long dark hair, her face obscured in his thick coat collar.

Rick's first thought was that his friend had been successful in finding a wife, and he grinned in return as he stepped forward to greet the couple. He discovered his intuition was correct when Jack slid off the horse with a girl-woman under his arm, introducing her, "Meet my wife, San-a-chi of the Skuleme Tutuni. I found her family living far away from their old village on the Rogue. They live in the hills near Chetleschantunne land—white man's Pistol River."

Standing shyly beside her man, the girl smiled hesitantly, speaking in a slow and practiced tone, "Hello, friends."

Shaking Jack's hand, Rick gazed into a pair of expressive brown eyes, warm and inquisitive. He decided they were her best feature as he scanned the homely young face of Jack's bride, its Indian caste seen in broadened cheekbones, wide pug nose, and a slightly flattened brow. He grinned suddenly, receiving a little response from the girl, and thought Jack no doubt considered her beautiful. She was a Tutuni.

"Hello, San-a-chi, welcome to the Sixes Valley and your new home. I am Richard McClure, and this is my wife, Julie. Her parents are John and Hazel Madsen, and this is her brother, Fred," he stated slowly, wondering how well she spoke English.

A brief look of puzzlement caused her to frown as she replied, "Thank you." Cocking her head to one side, she apologized to Rick, "My English is not good. My husband said his friend is Rick. I don't know 'Richer'. I'm sorry."

"Ha! Ha! You speak very well San-a-chi. Richard is my given name, but my nickname is Rick."

A bright smile lit the girl's face, and she nodded with a quick answer, "Yes, I see. Nickname me Sandy."

Julie now stepped forward quietly, kissing Jack on his cheek and offering a cheerful "Congratulations!" A growl from Sandy greeted her action, and she found an angry and flustered young woman looking at her.

Julie was taken aback momentarily, quickly covering Sandy's jealousy with an explanation, "Welcome San-a-chi...Sandy. Your husband is an old friend, and I greeted him in the white man's style," whereupon she leaned forward to bestow a similar buss on the girl's wooden cheek.

Somewhat mollified by Julie's words and their friendly tone, and after a moment of thoughtful deliberation, Sandy stood on tiptoes and kissed Rick's cheek, stepping back with a smile and a "there!" her glance toward Jack seeking his approval. His nod put her at ease, and she maintained her smile.

Rick gestured to the open door, "Come in and join us for dinner. You can both tell us your story."

Fred took the reins from Jack and shook his hand, offering, "I'll put up the horse, Jack." He turned a little pink as he felt Sandy's lips on his cheek, but he managed a grin and a simple "Welcome to Sixes, Sandy."

Jack laughed gaily, "San-a-chi learns quickly, but she hasn't had any white friends. You can help me teach her your manners and customs," and pausing, added, "San-a-chi has made me a very happy man."

Everyone shucked their coats as they settled about the dinner table, Julie staring at the girl briefly before glancing sideways to get her husband's reaction. Sandy was attired in a beautifully decorated buckskin dress, obviously her best outfit, and one which fitted her shapely figure very well. Catching his admiring gaze, she poked him with an elbow and complimented the girl, "Sandy, that is a lovely outfit for a bride. Jack, you're a lucky man."

Their neighbor beamed contentedly, describing his search for a wife. "Old John sent me to the Euchre River where an eighteen-year old woman lived, but she had married during the summer. Her family directed me to several families along the Rogue River, but there were no marriageable girls in that area—lucky for me. An old chief told me of San-a-chi's family on the Pistol River. He said his 'cousins' had a girl-child with them when they moved back to the coast two years ago. Well, Sandy had grown up since the old chief had seen her and turned into a beautiful woman. I fell in love. Her father agreed we could marry after her fifteenth winter, and besides, I needed to work to pay him for his daughter. Well, here we are."

Hazel blurted out the question on everyone's mind, "Fifteen? You're only fifteen, Sandy?"

"Hee! Hee! Yes, me young but Cha-qua-mi old," the bride answered artlessly.

Jack quickly added, "Sandy had several boys calling on her last summer, but she told me I was the only man she knew and agreed to marry me," and looking about the room he asked, "Where is Scott?"

✶ ✶ ✶ ✶ ✶

With Humbug towering over his left shoulder, Rick urged Main into the cold stream, following the wayward steer to the north shore. Johnny spurred his horse down the far hillside to meet the swimmers, complaining all the while.

"Why did you take our pay in this miserable beast? He's more trouble than he's worth. Why did we work our tails off at Mason's for three days just to chase this churlish dogie to the butcher?"

Rick chuckled as Main clambered up the low bank, retorting, "Ha! Ha! He's a full-grown steer, not a motherless calf, Johnny. I have a feeling he knows his fate. Wouldn't you get nasty in that case?"

"Ha! Ha! Yourself! Now I know why I'm a lawyer and you're a…. cowboy—or whatever."

Quick in repartee, Rick jibed, "And we're both working for peons' wages. Cheer up, my friend, you get to take the Tucker estate through probate court this week."

The two friends trailed the steer over the bluff and onto the sandy beach, continuing their comradely chatter into Port Orford.

✱   ✱   ✱   ✱   ✱

With a gunnysack full of supplies and the jingle of silver coins in his pocket, Rick left Hermanns' store and headed for the post office. Johnny spotted him walking along the street, and bidding good-bye to Louie Knapp, he scurried across the street to walk beside him.

No words were necessary as the men picked up their mail, Johnny receiving three official-looking missives which he ignored, and Rick a single well-worn envelope with his address written in Scott's familiar hand.

Ripping it to shreds in his haste for news, Rick extracted the page of notepaper and scanned it quickly. As relief flooded his features, Johnny grinned and said hopefully, "From the look on your face, it must be good news. Are Anne and Junior well?"

"They're over their bout with influenza, but Anne is still weak and grief-stricken with Albert's death. Dad says here that she's infirm. Does that mean she's bedridden or what? Anyway, she wants to come home, so Johann is handling her affairs while Dad brings her and Junior to Port Orford by ship."

Reading further, Rick added. "Young Kurt will take care of Rhine until we visit Salem next time. Hmn! Kurt was ill, too—really sick. He gave his horse to my father, so we have two horses to pick up. Well, we'll need them for summer work, but with Julie expecting, I can't leave the ranch."

Johnny quickly volunteered, "I'll do that chore for you. I have to check on Jack Sixes' land claim and follow up on a couple of cases Albert and I were pursuing. If you'll loan me Main, I'll leave as soon as I finish Billy's probate job. Say, you can use my place if Anne's too weak to travel out to the Myrtlewood Grove. I'll be in Salem for a couple of weeks."

"Thanks, Johnny, you have a deal if you'll let me reimburse you. And I'll help Jack and Sandy with your expenses on their behalf. You can't afford to volunteer all your time," Rick stipulated as he agreed with his friend.

* * * * *

Three haystacks stood in the east meadow as a monument to their work on this sunny day in June. Jack Sixes took his silver dollars in pay and hurried home to his wife. Strolling across the pasture in silent thought, Rick was concerned about the livestock—or the lack of it. *I wish we had a dozen more cows to feed. All this hay will go to waste on our small herd. Maybe I should start thinking about how to sell our next hay crop. We're going to need a cash crop this summer.*

New Salem trotted up to the rancher looking for a free handout, and Rick chatted with his old horse after he rubbed her muzzle, "Hello, New Salem, are you looking for a treat? I don't have a carrot, but I bet Julie does. What say we try the house for a handout? I can use a cup of coffee. Then we can go into town and see if our ship is in port yet."

The horse followed his coaxing voice to the yard, Rick feeling a little silly but fairly effective in so handling the old mare.

"No, my friend, stay out of Julie's garden," he admonished his horse as his wife opened the door.

She held forth a carrot to Rick and advised, "Here, Dear. That animal had better stay out of my vegetables if he knows what's good for him."

Breaking the carrot into two pieces, he fed one segment to the horse as he saddled up and put the other in his pocket. New Salem would have to earn that reward when they reached town. The old horse had turned lazy since she'd been put out to pasture but had to earn her keep again until Johnny returned with her distant cousins.

* * * * *

Rick rode the long way around, stopping at the lighthouse to contemplate the coming weeks. Julie's tummy was expanding as her time approached. Still ten or eleven weeks, she had told him, the pregnancy slowing her down nevertheless. The Myrtlewood Grove would be a bit crowded with Anne and Junior living in the house, but his sister would be good company while Julie was homebound.

His gaze swept the horizon as his attention wandered, a small steamer changing from a distant dot to a clearly defined vessel on course to port. *Hmn, with that heading I expect she's out of Portland. Maybe she's our ship.*

He remounted New Salem and spurred her along the trail to Port Orford. If he hurried he could be on the beach by the time that steamship rounded the Heads.

Once traveling the streets of town, Rick slowed the horse to a walk, waving to several acquaintances going the same way he was. Marshal Ashton called out from a storefront, "A steamer's coming in, Rick. Isn't Scott due back about now?"

"That's right, Lew, and with my sister and her son if all's well. Want to climb up behind me and ride to the beach?"

"Sure!" Ashton accepted as he placed his foot in the freed-up stirrup and heaved himself aboard. He was talkative this morning, rambling on about events in town and news from up north.

As they dismounted at the bottom of the bluff trail, he remarked, "Say, didn't you have trouble with some toughs up in Elkton? Three thieves robbed a traveling salesman near the Calapooya Pass and almost got caught by a party of hunters. Couple of shots fired and a merry chase down the Umpqua to Scottsburg were all for naught. The robbers passed through Scottsburg and disappeared, and the would-be posse gave up. I wish I'd been there. With a real lawman leading that posse, we'd have caught those bandits."

"If they're the same three roughnecks I saw along the trail, you might give them a careful look. They seemed just plain mean to me," Rick replied, promptly forgetting the robbers as the ship passed the Heads and plied the channel waters into the anchorage.

He espied passengers at the rail, his dad holding Junior in his arms as they exchanged a flurry of waves, but he couldn't see Anne.

Lew interrupted his search, offering, "Rick, I'll hold your horse while you meet your family."

Handing his friend the reins, Rick walked across the sand, absent-mindedly wading into the lapping waters of the port as he took Junior from his father with a concerned question, "Where's Anne?"

"Hello to you, too, Son. Anne's rests in her cabin until I return for her. Your sister's not at all well, Rick, but my grandson here is raring to see a real Indian. Isn't that right, Albert?" Scott asked in a teasing manner.

"Yes, Gumpa. Whah da Injun, Uncle Rick?"

"There aren't any Indians around right now, Albert, but that's a real marshal standing over by my horse over there," Rick offered as a substitute to the curious toddler.

Scott's smile became a frown as he reflected on his daughter's problem, "I don't think Anne is strong enough to ride out to the Myrtlewood Grove. Maybe she can stay with Mary and George or at Knapp's Hotel."

His son had a ready solution and quickly shared it with Scott, "Johnny's up in Salem on business and has offered his house to Anne. He had a notion she might be ailing. Bring her to shore, and we'll ask her. In the meantime, Albert and I will talk to Marshal Ashton and maybe look around for a real Indian."

Rick trudged through the loose sand to his horse and lifted Albert into the saddle. Taking the reins from Lew, he introduced his nephew, "Marshal Ashton, meet my sidekick, Albert Lee. He asked to meet a real marshal—that's you, and a real Indian. Seen any around today?"

"How do, young man. As Marshal of Port Orford I officially welcome you to town, and I saw Chief Old John over at the store earlier this morning," Lew spoke entertainingly to the lad.

"Ooo! Ooo! Ooo!" Albert gurgled in excitement, Rick glancing over his shoulder to see his father help Anne into the dory. The two-year old was absorbed with the marshal's badge and by his continuing chatter. As Albert quieted, Rick became aware that Lew had left them, scurrying up the bluff to answer a logger's call that there was trouble on the main street.

Turning his attention back to his sister, he studied her wan and depressed face with concern, giving her the warm McClure smile which always got a like response from her. He helped her mount New Salem behind her son and chuckled sympathetically, "It's good to see you, Anne. I'm sorry about Albert. He was a fine man and my friend as well."

Seeing tears form in the corners of her eyes, he digressed to his normal blunt manner, stating the obvious, "You look like hell, Sis. We'll have to fatten you up on the Myrtlewood Grove although Dad and I thought you might stay at Johnny's place while he's in Salem. You know, the Masters' house."

He was rewarded with a bright smile and an optimistic expression, her loquacious retort lasting all the way to the top of the bluff. Brother and sister paused to savor the view from the grounds of Old Port Orford, Anne still in a happier mood. In a quiet voice filled with wonder, she uttered, "It's so beautiful. I'd forgotten how much I love this country. Albert, see that mountain off there? It's called Humbug, and that's where Grandpa fought the Indians long ago. And the gray whales sometimes play in the ocean down there, too."

Rick's attention wandered from his sister's chattering. The sight of a stranger pushing Old John out in the street raised his hackles. Marshal Ashton's angry voice upbraided a somewhat familiar-looking man, the sound carrying to his ears, but not the words. He was in the process of dismissing the matter as the marshal's business when he caught a clear frontal view of the stranger.

His sister became silent abruptly as he seized his Sharps from the scabbard, casting a meaningful glance toward his observant father, before saying, "Take Anne and Albert to Johnny's along the bluff trail. I'll give Lew a hand."

He strode purposely forward, believing the marshal capable of handling the toughie facing him, but not his two thieving partners. Recognizing the stranger as one of the bushwhackers on the Elkton-Scottsburg Road, he figured the rest of the gang was nearby. Lew might pontificate about law and order and his role as defender of the people, but these scoundrels were more than he could handle alone.

Rick skirted a building to approach the confrontation in the street, and noticing Old John scooting away from Hermanns' with a fearful expression on his stoic face, he shifted his gaze in that direction. A second toughie stepped into the street from Hermanns' porch, his bandy legs spread in a wide stance as he pointed his rifle casually in the marshal's direction. Rick promptly swung his Sharps to cover Shorty, searching for the third thief as a voice sounded from the alley across the way, "Robbers, there's robbers in Hermanns' store."

The third member of the gang exited the open door with the tight grip of George's fist holding a gunnysack full of goods the toughie was carrying. The ugly bruiser backhanded George across his face, knocking him down the aisle, and Lew declared, "You're under arrest! Put up your hands. All three of you are going to jail."

Shorty leveled his rifle at the marshal, and Rick shouted a warning, "Drop the rifle, stranger!"

The rifleman was startled by the order, and his gun barrel wavered as he fired, Rick, in turn, lining his sights on Shorty's legs and squeezing the trigger.

No sooner had the shooter keeled over in the street, crying in pain as blood drenched his trousers, than Rick reeled from a smashing blow to his body, staggering against a wall as the force of the bullet pushed him backward. He heard a buzz over his head as two pistol shots rang out, a shotgun blast dwarfing their sound. He slipped down to the sidewalk with his empty Sharps as George emerged waving a smoking gun. The pistoleer and his gunnysack were sprawled in the dirt before Hermanns' store, no sign of life left in him.

Shorty cried out again as he struggled to reach his rifle, then Rick waved his Sharps threateningly, ordering in a croaking voice, "Don't try it fella, or else."

As the crippled robber hastily obeyed the command, Rick turned his gaze to the marshal and his prisoner, finding both men had pistols pointed at each other. Gathering his breath to strengthen his voice, Rick called out, "Drop it, you thief, I've got you covered."

Casting a vicious glance toward the menacing sound, the man took his eyes off Lew and was promptly buffaloed by the marshal's six-gun. Scott ran into the street and collected all the loose weapons, declaring with a touch of pride in his voice, "Son, you're no slouch in a fight. How's your shoulder? It scared me a mite when that son of a gun shot at you. And me without a gun."

I'm fine, Dad. Look after George. It looks like he's having second thoughts about killing that varmint," Rick replied as he struggled dizzily to his feet, needing a wall's support to stay erect, thinking perhaps he should have accepted his father's assistance.

Albert pulled back on his pole, spilling a six-inch trout onto the gravel before his crippled uncle, his enthusiasm not a bit clouded by its diminutive size. Sitting with his back to a driftwood log and his arm in a restraining sling, Rick praised his toddling nephew, "That's a boy, Albert. Throw him in the bucket with the other one you caught, and let's find another for Aunt Julie."

Rick had been loafing for a couple of days, ostensibly to let his gunshot wound heal. He and Albert had been spent yesterday watching Scott at work, planting more potatoes and onions, pruning the apple trees, and feeding the livestock. Today he was basking in the sun and entertaining his nephew while Gumpa fetched Anne out to the Myrtlewood Grove.

Albert's pole jerked spasmodically as he hooked a real trout, the boy yelling excitedly as he stepped into the pool and pulled hard on the line. Overwhelmed by the task of landing a big fish, he handed his pole to Rick who grinned and proclaimed, "Oh, no, Nephew. It's your trout. You haul him in. Come on, back up to me and keep pulling."

The lad grunted and groaned in his effort to land the behemoth, succeeding in beaching the foot-long trout on his third try. Rick threw his good arm over Albert's shoulder and gave him a congratulatory hug, chuckling at the boy's effervescence. Both Scott and Rick had failed to lure this denizen of their pool out of its hidden depths over the past year, a small lad successful on his first outing.

Albert needed help in lifting the trout into his bucket and was eager to throw his baited hook back into the river. Rick managed to convince the boy that he must show his catch to Aunt Julie. After all, she had to clean and fry the fish for lunch.

Taking his nephew's small hand in his own, Rick led the jabbering youngster up the path, unable to translate Albert's words but understanding their message nevertheless.

Across the field Rick spotted the movement on the knoll and soon made out the forms of three horses, Johnny astride

Kurt Gerbrunn's favorite riding horse, with Rhine and Main roped to the cantle of his saddle. Julie opened the door to welcome the traveler home, and after a few words, held the horses so that Johnny could run forward.

"What have you been doing? Fighting again? At least you're in one piece," Johnny shouted, remembering at the last moment not to hug his wounded friend in greeting.

"Lew and George were the heroes of the robbers' capture. I was just a helping hand. What news do you bring from Salem? Why are you riding Kurt's horse?" Rick queried with interest as he looked his old friend over.

Delivering Albert and his trout to Julie, the two men stabled the horses, talking rapidly to share their respective stories. Johnny had to repeat himself at the dinner table as Julie asked her questions, including asking about his riding Kurt's horse into the ranch.

"You say you left Salem Tuesday morning? And rode here in two and a half days? You must have been flying, it's over a hundred and fifty miles of roads—plus ferries," Rick burst out in near disbelief.

Julie chuckled at her husband's reaction, but agreed with him, "Hee! Hee! You must be joking, John Larson. Rick and I rode here from Albany, and it took us three full days. Ugh! I was sore for a week afterward."

Sporting an "I told you so" grin, Johnny explained, "I took four and a half days riding north on Main. Coming south I had three fresh horses."

Pausing to refresh his memory, he continued, "I started south at dawn, oats in one saddlebag, and sandwiches in the other. I had a canteen strapped at my pommel and a bedroll on my cantle. Let's see, I rode Main to Tangent and changed my saddle to Rhine, making another change to Berlin just north of Eugene. Darkness caught us in the middle of nowhere, so the horses and I had a nice campsite all to ourselves.

"I crossed Calapooya Pass the next morning and stopped in Elkton for a meal at that inn you recommended. Nice couple runs it, they treated me royally when I mentioned your name. In fact, Augie showed up just before I left. Told me about those three robbers working the Pass and the road and offered to ride with 'any friend of McClures', but I figured my horses could outrun any would-be thieves. I left Augie a bottle in your name and rode Rhine lickety-split for Scottsburg, changing there to Berlin and riding on to Coos Bay.

"There I heard about a regular little war in Port Orford, with Marshal Ashton capturing the three highwaymen everyone was looking for. Didn't hear your name mentioned though.

"Anyway, I rode down here at a dandy clip to get the story firsthand from Lew. Of course, I stopped by to see Anne and Scott since their ship was supposed to call at Port Orford a couple of days ago. When do you expect them?"

Rick was quick to answer, eager for more news, "This afternoon sometime. You might as well stay overnight with Dad. He'll insist on hearing all this news. Now tell us about Jack Sixes and his land."

"I filed all the papers and paid the bill with Johann's money. That state land clerk was afraid to say no to us lawyers, but he insisted his boss would have to approve any Indian claim to land. Johann suggested putting it in your name if Jack can't get clear title. He thought you could transfer it later without a fuss. I trust him to protect Jack's claim, one way or the other. You know folks, the Rogues seem to have fewer rights than other tribes, and none of them gets much respect."

Julie posed the question with which she was specifically concerned, "How is Kurt? He must be pretty sick to give Berlin away. I know how much he enjoys riding."

"Healthy enough, but that bout with influenza aged him considerably. His doctor told him to quit riding when Scott was up there, so he gave the horse to his friend as a gift." Johann quoted him as saying, " 'You two old friends of mine will get along just fine.' I don't think Kurt expects to live very long."

"Hmph! That tough old German will probably outlive us all," Rick murmured with psuedo-conviction, asking, "What's happening in the capital...and in the U.S.A.?"

The subject of state and national politics provided an hour of conversation, Johnny expressing chagrin that Hayes had declared he was not a candidate for a second term.

Rick was more interested in who might be Governor of Oregon than President of the United States. Washington, D.C. was too far away to stir his intellectual curiosity. He was concerned about Curry County and how things would be in the coming year.

Chapter Ten

The first sign of trouble came when a panicky voice called out, "Cave-in! Help, Adam and Jack are buried." Rick reacted quickly, grabbing a shovel as he ran toward the west pit, leaving the horses with the stable boy. Karl Hassler, the straw boss, burst out of the shed and followed him across the dune-like terrain. There were six men mining for gold in the black sands near Floras Lake, Jack Sixes included.

Johnny and the two neighbors had come up there last month, all three men attracted to jobs that paid cash wages. Court duties had called the lawyer to Ellensburg a few days ago, but his friends kept working.

Rick wondered how there could be a cave-in at the pit since the site was pretty flat. He was still puzzled when he topped the sandy berm separating the two working sites, his gaze sweeping over the four men digging frantically in the dune's slope underfoot. Jack's head and shoulders were clear of the shifting sands, but he refused to move, arguing, "No! No! Adam has hold of my ankle. Dig him out before he runs out of air. I'm all right."

Discarding the shovel, Rick drove flat over the sand before his friend, scooping sand away with his bare hands. As Jack reached downward with his hands and arms beside his body, Rick drove his hands deep into the alluvial grains, fingers stiffened rigidly to pierce the black sands. Fingers touched fingers, and Jack giggled nervously at their contact, moaning dispiritedly, "I'm stuck. Can you reach Adam's hand? It's just below mine."

Rick wiggled his fingers deeper in the sand, which felt damper and became harder to penetrate. The men around them followed Rick's example, dropping their shovels to push sand away from Jack, two scoops out and one scoop drifting back into his chest accepted as progress.

Feeling a foreign substance, Rick muttered, "Ugh! Oh, leather, must be your boot. Wait a minute, I've got a finger...it's moving...two fingers...good...Adam is alive." Pulling the fingers now entwined with his steadily upward, his elbow broke free of the sand, and he grunted, "Can you fellows grab Adam now?"

Several hands responded enthusiastically, the miners eager to help their comrade. As they heaved with strength and determination, a hand and arm were followed by Adam's head, face covered with his other hand. Sputtering for air and spitting sand from his lips almost simultaneously, the miner was very much alive.

Curiously enough only Rick paid attention to Jack as the turbulent eddy of sand spilled over his chest. The two friends appeared to wrestle each other for several moments before Jack emerged from his captivity and stood erect beside Rick.

Arms locked around each other, the two friends plodded over the berm and headed for the shed. Karl sent the four men back to work and helped Adam stumble across the yard to collapse in the shed.

The sand-covered miner was safe and sound but disheartened by his ordeal, muttering over and over, "I quit! I quit! I quit!"

Tending over the prostrate accident victim with a damp cloth and a soft touch, Rick tried to ease his concerns, "Easy does it, Adam. You don't have to work any more today."

"No! No! The hell with this Godforsaken wilderness. I'm taking my wife back to civilization. I can always get a job in a Portland mill," his voice strengthening with his resolve.

Energy flowing back to his reclining form as he revived himself with this decision, he struggled erect and all but yelled at Karl, "I want my pay," and in conversational tones he addressed Rick, "You want to buy my livestock?"

Laddie raced ahead, his barking muffled by the undergrowth as he gathered his stray charges and drove them onto the trail. The brown and white collie was still a pup by shepherding standards, but already his breeding was showing.

Adam had claimed Laddie was a very valuable working dog but gave him to Rick so the animal would have a good home.

Actually, the two ewes the collie was herding were Jack's, as was the milk cow roped to the Indian's saddle. Rick was carrying a lamb across his saddle, a present for Albert, and leading both his milker and his steer on short ropes. Their outbound friend had driven a hard bargain for the cows until he had all their wages in hand and then threw in the sheep and dog.

Following this example in bartering, Jack had accepted the smaller share of their spoils in exchange for a rooster and three laying hens from Julie's coop. Both men left Adam's now deserted claim near Myrtle Point with pleased thoughts of their good fortune, also happy to be finished with black sands mining.

They made camp that evening south of Bandon, eating sparsely of stale biscuits and fresh milk, Rick moaning a complaint, "Maybe we should have stopped in Bandon for food. I'm starving, and the Langlois place is a long piece down the trail."

"Nah, your shortcut saved us a mile or two," the less sociable Indian demurred, adding with a smile, "Besides, I'm in a hurry to get home and see San-a-chi."

By late morning Rick was complaining again, "Jack, my stomach is churning with all that warm milk. Hmph! Must be buttermilk by now. There's a farm over that away about a mile."

"Nah, let's keep on the trail. You can eat at Langlois'."

When that destination was reached, Rick's tummy really growled in hunger, but to both men's chagrin, no one was at home. Eschewing the possibility of a hot meal, Rick entered Langlois' kitchen in search of sustenance, finding a loaf of bread and some venison jerky in the pantry. Always nervous when entering a friend's empty house, Rick left a note of thanks for Mrs. Langlois before he left.

* * * * *

Meanwhile, Jack had borrowed a bucket of oats and treated the livestock, letting them drink their fill at the trough. It was still a long way home— for man and beast.

Twilight cast a darkening shadow over the Sixes Valley as the caravan crossed Cascade Creek, Laddie sensing the trail down the knoll as he herded his two sheep into the yard. The ewes' bleating and the collie's barking grew confrontational as the dog nipped their flanks, driving them away from the vegetable garden.

"Shoo, you sheep! Good doggie," came his wife's voice through the trees.

Rick called out as he was emerging from the forest, "His name is Laddie, Honey, and he's yours just as soon as he finishes his work."

Julie waddled forward to meet him, one hand supporting her distended abdomen. Rick could see his sister and little Albert in the doorway as he asked, "Where's Dad?"

No sooner had he said that Scott came than trotting over the field from his cabin, "I'm here, Son. Had to put my Sharps away after I recognized your horses. What do we have here? And hello to you, too, Jack."

Handing the spoiled lamb to his dad, Rick laughed happily, "Ha! Ha! Here's a pet for Albert, and behind are my wages as a miner, a milker for the baby and a steer to sell next winter. Jack owns the two ewes and his own milker. Oh yeah, plus a rooster and three good laying hens from our coop. Will you take care of our cows while Laddie and I help Jack home with his hard-earned livestock?"

He dismounted and embraced his waiting wife, asking his much-repeated questions, "Are you all right? How's the baby?"

"We're both as healthy as can be, Dear. Come along," she continued leading him to the chicken coop, "Let me show you which hens Sandy befriended last week. She's been studying our feathered friends with proprietary interest, so I'm glad you made a deal with Jack. And I hope you two miners are home to stay. Sandy and I need you more than we need your miners' wages."

Rick grinned and nodded affirmation, words unnecessary in their mutual love and understanding.

Rick corralled the chickens amidst considerable fuss and flying feathers, placing the cage atop Jack's pommel with teehees from his womenfolk.

Even the stoic Indian laughed outright as Rick sputtered a white fluff from his lips, teasing his friend, "Thanks for that lesson, Rick, but I don't see any feathers or down on Julie. I guess I'll let San-a-chi take care of our chickens."

The hapless chicken farmer had no retort, merely shrugging his shoulders in self-derision.

Julie changed the subject, asking curiously, "I thought sheepdogs were loyal. Will Laddie come home with you?"

"Good question, Dear. Laddie's had three owners, and he's barely over a year old. Collies are known for being family dogs, and he did come south with me. He'll just have to learn that he's a McClure and belongs on the Myrtlewood Grove."

The warm and sunny days of August passed fleetingly, Julie growing more and more uncomfortable carrying her unborn child to term. Anne was able to ease Julie's burden as her own health improved, and she could help with the garden and the chickens. One night his wife's groans awakened Rick, who quickly diagnosed her spasms as labor pains and excitedly called out to Anne. His sister was calmer and more correct when she identified Julie's condition as false labor.

As her anticipated delivery date came closer, her folks arrived for Sunday dinner, Hazel bringing a bundle of clothing and moving into the spare bedroom for the duration.

And so it was that Julie had plenty of tender care later in the week when Scott James McClure was born in the wee hours of August 28, 1880. The hale and hearty eight pounder cried in a lusty voice for his mother's milk and brought forth a comment from Scott, "Just like his daddy, by golly," and an invitation to Rick and Albert to share his cabin for a few days—gladly accepted by both.

With his grandson came the lamb, a constant companion these days. But Laddie showed he was Julie's dog by choosing to sleep on the stoop, alert to his mistress' every sound.

Fred joined the men in the cabin for two nights as he helped with the third harvest of their hay crop, spending his spare time being the proud uncle. Finally John came to collect his wife and son, plus a couple of gunnysacks filled with potatoes and onions. As the Madsens left for their Elk River farm, the Myrtlewood Grove returned to near normal operation, Rick experiencing the joy of rocking his son to sleep after his middle-of-the-night feeding. While changing diapers was accepted as a fatherly duty, Rick was less than enthusiastic in that task. Fortunately his wife and sister did most of the dirty work, leaving the new father an easier holding and rocking job.

Eventually the womenfolk found a chore which suited him fine, Julie sending him to town to announce little Scott's arrival. Rick relished the release from the humdrum work on the ranch, spurring Rhine into a brisk gallop along the trail to Port Orford.

Hitching his horse to the corner-post of a small building across the street from Hermanns' store, Rick inspected the town's latest claim to fame, reading the block letter sign on the window aloud, "The Port Orford Post, J.H. Upton and Son."

A bearded man in coveralls was visible through the glass, Rick recognizing the usually sartorially dressed publisher bent over his press. Rick knocked on the door, and at a nod from Upton, pushed it open to enter the newspaper office.

Rubbing his ink-stained palms dry on his smudged work pants, Upton stepped to the counter. Failing to recognize his visitor, the newspaperman asked, "Yes, sir! What can I do for you?"

Rick reintroduced himself with a smile and an extended hand, "I'm Rick McClure from the Sixes, Mister Upton. We met during your grand opening earlier in the summer. I was interested in your story on the Northern Pacific Railroad building near Portland and your editorial about the need for a rail line into Coos Bay and Port Orford."

"Of course I remember, you were most kind. Oh yes, you're the new father. Congratulations, Rick! Your father-in-law is mighty pleased with his grandson. He was in here three days ago with all the statistics. I'm setting the story in print right now. Want me to save you a few copies of this week's edition?" Upton asked with a knowing grin at the proud father.

"Ha! Ha! You bet, J.H., I'll buy a dozen copies. So John beat me to it, eh? Julie will be pleased with her dad. What's last week's news? I've been stuck on the ranch," Rick queried and then accepted a well-worn copy from Upton's ink-stained hand.

"All the local news plus an editorial on the Garfield-Hancock presidential contest. I'm not enthusiastic about either candidate. Hayes should have run again. Would you like to pay for the papers now?" Upton asked as Rick dug out a handful of change. "Twelve copies of the *Port Orford Post*, right? Keep last week's copy as a gift."

"Thanks, Johnny Larson will pick up the papers on his way out of the Myrtlewood Grove. Why don't you send me a copy each week?"

✱   ✱   ✱   ✱   ✱

Johnny became a frequent visitor during late summer, visiting Anne and her son as well as the rest of the McClure clan. Laddie was familiar with the family friend, but when Johnny first came to see the baby, everyone was surprised to see the collie challenge him, crouching menacingly before Scott's crib with fangs bared and an accompanying growl deep in his throat.

"Easy, Laddie, I'm not going to hurt the baby," Johnny spoke soothingly, chuckling as he asked Julie for help, "Julie, will you tell your watchdog that I'm a good guy?"

The young mother smilingly picked up her baby and stepping around the tense dog, she said, "Easy, Laddie," and then placed the bundle into Johnny's outstretched arms. The collie watched both Julie and Johnny, and sensing all was well, yipped once and lay down beside the crib with tail wagging in approval.

"Hello there, Scott James McClure. I see you have a watchdog to look after you. My, you certainly are a...err...quiet baby. Oops! I think you need your momma," Johnny cooed, and grinning red-faced, handed him back to Julie, wet diaper and all.

During the ensuing weeks, Johnny spent a lot of time at the ranch, visiting the baby and Albert, delivering newspapers, and helping with the harvest—all good excuses for him to be around Anne through her recovery. They had always been good friends, and Rick thought nothing of his constant presence until his wife called it to his attention. Lying beside him in bed, Julie murmured in a low voice, "Have you noticed that Johnny is spending a lot of time with your sister?"

Rick pondered her words for several moments before chuckling quietly and answering in kind, "Ha! Ha! I do believe you are on to something, Dear. The three of us have always been close, but he's feeling more than 'brotherly love'. Maybe it's her grief as a widow that holds him at bay. He's too decent to impose on her loss."

"Hmn, maybe, or maybe he's only confused because of that Barton girl's rejection. He can be sensitive about being part Indian," Julie whispered.

"I don't think Indian-blood has anything to do with it. He's just shy, but he did swear off women when Sarah jilted him."

Julie agreed in a final opinion, "Hmph! Good riddance, I still say. He's too good for the likes of her. Hmn, Anne and Johnny, I'll have to watch those two."

With a shrug of distaste, Rick warned, "Now, Dear, none of your female matchmaking. Let them do their own thing."

Johnny showed up for Sunday dinner with three California oranges, a rare treat purloined from a shipment bound for Portland. He also brought a peppermint stick for Albert, which nonplussed the adults gathered about the table because they were eager to hear his story of the oranges.

He finally sent Albert outside with the admonishment, "Don't run with that candy in your mouth."

Grinning at his anticipating audience, even Julie watching him from the stove, he began, "Captain Tichenor's back from San Francisco, you know. He went aboard a ship in harbor to visit an old mate and came ashore with a 'damaged' crate of these juicy citrus fruits.

"I was on the beach returning a client, a drunken seaman, to the ship from Marshal Ashton's custody, and there was our old friend struggling with his broken crate in the dory.

"After collecting two dollars from the mate and his wayward sailor, I offered to tote the captain's treasure horde up the bluff to his house. Besides a few splinters in my palm, I gathered the entire story from the retired mariner. It seems that his friend couldn't allow an open container in the ship's hold, and when they 'found' a splintered crate, Captain Tichenor volunteered to relieve his old friend of the burden. No wonder

George Hermann pays such high rates for hauling his supplies from San Francisco.

"Anyway, I was offered a reward for my strong-backed work, and upon telling the good captain that I was visiting the McClures, he gave me these three oranges which I brought for dessert."

Anne smiled in amusement, both at the yarn and Johnny's recital of it. He seldom was given to storytelling, and she commented, "John Larson, I do believe my brother Richard has been leading you astray. That tale is about as fanciful as he tells. Now give us real news, like how are Ellen and all her daughters? Captain Tichenor must have talked about his granddaughters."

"He talked more about the oranges and his sea voyage than his daughter, but he did say her family was well. You know, he asked about the mill on the Sixes. How that man knows everything that's going on in our end of the country, I'll never figure out," Johnny said.

"Mill? On the Sixes?" chorused everyone around the table.

Johnny laughed playfully as he continued, "Ha! Ha! Yes, I was dumbfounded, too, so I rode by it today. Met a man named Girard just below the Sixes Crossing. You know, where that slough is located downriver from the old Indian hunting village. He told me he's making a millpond out of that backwater and setting up a small mill next to it. He plans to cut lumber for local farmers, and he has a contract with one of those black sand mining outfits. Have you heard of one near Denmark?"

Scott shook his head, remarking, "That's news to me, but I shouldn't be surprised. Mining seems to be returning to Curry County. I saw a couple of prospectors on the north side of the Sixes Estuary last month. I thought those sands had been played out years ago."

"With your horses, you could go back into the freighting business, Scott. Someone has to deliver cut lumber to Girard's customers," Johnny suggested.

Rick quickly inserted, "I'd rather sell him some timber. Dad and I will have to ride over there tomorrow and see this Girard fella."

Nodding agreeably, Scott commented, "I haven't thought that much about timber since the big fire, but Buzz and I spent a lot of time trying to make a dollar or two on our logs—wasted time actually. Hmn, come to think of it, Jack Sixes asked me about lumber the other day. He wants to build onto his lodge. You're right, Son, we'll pay Girard a neighborly visit."

★ ★ ★ ★ ★

Father and son rode up to the industrious man slowly, making enough noise to announce their arrival at his campsite. Next to the canvas tent, which was a type commonly seen in mining camps, was a series of postholes. A dark-haired and broad-shouldered man was digging in the loose soil, suddenly using his spade handle to push himself erect and turn toward his visitors. Brown eyes studied them from beneath shaggy eyebrows, his big nose set slightly askew, suggesting it had been broken in the past, both features combining with a square unbearded chin to make his face appear stern. Stepping forward and straightening his back, the stranger grew taller than he had first seemed, and as he flashed a warming smile, his countenance became friendly.

"Welcome, neighbors! You must be the McClures. John Larson described you quite well. I'm James Girard, up from Crescent City. Light down and get acquainted," the stranger invited, remarking as they did so, "Those horses you're riding are fine animals. Are you interested in hauling my machinery and supplies up here when my ship comes in?"

Scott was first out of the saddle, stepping toward the man with an extended hand, introducing himself, "Welcome to the Sixes River, Mister Girard. I'm Scott McClure, and this is my son Rick. We have a ranch upriver a couple of miles. Johnny told us of your plans."

Rick shook hands with Girard silently, letting his father carry the conversation, Scott asking, "Is your mill due in Port Orford soon?"

"Yes, any day now, but I don't have any horses or crew to transport it here. Are you interested?" Girard repeated his offer.

Scott glanced at his son for a nod of approval and then agreed, "Yes, we'll take the job, but we'll have to have some help. Did you say you're looking for a crew?"

"Yes, what do you think of Bill Tucker? John Larson recommended him and said you'd do the same," Girard asked openly.

Scott nodded, suggesting, "Bill would make a fine straw boss. He knows every logger and mill worker in the area. His late father was a good friend of mine, and so is he. In fact, my son was best man at his wedding this past summer. He's a good dependable family man."

"So John said. I'd like to talk to him. And I'll need two other men to build my mill. Maybe we can share labor and save me some freight costs."

Scott and James dickered over prices during the ensuing hour or so while Rick rode into Port Orford to talk to Bill Tucker and check on sailing arrivals. He returned with a pail of beer, having heard from George that Girard liked the beverage, and the three men sealed their deal with a drink. Rick told James that Bill would be out at the end of his shift, and he reported there were no ships in the harbor.

Sunshine brightened yet another day of Indian summer as Rick carried his fishing pole and a bucket of small trout through the myrtlewoods. Walking up to his father perched astride the corral fence contemplating a pair of cows about ready to calve, he complained, "We won't see decent fishing in the Sixes until there's more water in the river."

Scott glanced into a pail and laughed at his son's comment as well as his paltry catch, stating philosophically, "Ha! Ha! You can't expect the best of both worlds, Richard McClure. When the rains come, you'll have a bank-full river, but we're not likely to see this kind of balmy weather again until spring. Don't wish our sunshine away. Winter will come soon enough. Now you'd better make peace with Albert. He's up from his nap and fussing because you went fishing without him."

Before Rick could think of a suitable retort, the hollow sound of hooves on the Cascade Bridge reached their ears. "Who's coming for Sunday dinner? It's a good thing Julie has a pot of venison stew on the stove since your catch is so small," Scott continued teasing as he dropped to the ground beside his son.

They walked forward to greet their visitor, recognizing James Girard as he rode into the yard, his eyes appraising the ranch until settling on the advancing duo. Scott welcomed the man, calling out; "Light, James, and Rick will introduce you to our family while I tend to your horse. You can stay for dinner, can't you?"

"Why, thank you, neighbor, a home-cooked meal is just what I need," James said as he dismounted and handed over the horse's reins.

Anne appeared in the doorway with Albert, who ran directly to Rick's bucket before he reverted to his normal shyness around strangers, hiding behind his uncle's leg to study the man.

"Albert, say hello to Mister Girard," Rick said as he patted his nephew's head reassuringly, and turning to Anne, he introduced her to their neighbor. "Our guest is James Girard, the gentleman who is building a mill downriver. James, meet my sister, Anne Lee, and her son Albert. And standing behind Anne is my wife, Julie. My son Scott must still be napping."

"Welcome, Mister Girard," the ladies chorused, Anne quickly adding, "How is your mill coming along?" She had several more questions on her mind as she shook hands with their neighbor and led him to Julie. Both women were eager for news from the outside—even Crescent City seeming as interesting source.

Girard bowed slightly as he nodded to each woman and answered with a happy look, "Missus Lee, Missus McClure, please call me James. I received good news an hour ago. Johnny Larson rode out to inform me that my ship is in the harbor unloading mercantile supplies. My mill machinery will be offloaded tomorrow morning, and we need to move while the Elk and Sixes Rivers are low."

Turning to Rick, he asked hopefully, "Can we move it tomorrow?"

Scott interjected an agreement as he entered the door, "Yes, of course, James. I'll ride up to Jack Sixes' place after dinner and collect him and his horse. Julie's menfolk will help, too. Where's Johnny?"

"He returned to Port Orford to handle the delivery for me. He'll meet us on the beach at dawn," James answered.

Scott nodded thoughtfully and looked at Anne with a questioning stare, raised eyebrow and all.

Before he could speak, she laughed and volunteered, "Sure Dad, I'll take care of the chores. Now let's stop talking business, so Julie and I can visit with our guest. Besides, dinner will be on the table in five minutes."

The mill owner produced a well-worn leather money sack and untying its drawstrings, commented, "My father's old purse is antiquated but still trusty," and as he extracted two gold coins, he added, "Forty dollars now, and the balance after my mill is producing lumber. Is that correct, Scott?"

"That's right, neighbor. Give the money to Julie; she's our family banker. Maybe she'll find some brandy for an after-dinner toast," Scott acknowledged.

His silent thoughts were that having cash in the house would make winter months more comfortable, and with so many young men in the crew, his tired old back should manage nicely. He and John Madsen would supervise the transportation operation and tend the horses while the youngsters did the heavy work. And maybe he should talk to James about selling him Myrtlewood Grove logs.

The false dawn came and went while they saddled their horses and tied on packages of leather and rope. Jack Sixes rode ahead to fetch the Madsens for their hauling job, and soon Rick and Scott set out. They found James Girard waiting at the Sixes crossing as the deep blue of the eastern sky lightened. With a brief exchange of greetings, the trio pushed on, crossing the Elk River and carefully spurring their horses along the trail.

The sun's rays topped the white sails of an incoming lumber schooner as she approached the snug harbor, men and horses skirting the old parade grounds and starting down the bluff road. Johnny Larson was standing beside a horse and wagon on the sandy beach, watching a steamship anchored offshore unloading crates into a lighter. At the sound of hooves he glanced their way and waved, his attention quickly returning to the ship.

"What's coming ashore first, Johnny?" James asked curiously, unable to discern shapes in the early light.

Johnny shook his head in a show of frustration, replying, "I don't know, James. According to the mate, your mill is all that's left to unload. Those crates seem real heavy, but I can't make out the details."

"Uh huh, it may be my tools or the finishing saw. I wonder how they'll get the big blade ashore? It's awkward and weighs a lot. How will we move it to the Sixes?"

Scott soon realized everyone was looking at him, and with a small grin, outlined his plan, "We'll stack the mill equipment right here – above high water level. Johnny's borrowed his dad's wagon, and we hope the road is good enough to let us take the blade directly to the mill today. The Madsens and Jack Sixes will load two horses with smaller stuff and follow. In fact, I think John should stay here to watch the crates being unloaded."

"Can we finish today, Dad? I see clouds to the southwest and the wind is picking up," Rick wondered in a worrisome voice.

"I doubt it, Rick, but it depends on that wagon carrying the big blade on that rough road. If we can take a second trip with crates today, we won't have to worry so about the weather," Scott explained further. A round of nods expressed both hope and agreement that they should finish before any rain fell.

The first lighter was halfway to the beach when the two Bills ran and slid down the sandy bluff. Bill Tucker and his buddy, Curly Bill, had been working for Girard on his mill platform, and along with Jack and Johnny would help him finish building the mill.

Scott's would-be teamsters and the ship's sailors formed a good team, unloading and stacking equipment, the third delivery on shore being the big blade. Johnny's wagon moved up the hill before ten o'clock, four horses roped to the box and Curly Bill continuously checking the lashings from his seat in the wagon. It was well out of town on the road to Sixes before the next load of crates reached shore.

Jack and Fred led their pack horses past the wagon as it crossed the Elk River without incident, the two young men returning in time to help the wagon descend the Sixes grade and cross the river.

With ropes lashed between saddles and the wagon box to provide support for the Hermann's horse, Johnny twitched the reins and spoke soft encouragement to the animal. Working together men and horses dragged their awkward load into the gravelly streambed; water running through the wheels spokes axle-high.

Curly Bill braced himself against the sideboard and leaned forward to check the lashings binding the serrated steel blade in place. At that moment the front left wheel rim slid off a slick boulder buried in the loose gravel, the wagon suffering a jarring impact, accompanied by the distinct twang of rope splitting the air. The logger reached quickly for the loose end, seizing it adroitly and crawling to the left sideboard to rescue it.

"Damn!" came Johnny's exclamation of impending disaster as the same wheel crashed against another hidden obstacle, the horse and wagon coming to a total stop. Curly Bill's right foot slipped out from under him at the same moment another rope twanged, and the blade shifted position into his ankle.

"Ahhh! Eiyah!" Curly Bill screamed in agony as the steel teeth sliced into his booted ankle before coming to a stand still, the logger mercifully unconscious.

Scott surveyed the situation in that instant, and freeing his towrope; he cast it over the circle of steel, carefully slipping the hemp line between sharpened teeth for a more secure purchase. He backed Berlin up the river bed, calling out, "Go ahead, Johnny, we can't help Bill until the wagon's on solid ground, If we try to pull that blade off him now, it might kill him."

Trusting the senior McClure's orders, Johnny snapped his reins, and the wagon broke free of the rocks and climbed the low bank onto a level spot. Rick leaped directly from his saddle onto the wagon, grabbing a peevee to lever the blade away from the injured man's leg. Johnny dragged Curly Bill free by the collars of his shirt and longjohns. James Girard and Bill Tucker lifted the injured man out of the wagon bed and laid him on the grass, a low moan emanating from their friend's lips.

Scott hurried to the prone figure, pulling his leather belt free from his trousers, and with a firm grip, straightened Bill's bloody leg, grimacing at the shattered bones extruding from torn skin and sliced leather, He strapped the belt around the thigh until the bleeding stopped, and then fell back on his heels.

Watching the probing fingers of James and Bill, he asked, "Any other injuries?"

Bill shook his head and moved backwards, and when the mill owner concurred, Scott ordered, "Rick, get up on Rhine, you and Fred will take Curly Bill into the hotel, Louie will know if there's a doctor about. Remember to loosen the tourniquet regularly."

Looking to James, he added, "Let's cradle him up to Rick on the count of three. One, two, three! Ugh!"

Rick accepted the limp form in his arms and gripping him firmly, grunted, "Let's go, Fred. Bill can't feel anything and he needs care immediately," and followed his young friend across the river and up the grade toward Port Orford.

Rick's mental confidence was confused by the tragedy and his lack of experience in dealing with such a grievous injury; He operated by rote and discipline, following his Dad's orders as he galloped to the Elk River. After crossing the shallow ford he paused to loosen the tourniquet and allow Bill's blood to flow. Cinching it tight caused the man to groan in pain, his eyes blinking and rolling in a semi-conscious condition.

Fred helped as best he could, holding the patient steady during the ministration of rudimentary first aid. His only comment was "Maybe we should ride slower if he's in pain."

Disregarding his partner's sympathetic advice, Rick muttered, "We'll do as Dad suggested, and ride like hell for Louie's place. Move out, Fred,"

Their galloping entry into town did not go unnoticed, and Louie was in the street being briefed by Fred as Rick neared the hotel.

The innkeeper waved him off, pointing to the harbor as he shouted, "Take him to the beach, I hear there's a doctor aboard the ship unloading Girard's mill. Hurry, they're ready to sail. It's Curly Bill's best chance to save his leg."

With a nod of understanding and a touch of the reins, Rick directed Rhine to the bluff road at a weary trot, Rick thought, a frontier town is no place for a man with a crushed ankle, but I doubt even a good doctor can save Bill's leg. However, I'd want to give it a try, if that were my ankle.

The Madsens had an empty lighter waiting in the now-choppy waters of the harbor; two volunteers at the oars as Rick rode into the surf. Fred held Rhine's reins while John's arms circled Rick's waist so he could dismount with Curly Bill in his arms. He staggered in maintaining his balance on shaky legs.

Bill groaned as his injured ankle brushed the pommel, and again as Rick stumbled into the rolling boat. Before they could pull away, Fred asked, "Shouldn't we loosen the tourniquet again, Rick?"

Nodding in agreement, Rick ordered the oarsmen, "Hold it, men, Fred's right. He needs to let a little blood through that leg," and as red drops trickled onto the slatted floorboards, he added, "Sorry about that. Tighten it back up Fred,"

Fred quickly complied, and stepped away with his hands clear. John immediately shoved the boat out to deeper water, and the two crewmen rowed furiously toward the waiting steamship.

A bearded gentleman standing beside the mate at the rail called out; "I'm Doctor Stephenson. What happened to that man? What kind of injury does he have?"

Taking a deep breath, Rick answered in stentorian tones, "A mill blade crushed his right ankle. It's messed up pretty badly below his knee. We left his boot on."

"Did you check for other injuries? How long has he been unconscious?"

Rick nodded in affirmation, and replied, "Ever since that steel blade rolled aver his ankle - maybe an hour. We couldn't find any other injury."

The lighter bumped against the ship's hull, Rick standing on wobbly sea legs to raise his burden high, three seamen grabbing limbs and the doctor grasping the damaged leg with gentle hands.

Rick breathed a sigh of relief, tension every bit as wearying as the physical drain, and handed Girard's tattered purse to the mate with an explanation, "His boss sent payment for passage and medical care, but he wants his purse back, The patient's name is Bill Collins, and he has a brother in Oregon City. Take good care of him. He's our friend."

The mate nodded as he emptied the leather pouch and handed it back, stating simply, 'We'll get him to a hospital as soon as we dock in Portland." Turning his head forward, he shouted, "Up anchor, Jonesy," and swinging around to face the helm, he added, "Ready for sea, Captain."

Rick handed the nearest oarsman a silver half-dollar and thanked the pair, "Good work, men. Buy yourselves a beer on me."

The steamer was plying waters clear of the Orford Heads as the three teamsters built a fire to dry their stockings and warm their chilled toes. The sun had disappeared behind white puffs of vapor, darker rain clouds visible in the southwest.

Louie Knapp made his way down the road to the beach, a coffeepot in one hand and four tin cups in the other.

John spoke as he crossed the loose sand, "Bless you, Louie, you read our minds."

"Mother watched you and the ship from the hotel while I went over to George's and I told him what was going on. She figured you needed looking after, so here I am with hot coffee. Can I leave the pot in the coals?" Louie asked rhetorically after everyone had filled a hand-warming cup.

Dry socks and warm tummies abounded by the time Louie traipsed up the bluff with empty cups, the tree men busily loading their horses with odds and ends of mill equipment. Rick packed the lighter canvas bags on Rhine, giving him a rest from heavy cargo. By the time Scott rode into town ahead of the returning wagon, they were ready to travel.   Rick briefed his father on Bill's condition and departure for Portland, while the Madsens rode ahead to tell the rest of the crew.

Rain was falling by late afternoon, and Johnny returned the wagon to the Hermann barn. It was well after dusk when the last loaded horse crossed the rising Sixes River and completed the hauling job. Tomorrow was soon enough to unpack the freight boxes, and start putting the mill together. James and Bill elected to stay in the tent, John headed home to his ranch, and everyone else accepted Scott's invitation for a dry bed and a hot supper. Rick hoped Julie and Anne had enough food to feed so many hungry workers. With the rivers up, there would be several more days of work at the mill.

Chapter Eleven

Falling snow blanketed the Myrtlewood Grove, obscuring Rick's view of the house and corrals. He kneed Rhine into motion, herding the cattle across the east pasture toward the open corral gate and brandishing a willow switch when encountering a recalcitrant steer.

"Move along, little dogie!" he growled at a confused calf, motherless for the moment since all the cows were in the barn with Scott's young bull.

The snowfall diminished for a moment, and Rick could see his father sitting astride the corral railing, watching the always-hungry beasts enter the gate to reach piles of newly strewn hay.

Rick's attention wandered as he rode to and fro behind the cattle, his memory calling up a picture of sunshine and blue skies, similar to the pleasant fall weather during their mill-hauling job.

I wonder if Johnny is working over at Girard's today, he thought. *For that matter, I wonder if anyone can make it over to Julie's big dinner—tomorrow's Christmas. This blasted snowfall is downright disruptive.*

Gee, she's worked so hard to impress her folks and the Hermanns that she'll be disappointed if everyone is snowed in. Besides, this is the first year we can afford a little luxury.

"I still think I'm right. We should buy that land along Cascade Creek," he muttered aloud as he drove the last steer into the fold.

"Then we'd better tell Johnny to buy that parcel for us, Son. How long have you been fretting about that land?"

Rick grinned at being caught daydreaming but answered soberly, nevertheless, "All month! Ever since Hughes added a couple hundred acres to his place, I've been figuring we ought to fill in our boundaries. You know what I mean, Dad."

Scott smiled with pride as he nodded, retorting, "Neat and tidy is what you mean. Just like your old man. As I get older, I forget youthful ambitions too easily. My vision of the Myrtlewood Grove becomes simpler, while yours has the energy of older days. Carry on, Rick, and follow our dream for the ranch."

He paused in thought, chuckling as he continued, "Ha! Ha! Besides, Girard is buying our logs, and we have our new lumber hauling business. There's plenty of money for the first time in many years."

Scott's tracks to his cabin were all but covered by new snow as Rick trudged into the blowing storm after having stabled Rhine. He stomped his boots on the ground before entering the toasty warm house.

"Albert, close that door! I told you to...ooops!...is that you, Rick?" Anne blurted out as she stood over a boiling pot on the stove. Cheeks grew pinker as her brother laughed at her gaffe, and she quickly added, "Well, it's your fault for being bawled out. You promised your nephew you'd build a snowman together, and he's been waiting for you to come home ever since."

Albert appeared at his bedroom door, fully clad for the wintry snow. Yawning and rubbing his sleepy eyes with mittened hands, he asked, "Now, Uncle Rick?"

As an early dusk enshrouded the yard where the two snowmen builders were completing their task, Johnny rode through the blinding curtain of flakes, roaring lustily, "Hello, the house! Anyone for a snowball fight?"

The words were no more out of his mouth when they were replaced by a clod of soft snow. The challenger slid out of his saddle, brushing the icy debris from his face and searching for his opponent. Catching a glimpse of movement by the now-seen snowman, he threw a hastily prepared missile with deadly accuracy—hitting Albert in the chest. The startled boy's face became a kaleidoscope of expression, surprise to tears to giggles all preceding in his efforts at retaliation. His arms flailed the air with handfuls of snow to no avail, but with joyful gusto as he joined the playful melee.

Scott ambushed Johnny from the rear as he sneaked around his horse to lambaste the younger man with a huge snowball, only to feel a shower of the ice crystals slide down his neck as Anne entered the fray. Snowstorms were few and far between along the Oregon coast, and combined with the holiday season, made such horseplay a rare treat.

Anne soon rescued Albert and pulled him inside the warm house—much to his chagrin. Her lightly dressed father skedaddled across the yard to enter the open doorway. When an arcing shot fell upon the previously untouched Rick, he called for a truce, and the two friends retired to the barn and tended the horse.

Scott was absorbed in the latest copy of the *Port Orford Post* and barely glanced up when his son burst into his small cabin.

"Close the door, Rick," he complained as cold air blew through the opening.

Johnny staggered inside, slamming the door behind him as he apologized, "Sorry, Scott. I slipped in the snow and fell down. Rick thought I was only a step behind. Say, that wind is really blowing out there."

"Ha! Ha! That's why I'm sitting in here. I came to my cabin to stoke the fire and read my paper," Scott retorted with humor and a veiled hint that he wanted to be alone.

Ignoring his father's comment, Rick seated himself on the floor next to the warm stove and asked, "What does Upton have to say this week?"

"Well, this story on Girard's mill is interesting. Johnny, your name is included as a crew member, along with Billy and that new fellow, Rod Bishop. Isn't that the man that replaced Curly Bill? There's also a footnote that Bill lost his leg after all. He's been fitted for a peg leg in Portland."

As Scott paused in his narration, Johnny inserted a thought, "Speaking of Girard's mill, Jack Sixes made a deal with James for logs. Rick and I thought we could help Jack float them downriver to the millpond. Maybe you could sell a few logs yourself."

"That's mighty tough work. Delivering logs on the river, I mean. Who's going to ride those logs?" Scott pondered aloud, his mind half buried in thought.

Rick replied, "You tried it one time, Dad. And Billy has some experience. Maybe you guys could teach Johnny and me."

Laughing at himself, Scott admitted, "Ha! Ha! I was too scared to ride the river. I'm a rowboat man myself. It's too dangerous to fool around without knowing what you're doing. My old friend Jacques was the courageous hero in our attempt. You know, Johnny, your mother's first husband. Anyway, we'll need to hire an expert to help Billy. Didn't that new mill hand say he was a logger and a boom man? Maybe he's ridden logs downriver before."

★   ★   ★   ★   ★

Mid-morning arrived before the last snowflake had fallen, a solid carpet of white covering the Sixes Valley. Rick lunged forward to cast his last pitchfork shock of hay over the corral fence and wheezed, "Whew! I'm sweating under all these clothes, but I'd probably freeze without them. Say, am I crazy or is it warming up?"

Scott unbuttoned his coat, demonstratively, agreeing with his son as he answered, "It's warmer now than early this morning, all right. The wind is blowing out of the southwest, which could mean rain. Maybe we'd better admire our wintry scene before it disappears. White Christmas is sort of unique in this country."

Rick pointed skyward in the direction of the ocean, remarking, "I see a patch of blue up there."

"And I see that the barn eaves are dripping," Johnny observed thoughtfully, adding, "I wonder if my folks will come to dinner."

"I hope not, Johnny," Scott replied in a worried tone, explaining, "The Sixes will be roaring by nightfall if the weather continues to warm. Doubly so if rain falls in the next day or so. In fact, maybe your in-laws will stay home, Son. Traveling could be hazardous for a few days."

Rick suddenly grinned and gestured to the knoll as he retorted, "Maybe they can stay awhile...now that they're here."

The trio hurried into the yard to greet the Madsens, Scott managing to reach the shivering Hazel first. He lifted his arms to catch her shoulders as she dismounted awkwardly from behind John. Both horses were wet, and their riders all soaked from the waist down.

Julie rushed outside to assist Scott, brace her stumbling mother, and support her walk to the house. Scott spoke tersely over his shoulder, "You men get inside and dry off. Rick and Johnny will tend your horses."

"Ha! Ha! Merry Christmas to you, too, Scott! I accept your offer willingly," John retorted as he tossed Ariane's reins to Rick.

The horse nuzzled her former owner affectionately and was rewarded with a thorough rubdown and a spirited conversation. Johnny completed a similar chore with Smokey, sans pet talk, and scooped a handful of oats into each of two nosebags. Handing one to Rick, he strapped the other on the gray mare and strolled to the barn door.

Rick was surprised when his partner swung the door wide and led another horse inside. Jack and Sandy followed to greet their friends with a "Merry Christmas" and a shy offering of smoked salmon.

The table was set when the foursome arrived from the barn.

Julie gave Sandy a hug and greeted her latest guest, "Merry Christmas. Scott saw you coming so we decided to eat now. My folks need to leave early if they're going home today. Did I see sunshine on the south ridge?"

Jack nodded affirmatively, remarking, "The snow is melting already, and there is some blue sky overhead. What will those dark clouds to the west bring? Rain?"

"That's what Scott predicts, Jack...and a wild river by nightfall," Julie replied, speaking to everyone as she gestured at the table, "Sit down, please, Anne and I will serve. Oh! Not you, Dear, you have to carve the roasting hens—both of them, if you please."

After dinner the women alternated between cleaning chores and pampering Baby Scott, who was awake but not yet demanding his Christmas dinner. Sandy paid close attention to the baby and his mother, saying little as the women gossiped about Port Orford events and people.

Noting the Indian girl's interest, Julie offered, "Would you like to hold Scott, Sandy?"

Nodding happily, Sandy held out her arms to accept the baby, cradling his small form with expertise as she confided, "Thank you, Julie. Many brothers and sisters in a big family."

The young mother watched for a few moments, and as she turned away to answer a question from her mother, she all but missed Sandy's quiet announcement, "I have baby next summer."

However, her husband heard her across the room and un- abashedly proclaimed, "And I will be a father!"

Congratulations prevailed through both groups, the ex- pectant mother modestly glowing with the attention while her husband became uncharacteristically emotional, actually buoyant and talkative in his pride at being a father.

Rick's eyes met his wife's glance in meaningful under- standing, and his nod brought a smile to her lips as she told Sandy and all those gathered in the room, "I am pregnant, too, and expect a baby during the summer. Our children can be playmates and good friends."

The two mothers-to-be embraced in mutual joy, Sandy ut- tering a deep-felt feeling, "We friends, too, Julie."

Rick helped Jack peavey the last fir log into place beside the turbulent Sixes River, the proud owner counting loudly, "And ninety-two. That's one hundred and eighty-four dollars!"

"Ha! Ha! That's the way I figure, Jack, but don't count your profits until the logs are in Girard's pond. That's the deal," Rick reminded his neighbor.

Nodding jerkily with understanding if not total agreement, Jack bemoaned, "I know. I wish I could ride the logs downriver tomorrow, but Bill is my friend and will do a good job. When's Johnny coming?"

Rick grinned as he teased the newlywed, "You've been too busy counting Cha-qua-mi of the Tutuni tribe—turned Jack Sixes, a rich man. Johnny's been talking to your pretty wife for five minutes. Hee! Hee! You'd better join them while I tend our horses. Any oats in the bin?"

Entering the lodge after washing in Jack's crude horse trough, he found supper on the table and his friends taking seats. He gibed, "At least you could wait for me—the only working man on the farm. Why it's not even dark out yet."

San-a-chi passed him the meat platter first, replying with tact if not humor, "Richard good worker…but sun down. All men eat…go bed soon."

After eating seconds of the mashed potatoes and gravy, one of the dishes which Julie had taught Sandy to prepare, Johnny leaned back with a grin of beneficence and announced, "Well, folks, I have good news from Salem. The lodge and land around it are officially yours, Jack. Here's the deed."

Jack accepted the paper with trembling fingers, emotion overriding his usual stoic visage for the second time this winter. He exclaimed, "We're landowners, San-a-chi. Just like my grandpa in the old days."

Reading the official form slowly, a perplexed look crossed his face as he asked querulously, "Where does it say Cha-qua-mi of the Tutuni owns this land?"

Johnny produced a second document, shrugging his shoulders as he replied philosophically, "I had the court change your name to Jack Sixes so you could own land. And I named your wife Sandy in the records to protect her rights. Your Tutuni name caused concern in the white man's court."

Jack was nonplussed, his tongue tied in its effort to find words, but his wife was more practical, stating a simple truth as she saw it, "Then son's name be Jack Jack Sixes. We live with white man's names."

Nodding in semi-approval, the Indian nevertheless muttered, "But his tribal name will be Hi-to-mah."

"Congratulations, Jack and Sandy, and you, too, John Larson. How did you manage this coup?" Rick queried in curiosity, aware of his difficulties in legal work on the case.

Johnny commenced his story modestly, relating his lack of success during months of work in the Salem courts. Finally his face beamed with unmitigated pride for his unique achievement as he explained, "I've had enough time on my hands to read every law journal, book, or finding which Johann keeps sending me. I found an interesting case filed after the Indian wars on the plains. A Ponca chief named Standing Bear asked for a writ estopping the Army from harassing him."

As he paused to sort out his memory of the findings, Rick prodded him with a question, "Does a writ in another state apply to Oregon?"

Nodding yes, Johnny continued, "It does if it's a federal writ, but the sad part is that the Ponca's writ was denied by the United States government because the Indians 'were not persons within the meaning of the law'—not too different than the treatment of the Tutuni at Fort Orford in 1856.

"Anyway, I kept reading articles until I came across one which I could use in Salem. In 1879, a Judge Dundy reversed the Ponca decision and declared 'an Indian as a person', and thus having rights.

"I used that ruling in my argument, with the changed name of Jack Sixes and spiked any argument from the government attorney. Not bad, eh?"

"Ha! Ha! Proud of yourself, aren't you? Well, you certainly deserve credit for your legal finagling. Only a lawyer could think up such a story to save the day. I'll buy you a beer after the log drive tomorrow. Your narration wasn't exactly a bedtime story, but I'm going to hit the hay. My blankets are in the barn. Thanks for the delicious supper, San-a-chi," Rick concluded as he and Johnny left the Sixes alone to revel in their new status as ranchers.

✷ ✷ ✷ ✷ ✷

The verdant forest brightened to kelly green as morning sunlight swept down the lofty ridges surrounding Jack's lodge, heralding fair weather for their log drive. Billy Tucker and Rod Bishop left the breakfast table with Rick and Johnny to join Jack on the river landing. He was pacing beside his three tiers of logs, eager to be underway.

"Sun's up! Girard told us to dump these logs at dawn," Jack called out to his approaching crew.

Rick laughed in high humor with his friends joining in, "Ha! Ha! That's right, Jack. Come on, men; let's dump 'em. Dad and Fred will spill our stack into the Sixes when Billy and Rod pass the Myrtlewood Grove."

With a practiced economy of effort, the five men levered each stack into the swollen Sixes, the thunder of rolling logs mixing with heavy gurgling of turbulent waters. Rod jumped aboard a massive fir log, cleated boots gaining purchase on its thick bark with ease. In his hands he gripped a peavey, the tool serving as a balance as well as a lever to free up the logjams as the drive floated downstream.

Soon Billy followed suit on a second fir, and Jack ran to his waiting horse to ride downriver to Girard's mill to help corral the incoming logs.

Rick and Johnny peaveyed the remaining timber over the bank, freeing a pair of logs from a snag before they raced over to their horses. Johnny galloped away as he shouted, "See you at the mill. Be sure to check the bend west of here." The latter reference was a reminder for Rick to check the riverbanks for jammed logs on his ride down to meet his father. The McClures would follow the logs to the mill, ensuring a maximum number of logs made it to Girard's.

Riding drag proved easy, Rick spotting two logs hung on the south bank, which he bypassed. He freed a single log on Johnny's bend of the river before riding up to his father at his own landing.

"Everything is going well, Son. I sent Fred to work on the millpond when Johnny rode past. Let's finish our chore along the river," Scott said hurriedly, both men spurring their horses through the yard toward Slide Ridge—the next likely jam site.

Bill was visible breaking loose a logjam under the bluff, Rick reining in his horse and waving Scott ahead. *This is the same spot where the Madsen cow went in the water,* Rick thought as he scrambled down the slippery bank. *I guess I'd better clear that log wedged into the rocks,* Billy's signal confirming his intent.

Rick levered the troublesome log loose and jumped backward as the jam burst free of its stopper, like a cork pulled from a tilted bottle. Billy nonchalantly waved good-bye as he poked and pushed his entangled raft clear of the gap, riding his own log with the skill of a veteran logger.

* * * * *

By the time Rick was on the trail again, the logs were out of sight. He rode past the crossing and skirted the blackberry brambles, the mill all but in sight when he found Scott afoot below the riverbank, fending off a half-dozen logs. Seeing his dad had the situation in hand, Rick continued on to the mill.

Dismounting before the mill office bunkhouse and still toting a peavey, Rick paused to survey the situation. Girard had tied a boom across the river aslant of the pond, anticipating the drift necessary to channel incoming logs toward Fred and his father. He and Rod were astride logs in this retaining wall, funneling the drive through a gap in the riverbank to the pond.

Rick leaped into the bottleneck beside Fred, manhandling logs to relieve pressure on the boom. Thirty some logs crowded the funnel, Billy riding his log platform in an effort to clear the congestion. Slowly a fir butt slid over the center of the boom, snapping a strand of rope with a threatening twang as James called out in alarm. He leaped into the shallows and waddled ashore, Rod shuffling toward the south bank as fast as he could go.

In those ensuing moments, a dozen logs were herded through the bottleneck, including Billy's own, but when the boom split asunder, an equal number slammed through the retainer and spilled downriver. The ripple effect on the boom log spilled Rod into a torrent across the way.

Scott thundered by the mill on Berlin, heading for the Hughes pasture where he could rescue the dazed logger, who was visible grasping a loose log as if his life depended on it. Rick was quickly in mounted pursuit, both men carrying their peaveys high—much needed tools for a rescue.

Luck was smiling on Bishop as his lifesaver of a log drifted close enough to the north bank for Scott to snag, Berlin's haunches deep in the muddy water before the logger could reach the stirrup. The three men ignored their peril as they secured seven logs to the bank. They could pull them upstream later, but no one suggested they chase the ones that got away. The Pacific would claim them on the outgoing tide.

Blue skies had turned a surly gray by late afternoon as the four horses, heavily laden with lumber, were led in caravan-style across Slide Ridge toward home. Scott looked over his shoulder at the incoming storm clouds and waxed philosophical, "Cheer up, Jack! We were lucky to finish that drive in sunshine. Tonight's weather won't lose us any money, Rick's promised to help you stack it in your barn before rain falls."

"I know, Scott, but I only have eleven dollars in my pocket to show San-a-chi," Jack bemoaned.

From the rear of the column Rick laughed, calling out his opinion, "Ha! Ha! Better than nothing, Jack. You have enough lumber to add a bedroom on your lodge, and we have a little cash. Not bad, I say. Besides which I warned you we'd lose a few logs."

Scott inserted, "Yeah, we could have lost them all, like Buzz and I did years ago. Girard paid us for eighty-seven delivered, and he'll give us a dollar a log for those dozen or so that he'll salvage. I think it's been a good day's work."

Johnny added in subdued tones, "We volunteers appreciated the day's pay as well. Maybe your folks can sell Girard another log drive in the fall."

"And you get a supper as well as wages," Rick called again with good humor, kidding his friend with a rhetorical question, "Is Anne cooking?"

Johnny refused to rise to Rick's baiting, Scott exchanging knowing smiles with his son as they shared a silent thought. Anne and Johnny were becoming close, evidenced by his constant presence on the ranch.

✶ ✶ ✶ ✶ ✶

Spring arrived with a flourish of colors amidst the greenery of the myrtlewoods and the white apple blossoms. Nature's flora and fauna thrived during the sunlit days, the warming soil becoming a haven for both existing plants and the new seeds sowed by father and son farmers. A doe and her fawn joined three calves, a score of baby chicks, Albert's maturing sheep, and little Scott in the sunlit yard one day. Laddie and the women loafed with the menagerie after planting their small vegetable garden. Of course, the dog allowed no one into the freshly turned soil except for Julie and Anne.

Prosperity appeared inevitable as bright blue skies reinforced the McClures' optimism. When Johnny brought word that Hughes was buying more land, Rick and Scott began cutting timber for the second log drive. Rick had studied land plats on the north hillside until he'd found another parcel to buy, and their log sales would pay for it.

Scott had long since acceded to Rick's aggressive planning, letting him ape Patrick Hughes' expansionism, knowing from experience that investing the ranch's surplus cash was a worthwhile enterprise. The Myrtlewood Grove was supporting an ever-growing family.

"Patrick told me there are gold miners working the sands of the Sixes Estuary. Come to think of it, I've noticed several strangers in town—probably prospectors," Johnny mentioned one evening at the supper table, then continued with a smile. "He said to tell Scott that he'll sell them supplies and make a few dollars. Scott, you're welcome to all the prospectors who head upriver."

Chuckling in good humor, Scott explained to his family, "The first time we spotted prospectors in the Sixes Valley, Hughes was worried about strangers on his land. Well, I saw it as an opportunity to sell our extra produce and beef—even venison. We both made a pretty penny from their presence in the area."

Rick nodded in recalling his youthful memories, but Anne had to ask, "Didn't some of those men work for you and Buzz? I seem to remember a lot of field hands harvesting hay."

"That's right, dear," her father agreed, "They were a big help when Melissa was like Julie is now, a young mother and pregnant to boot. The funny part was that I was just like Rick is today; I'd rather have the money they owed us than their work. Ha! Ha! I can still see old Buzz putting our 'hands' to work and going off to fish. Now I appreciate his common sense."

"Ha! Ha! Indeed! Is that why I found you fishing this afternoon instead of trimming our logs?" Rick teased, fully aware that his father had responded to his wife's request for a change in their diet.

Scott simply grinned dotingly at Julie, no retort necessary when she favored him with a return smile, everyone recognizing the mother-to-be rated preferential treatment. She was barely showing her condition, a small potbelly the only sign of the next McClure child.

Julie was alone in her garden, propping up her rapidly growing string bean vines when Laddie growled deep in his throat and flicked his ears. His challenging bark carried across the farm as he raced to the foot of the trail, responding reluctantly to his mistress' command to stay.

"Hello, the house! Anyone home?" A young man's voice called out from atop the knoll.

"Yes, come on down. Laddie is well-trained and won't bite," Julie shouted, standing erect with thickened middle causing a slight strain as she waited.

Two men soon came into view, emerging from the forest before her, both moving slowly and carefully. The taller man was clean-shaven and carried himself with grace and strength, while the older man seemed covered with brown hair and appeared almost frail in stature. Neither saw her standing in the garden, their questing gaze centered on the house and the corral.

She waved a casual greeting, catching their eye as she said, "Welcome to the Myrtlewood Grove, gentlemen. I'm Julie McClure."

The men doffed their scruffy hats and walked into the yard, hesitating when Laddie snarled threateningly.

"Laddie, stop that!" Julie ordered, and addressing the strangers, offered, "Would you like a cup of coffee?"

"Yes, ma'am, thank you kindly. I'm Phil Smythe, and my partner is Ezra Drake. Could we buy a meal from you? We missed breakfast this morning," the younger black-haired individual asked courteously.

Julie looked the pair over carefully, noting backpacks filled with placer equipment as well as their frayed and patched clothing. She nodded and walked toward the house, motioning for them to follow.

Over her shoulder she asked, "How about fried eggs and venison steak?" When they nodded eagerly, she smiled and added, "But I can't charge for a neighborly meal. It looks like you men are prospectors. Heading up for the Sixes?"

Rick had witnessed the prospectors' arrival from the barn and now strode briskly forward to meet them, cutting off the spokesman's reply as the pair hesitated on the doorstep.

"Howdy, stranger! I see you've met my wife. I'm Rick McClure. Thought I'd join you for a meal and the latest news from the 'gold fields', or is it 'gold sands'?"

Relaxing with a chuckle, Phil quipped, "Ha! Ha! More like just plain sands, Rick. As you can no doubt tell, Ezra and I haven't discovered any bonanza. Didn't I see you down at the Hughes place last week?"

With a shake of his head, Rick answered quickly, "No, you must have seen my father. He mentioned running into an old acquaintance from his prospecting days when he delivered our milk to Patrick." Pausing to point behind their visitors, he continued, "Here he comes now, looking for his midday meal."

Walking into the yard from the direction of his cabin traipsed Scott, all three men aware of the Sharps cradled in his arm. Smythe and Drake laid their rifles against the wall and turned to meet the elder McClure. The word in the Sixes mining camp was that the Myrtlewood Grove welcomed friends—enemies received harsh treatment.

Julie stashed the handful of silver coins in her cookie jar and smiled at her husband approvingly as she spoke, "They didn't have but a dollar between them, but I'm glad you offered to help them with supplies. They seem like nice, honest prospectors."

"Not only that, but Ezra is a boom man, and Phil is very strong. We have our crew for a log drive. Dad went downriver to the mill to tell Girard forty some logs will be coming into his pond tomorrow morning. The number depends on how many Jack is ready to put into the river. We only have eleven," Rick explained his jury-rigged operation to her.

"Well and good, Dear. When you ride up to the Sixes to introduce Phil and Ezra, tell Sandy that Anne and I expect her to stay with us after the Fourth of July party. Our babies are both due in mid-July."

"I know, Julie, and your mother and my sister are going to be mid-wives. Hazel has already pre-empted Dad's cabin for a men's bunkhouse," Rick muttered in psuedo-complaint.

"Hee! Hee!" Julie chortled in high humor, "Would you rather deliver our baby yourself, Richard McClure?"

Grinning abashedly at such a thought, the father-to-be hastily retreated in unconditional surrender, "No! No! Your mother is more than welcome to our home, Sweetheart. We men will stay out of her way."

Chapter Twelve

Oh no, not a cloud! Rick thought and then straightened his slouching form to glance skyward. Seeing a fluffy patch of white sliding over the warm September sun, he nodded approvingly and returned to his afternoon dreaming. Fishing was more pleasant when he could let his mind wander.

Laddie's barking drew his attention to the boys' antics under the nearby myrtlewood. Albert was racing incessantly around the bole of one old giant, expending energy as only a three-year old could do. Wait, he would be three and a half next month—as he told everyone who would listen.

Little Scott toddled after him, bubbling happily at play, always cheerful with his older cousin. The dog pranced about the lads with seeming abandon, but whenever Scott wandered off course, Laddie herded him back to the tree trunk. Rick marveled at their collie's devotion to the children, and with confidence in both Laddie and Albert, he gazed anew into the swirling waters of his fishing hole.

Laddie's a fine watchdog for my family, he thought drowsily, *and for the livestock, too. He even spotted those three prospectors who tried to slip past the ranch two days ago. Said they didn't want to bother us, but I bet they're up to no good. Dad was concerned enough about those fellas that he rode upriver to warn the Sixes and Phil and Ezra about strangers in the valley.*

I wonder how little Jack is doing? I haven't seen him in a month. I bet my daughter is still bigger, even if she is a few days younger. Upton wrote a real nice article in his paper about the birth of our babies. Of course, my father-in-law made sure his granddaughter's name was spelled right, Jane Hazel McClure, born July 21, 1881. J.H. had some trouble understanding Sandy's name for her son, Jack Jack Sixes, born July 16, 1881.

Just like his trouble with the Northern Pacific story. The railroad is delivering freight and passengers to Kalama, not to Portland yet. Wonder when the line will be completed? I bet Uwe is making money hauling goods into Portland for the railroad.

Johnny got a letter from his sister Angie last week, saying business was great, but Kurt's health was poor. Maybe Dad should visit the Gerbrunns after harvest. He can afford it.

Anyway, his plan to visit San Francisco is on hold. George's many newsy letters tell him all about China and lots of people in need of Christianity, but never mention returning home. Dad sure misses him—we all do.

Laddie erupted in a paroxysm of threatening barks, no longer playing as he challenged something in the woods upriver. Heeding his warning without hesitation, Rick leaped to his feet and cast his pole aside. Gathering a boy under each arm, he hurried up the path toward the house, Laddie backing away from the intruder as he followed his charges home.

Julie appeared in the doorway with Rick's Sharps, wondering loudly, "What's wrong? Why is Laddie upset?"

Rick set the crying boys on their feet and took the rifle from his wife, pocketing a handful of bullets while she comforted the boys. With a purposeful stride, he went to the corral and climbed atop the fence, watching the trees along the river for movement. He soon spotted the three mysterious prospectors hurrying westward under the myrtlewoods. They ignored his presence, moving at a rapid pace straight downriver. Soon they passed the potato patch and were out of sight.

Moments later Scott rode through the myrtlewoods astride Berlin, obviously following the route of the trio. He waved to his son but continued to track their unwelcome visitors, returning through the apple orchard a few minutes later.

Clambering down the pole fence to seize Berlin's reins in his fist, Rick asked, "What were those yahoos up to, Dad?"

Dismounting with a tired sigh, he cast a glance over his shoulder before replying, "I don't know, Rick. They gave Sandy a real scare, but I can't say they did anything. Mostly it was how they looked at her and spoke to her. The three men left when Jack came home, but he told me Sandy was shook up enough that she had to explain in Tutuni. She was confused by their manner, offering to buy something with a leer or two. She wasn't sure whether it was food or herself."

"Hmph! Sounds bad to me. I'm going to ride into town and visit Marshal Ashton. Maybe he knows them," Rick decided as he led Scott's horse into the barn.

He emerged moments later aboard Rhine and waved good-bye to his father and the women who were engrossed in the retelling of the story.

$$* \quad * \quad * \quad * \quad *$$

"Hey there, Rick McClure! You look a might distracted, lad. Gosh, I haven't seen you in a month of Sundays," William Tichenor called from the doorway of the newspaper building.

Rick reined his mount over to stand before the old seaman and smiled as he replied, "That's right, Captain. Haven't seen you since your wife's funeral last year. We all miss Elizabeth."

"So do I, Rick, but life goes on, you know. How is your family? Oh yes, Ellen sends her greetings to all of you," Tichenor said.

"We're all fine, sir. Little Scott is toddling about the ranch, and his baby sister is growing fast. Time does fly, doesn't it? I apologize for riding past you just now, but I've got a problem on my mind. Three yahoos we distrust crossed the ranch heading for town," Rick declared with a baffled shake of his head.

"Well, there are a lot of strangers in town, but I don't recall seeing three suspicious rascals. The only such character I saw was on the beach when I got home. Reminded me of a sneak thief whom Scott and I knew in the old days—name of Burton. But he was too young. When I accosted him on the bluff, he told me his name was Jones."

"Heh! Heh! Not his real name, though. It took his buddy calling 'Jones' three times before he answered to it. Later the mate mentioned they were both prospectors heading for the Sixes River. But there were only two of them, and they left town yesterday," Captain Tichenor concluded, always ready to show off his knowledge of local people and events.

"Hmph! We had trouble with a nephew of Weasel's a couple of years ago, but I didn't see him along the trail. For that matter, I didn't pass those three yahoos either. Well, I see Marshal Ashton down by Hermanns'. I'll ask him about them all. Thanks for the information, Captain Tichenor," Rick said as he nodded good-bye and rode away.

George and Lew beckoned him in unison, both friends eager to give him the news that Ray Burton, alias Ray Jones, had returned to Curry County. George avowed, "He's up to no good, Richard. He didn't dare show his face in the store. His partner bought supplies enough for a half a dozen prospectors."

Lew added his two cents' worth, "I talked to him yesterday. At first he claimed to be Jones, but finally admitted he was Burton. Said he didn't want any trouble so he was avoiding 'people'. He hadn't committed any crime, so I let him go about his business."

"Captain Tichenor saw him, too. He heard they were headed for the Sixes gold country. I'd better get home. Doggone! I was looking forward to one of Mary's meals, too," Rick lamented with a playful scowl.

"Well, Mary will be sorry she missed you. Johnny is due back from Ellensburg for Sunday dinner. Why don't you gentlemen join us? Bring your family to a party, Rick, and Anne and Albert, of course," George said with a knowing smile and a raised eyebrow.

Returning the old man's look in kind, Rick shrugged and retorted, "You know as much about the romance as I do, George. Neither your son nor my sister will discuss the matter with me."

As Rick reined his horse about, Lew called out, "Give a yell if Burton—Jones becomes a nuisance, Rick. I'll be out to Mason's place on Humbug for a day or two. The sheriff and I are meeting to discuss law enforcement and do a bit of fishing. But I'll be back in plenty of time for one of Mary's meals. Remember, Burton and his friends haven't broken any laws. Maybe they'll behave themselves."

Rick grinned ruefully at the latter comment as he touched the brim of his hat in a good-bye salute, heading Rhine toward home. *Yeah, like a weasel won't bite you when he gets a chance*, he thought. *Burton's shifty and mean, and up to no good.*

Topping a bare ridge south of the Elk River, Rick reined his horse about and scanned the countryside for several minutes. *Hmph!* he thought to himself, *A campsite could be hidden in*

any of the forests around here. There's not a sign of any prospectors—not even a wisp of smoke. Maybe I'd better ride up to Julie's folks and pass the word about Burton's gang.

So inclined by this latest notion, he pushed Rhine ahead at a gallop, following the trail branching up the Elk. He arrived in the Madsens' yard several minutes later to find the farm deserted, horses gone from the barn and no one at home. Concluding that his in-laws were visiting the Myrtlewood Grove, Rick backtracked to the main trail and headed north to the Sixes River.

As he rode off the knoll into his yard, he saw John and Fred with his dad in the corral, looking over their young bull. Rick smiled with a welcome as he called out, "No wonder your farm was so quiet. You came over here for one of Julie's chicken dinners. How are you, John? Fred?"

"Fine, Rick," John replied as his son grinned his greeting, continuing, "Nice bull your father got from Mason. Scott promised me that my cows will get a visit next spring."

Scott interrupted his friend to share a bit of pressing news, "John saw five men sneaking up the Elk River. He thought one of them was Ray Burton."

Rick's gaze returned to meet John's eyes as he averred with certainty, "I did, and that rascal saw me, too. I was sitting on a stump waiting for the elk to cross that glade a mile or so upriver from our place. Suddenly there was movement in the firs on the south side of the clearing, and five men appeared. I figured the gang skirted the farm, and I was a bit mystified by it all—until I recognized Burton. He saw me as I dropped off the stump, and he didn't look happy at being spotted. Got any idea what he's up to?"

Rick nodded as he answered, "Captain Tichenor heard they're prospecting on the Sixes River. George warned me they headed this way yesterday. Hmn? Dad, have you ever crossed Cougar Ridge from the Elk to the Sixes?"

"No, but others have. It's a rugged trek, but Burton's gang might try to avoid Laddie's barking. Were those the three fellows I saw this morning with him?" Scott asked.

Nodding thoughtfully, he responded, "I think so. Yes, it makes sense. I'd better warn Jack. Lew said he was using the name Jones in the harbor but admitted to being Burton when questioned by the marshal. Claimed he was avoiding trouble and hadn't broken any laws. Lew let him go."

"He's a scheming no-gooder, Son—like his uncle. You'd better warn Phil and Ezra while you're up that way. Watch your back trail if you're gone very long," Scott continued.

Fred climbed over the corral fence, hurrying to the barn as he offered, "I'll go with you, Rick. Wait until I saddle my horse."

Scott pushed his chair back from the dining table with a smile of satisfaction and told his hostess, "You're still the best cook in Curry County, Mary Hermann, but that second piece of apple pie does it for me—I'm stuffed. Besides, I have to get home. I promised Phil and Ezra I'd have their supplies at the ranch today, and I'm leery of being absent with Burton and his cronies wandering about."

Lew Ashton quickly asked, "Has anyone seen them since John Madsen spotted them going up the Elk River, Scott? Come to think, maybe I should tag along and keep you company. Rick and Johnny can finish that pie and visit awhile."

Quiet laughter echoed from the diners' appreciation of Lew's attempts at humor, Scott's response coming afterward, "No, Marshal, and you're welcome to ride with me. If all's well, we can manage a little fishing while the sun is still up."

Scott stood erect and reached across the table to accept a document which George extracted from his shirt pocket.

The merchant explained, "Phil and Ezra have one hundred and twenty-one dollars' credit at the store. That's after paying for the supplies you are delivering to them. I figure they're smart to send their dust into town. Avoids temptation of thievery by other miners."

Rick suggested, "Dad, you might check the cattle in the east pasture before going fishing. The rest of us are dropping by the Madsens' place. I'm interested in what Fred saw when he tracked Burton's gang up the Elk River."

"Sure thing, Son. See you all later," Scott said over his shoulder before he and the marshal exited through the kitchen.

Twilight was at hand as Rick led his family into the ranch yard, Julie quick to spot the two figures carrying their catch of trout up the path from the river. She shouted in a humorous voice, "Are those fish properly cleaned for supper, gentlemen?"

Rick blurted out an anxious question posed to his father before he could answer Julie's, "Did you ride up to see Phil and Ezra already, Dad?"

Scott responded to his daughter-in-law first, smiling at his son's concern, "Yep, Julie, they're ready for the frying pan." Holding forth a string of trout, he offered, "Here, ladies, you take the fish, and we'll put up the horses."

Swinging his gaze to Rick, he stated simply, "Phil was here to collect his supplies. He had an interesting story to tell."

Julie had dismounted, but held on to her reins stubbornly, curiosity piqued as she insisted, "Anne and I want to hear this story, too. I'll fix supper afterward. Has Phil seen those nasty men?"

Scott nodded, and after a pause recounted the prospector's tale, "Phil was waiting right here in the yard when Lew and I rode in this afternoon. He looked a mite unhappy and was impatient to get back to Ezra with his supplies. Lew asked him what the rush was since there was plenty of daylight left for his return trip to camp."

Lew interrupted his friend, concurring with Scott's conclusion, "Yes, I thought he was kind of nervous, so I asked him if he'd seen Burton and his partners. Whew! That got him talking, all right."

Scott nodded and continued his narration, "It seems those five fellas stopped by their camp and nosed around some. Burton claimed he wanted to buy flour and beans, even though their pack horse appeared well loaded to Phil. Phil was careful to tell them about depositing their gold dust with George Hermann, and then he complained about how low their supplies were. Ezra fed the gang a meal of venison and biscuits, and with nary a thanks, they headed upriver."

"I asked if they had behaved themselves and didn't cause any trouble," the marshal inserted during a pause.

"That's right, and Phil sounded worried when he answered. He'd tracked them until they doubled back, skirting the camp and headed toward the Sixes family lodge. Ezra wanted to move camp, but their claim was producing gold dust, and they couldn't give it up. He did say that he didn't trust that bunch because three of them were around for a couple of weeks without turning a pan of gravel. He figures they act more like claim-jumpers than honest prospectors. Phil plans to sleep with his rifle while they're in the valley."

Lew shook his head in exasperation as he pondered, "They haven't done anything, but George may be right that they're up to no good. What Phil said as he left bothered me."

"It reminded me of Sandy's fright last week," Scott recalled, "Those three fellas accosted her at the lodge. Well, Phil was worried about 'that Indian woman' because she was 'mighty fetching'. One of the men made that comment before the others shushed him up, and Phil and Ezra are concerned for her well-being. That's why Lew is staying over. We'll wander up that way tomorrow. Maybe we're all imagining things, but Burton's a shifty character, and his partners are no better."

Rick nodded his agreement, commenting, "Burton's disrespect and dislike of Jack Sixes could cause problems. I'll ride with you two—at least as far as the lodge."

Rick and Scott were finishing morning chores while Lew was saddling horses when Jack Sixes rode up to the barn. A grimace creased his usually stoic countenance, and his manner was agitated as he greeted the trio, "Hello, Scott. Rick. I'm glad to see you, Marshal Ashton. I need your help. Those men are back again and hanging around my lodge. I've seen their tracks, but they've avoided me. There seems to be more than three men, however."

Lew answered thoughtfully, "Jack, there are five men and six horses in that bunch. Did you know that Ray Burton is back? Well, he seems to be the boss. Have they bothered your wife?"

"That explains it. Yes, to both questions. Sandy met two men in a blackberry patch. One of them she knew from last week and the other fits a description of Burton. They said something about her pretty legs when her skirt snagged on a berry vine. She said they gave her, a 'man's stare', and she ran home scared. I should hunt them down and shoot them, but I'm a Tutuni. Any Indian shooting a white man would be hung. You're a fair man, Marshal Ashton. Make them go away from my lodge," Jack concluded in a cry of despair.

"Let's go up to your place, Jack," Lew offered as he mounted his horse. Turning to the McClures, he asked, "Are you to ready to ride?"

Rick shook his head, suggesting instead, "Go ahead with Jack and Lew, Dad. I have to put our bull in the barn and finish feeding the livestock. I'll catch up with you."

A quarter of an hour later he galloped through the east pasture en route to Jack's ranch, his eyes ever busy scanning the trail and forest before him. He saw the Sixes' smoke drifting amidst the firs before he saw their lodge. Hearing no sounds and seeing no movement as he neared the clearing, he grew cautious and dismounted, entering the yard. He looked over the quiet surroundings from behind a massive fir, mystified as to where his friends had gone.

A rifle shot echoed from upriver, Rick moving forward on foot to inspect the buildings. Fingering the Sharps breech nervously, he noiselessly crossed the yard. The cabin door opened suddenly, and a gasp of fear and alarm came from a surprised Sandy. She clutched her torn blouse across her chest and jerked backward, her bruised face evident that she had endured recent violence. A full moment passed before she recognized Rick and sagged against the doorframe in obvious relief.

"San-a-chi, it's me, Richard McClure. What happened to you? Where are Jack, Dad, and the marshal?"

Still holding her shirt about herself, Sandy stepped outside, stuttering in English between tears, "Bad men come...take food...grab San-a-chi...tear clothes, laugh...San-a-chi fight. Big man hit San-a-chi...call 'Injun Hor'...San-a-chi run...big man hit hard...Jack come...men go away."

"Are you all right? Can you stay here by yourself?" Rick asked with concern.

"Yes, Jack say stay. He go shoot bad men. You go?" Sandy replied.

Nodding assent, Rick swung into the saddle and spurred Rhine up the faint trail, lifting his rifle barrel as he rode. He pulled the trigger as the sights fell on the blue sky and then honed on the answering shot. His recognition of a Sharps firing was confirmed moments later as he found his father waiting for him in a small glade by rushing Sixes waters.

"Pull up and rest your horse for a minute, Rick. Lew and Jack are following sign up that away," Scott declared, motioning in an easterly direction before adding, "How's Sandy? I worried about leaving her alone after her ordeal."

"Well enough to send me upriver, Dad. She's got plenty of spunk. What's Lew planning to do?"

Scott shook his head with an expression of awe, "Our marshal is tough when aroused, and he's madder than hell right now. Says he's only a town marshal and an honorary deputy sheriff, but it's plenty of authority to arrest those yahoos or shoot 'em, whichever they prefer. Your job is to follow the north slope below the ridgeline, and mine is to do the same along the south side of the river. Lew doesn't want them to double back, but be careful, my boy, remember the last time you helped the marshal. He ended up without a scratch, and you were banged up some."

Grinning cheerfully at the gibe of warning, Rick reined his horse away from the river and climbed the northern slope, guiding on a lone crag of rock topping the skyline before him. He wended his way through the pristine forest for the better part of an hour, finally topping a bare hummock before gaining a viewpoint of the upper Sixes Valley. To the east he saw smoke marking Phil and Ezra's claim site, and below the three hundred foot bluff at his feet was a broad gravel bar in the river bottom.

He spotted the movement of a man climbing atop a scrubbed deadfall at the west end of the bar at the same moment he espied two horsemen driving their mounts up the old burn across the way. He concluded that he'd found their quarry, but where were the other two men?

There! On the hillside, but no, that has to be Dad, he guessed silently. *Hmn, I reckon he doesn't see those yahoos near him. I'd better warn him.*

With that thought in mind, Rick leaned his Sharps across a knot in the fir beside him and steadied his purposefully. He sighted ahead of the two riders and to their left, away from his father, and squeezed the trigger. Even at a half-mile distance, his wandering bullet had its desired effect, striking rock shale twenty feet from the pair of fleeing riders. Their skittish reaction to the surprise shot alerted his father to their position, and he went to ground behind a rock tor, his rifle sounding a second warning to the pair.

The man on rear guard ran to his horse and mounted, riding to meet the two retreating horsemen coming off the south slope. A single rider galloped out of the woods below Rick, all four men spurring their horses up the river toward the gold placer mine. Lew and Jack trotted their horses in leisurely pursuit, the marshal signaling five men who were in the party ahead.

Receiving no other instruction, Rick continued along the north slope, parallel to the gang's line of flight, hearing an occasional shot from the valley floor. Eventually he drifted lower, guessing where he had seen the smoke earlier. Phil and Ezra had doused their fire long since, but Rick's sense of dead reckoning was on target as he emerged from the forest above their camp.

"Halt! Who's there?" an excited voice called from a copse of young firs ahead.

Recognizing Phil's voice despite its high-pitched agitation, Rick replied hastily, "Rick McClure! Can I come ahead, Phil?"

"Sure, Rick. Come on over, but watch for a shooter near our camp. Well, he may have pulled out after that Burton fella shot Ezra. He's hit in the shoulder and bleeding some," Phil rambled on.

Seeing Lew and Jack ride into the camp, allowed Rick and Phil to carry the unconscious prospector down to his sheltered bedroll. Scott came over to help Phil minister to Ezra's wound, and both agreed it was not serious enough to move the miner to Port Orford. Ezra agreed whole-heartedly when he regained his senses, punctuating his feelings with hearty epithets as to Burton's ancestry still resounding through the glade as the four-man posse rode east.

"What's up ahead, Dad? I've never hunted this far upriver," Rick queried.

"Me neither, Son. What about it, Jack? Have you been here before?"

Jack spoke without turning, "One time I followed old trail my grandfather told me about. I went behind that mountain north of us until I could see into the next valley—Coquille River, I guessed. There is white man's town down there, so I decided I had gone far enough."

Lew surmised, "Burton and his cronies will get away if they cross into the Coquille Valley. That's Coos County and out of my jurisdiction, but more importantly, they can reach Myrtle Point where three or four routes lead out of the country."

Scott shrugged eloquently and suggested in a matter-of-fact voice, "Well, let's cut them off before they crest the divide. I suppose we can shoot back, don't you think, Lew?"

Without further ado, he led the way forward at a pace more safely designed to avoid pitfalls of the rugged forest floor than the rifles of the pursued. When he heard the buzz of a bullet, he dropped to the ground and returned fire, the two shots sounding like twins in his excited hearing. His shot was intended more to discourage the shooter's aim than find its target.

Jack pushed his horse through the brush beside the streambed and then followed Scott's example when he drew a wild shot.

Lew drove down the open trail, Rick following on his heels as retreating hoofbeats sounded ahead of their charge. He yelled, "I saw two riders, Rick. They're running, so let's chase them for awhile."

With Scott and Jack well to the rear, the posse rushed on, drawing a random shot every now and then. Lew's horse stumbled in the rocks lining the bed of the narrowing Sixes River, but Rhine was more agile and carried Rick to the forefront.

Galloping over impossible terrain occupied the young man's full attention for the next five minutes. When he emerged into a sunlit meadow beside the river, he found his pair of yahoos waiting for him with leveled rifles. His luck held, however, as his horse's speed caused both shots to go astray. Rick's snap shot in return dropped both horse and rider, and the second man skedaddled into the forest. Lew's following shot thunking into the bole of a stout fir.

Rick raced in pursuit, Lew close behind as he shouted over his shoulder, "Scott, tend to the downed man."

Spotting his fleeing rider take a wrong turn into an obvious cul-de-sac, Rick signaled to Lew, who called out another order. "Jack, take care of the second rider."

Moments later Rick rounded a bend in the now-small creek bed and ran smack dab into three milling horsemen less than a hundred feet away. He swung his Sharps into line and snapped a shot at the left-most rider as a crushing force lifted him clean out of his saddle. Landing on his back in a helter-skelter heap in a shallow creek, he heard Lew's rifle crash overhead, and through dimming vision saw Burton's face shatter gorily, his lifeless form sliding from his horse onto the gravel. The other two riders melted into the forest even as Lew scrambled to the side of the senseless young man. The posse's chase was over.

Chapter Thirteen

Consciousness returned with agonizing pain rocking in his chest, breathing a physical effort seemingly not worth the exertion. His discomfort was quickly suppressed by the anesthetic shock to his nervous system, and a small boy's eyelids fluttered open to behold his father comforting him. Rick divined that he was no longer a lad, but the dreamlike quality of his mind would not be denied. Scott's eyes bore into the childlike rapture of his trance, his commanding plea unheard by deaf ears, "Hold on, Son! Just hold on!"

His corporeal being felt the gentle rocking motion of the horse and the comfort of his dad's arms as he mutely surmised that Daddy was carrying him home. He closed his drooping eyes, deciding to sleep the rest of the way to his bed.

A recurring sensation of patches of light accompanied by fuzzy faces, both appearing out of a darkened abyss haunted Rick's consciousness. Words and features never emerged until one such ethereal vision formed into an angel hovering over him. Rick's recognition of his wife was fleeting as well as confusing, drowsiness claiming his silent thought, *Wait, she looks a lot like Julie.*

Awakening somehow mentally refreshed if still physically numb, Rick opened his eyes wide into a sunlit world, staring at the familiar ceiling and reasoned astutely that he was in his bed and it was late afternoon. Distressed that he could barely move his muscles, he was also amazed that his mind was unclouded. *Golly, I've been sick for awhile—maybe a whole week. Was I shot in the fight with Burton's gang?*

He rolled his eyes toward the sunny window and saw Julie slouched in their myrtlewood rocking chair beside his bed, peacefully asleep. Children's voices could be heard outside, followed by his sister's low voice calling out, "Albert, go find Grandpa and tell him supper will be ready in five minutes."

Julie awoke with a start at the sound of Anne's voice, her expression reflecting a hint of guilt and confusion as she straightened up. Glancing at her husband's still form, she met his gaze for a prolonged moment before she gasped in startled cognizance that he was watching her also.

"Oh, thank God, Darling. You're awake!" she murmured in a subdued voice, her practiced bedside manner surfacing despite her surprise. He managed a wan smile, but only a croak issued from his throat.

Anne heard the sound of her exclamation and queried from the other room, "Is something wrong, Julie? Do you need help?"

"Oh, Anne, Rick is conscious. Quick! Come see!"

However, Rick's smile faded, and he drowsed off before Anne rushed into the room. During the night he awakened in candlelight to find the rocker occupied by his attending sister, her somnolence akin to his wife's. As he watched her weary countenance, he thought, *Both women seem tired. They must have been nursing me around the clock, and I bet Dad has been busy doing all the chores.*

But before he could work up a good case of self-guilt, his feeble physical condition claimed his consciousness. His eyes closed as he drifted off into deep sleep again.

He felt a gentle touch on his cheek, Julie's repetitive and persistent caress accompanied by a loving yet demanding voice, "Wake up, Darling. You need to eat a little breakfast. Wake up, Sleepyhead. I know you can hear me, Richard McClure. Oh please hear me, Rick. You need nourishment to get well. Come on, Darling, open your eyes."

Rick felt he couldn't refuse his sweetheart's plea, and when he opened his eyes as ordered, he was rewarded with a light kiss of relief. Julie's eyes misted as she chattered gaily and spooned water into his mouth, followed by hot milk and then a small helping of thinned porridge. As she reached for a crumb of jellied toast, he managed to muffle, "Nah, enough." His stomach felt full as it gurgled contentedly.

With great effort willing his muscles to move, he laid his hand on hers and smiled blissfully as he fell asleep.

A ravenous appetite titillated by his active sense of smell, his nose discerning a wonderful aroma made up of several dinner orders, awakened him as the noonday meal was finished. He heard his father say, "I'll be in the east pasture, Julie. Send Albert after me if Rick wakes up."

Julie's head appeared as she leaned around the doorjamb, a quick smile lighting her face when she saw his eyes open. "Ready to eat, Dear?" she queried hopefully.

His croaking "Yes" was sufficient response to initiate a flurry of activity in the kitchen, both women's excited voices carrying to the patient. Albert and young Scott came into the room to stand at the foot of his bed and stare in curiosity at Rick.

"Hello, boys," came out a light whisper, but the pair reacted with naïve understanding, his nephew stated the obvious, "You've been sick, Uncle Rick."

A fleeting impression crossed the man's mind. *The boys seem bigger—Scott is much bigger.*

All his attention returned to his hunger as Anne bustled into the room carrying a tray with two steaming bowls. Setting it on the nightstand, she leaned over the prone form to buss Rick's brow, murmuring, "Get well, Brother."

The boys abruptly scooted from the room, his sister's unspoken command of one meaningful look enough signal for their prompt obedience. Julie stepped around the lads as she entered the room to trade places with Anne. She kissed him lightly on his lips and then placed her hand behind his head to raise him to her breast, where she could give him a drink of cool spring water.

Rick thirstily gulped the offering until his wife replaced the tin cup with a steaming pottery mug. Admonishing her husband gently, she suggested, "Not so fast, Rick. This broth is hot."

He consumed the thin soup completely, his eyes looking at the other bowl with hunger. Julie laughed happily at this healthy sign of appetite and called out gaily, "Anne, come help me feed this starving man of mine."

Unable to spoon-feed Rick as she held his head to her body, she let Anne dole out her brother's first solid food since awakening. However, his eyes closed all too soon, Julie's comforting caress, Scott's panting but tardy arrival, and Anne's largess of venison stew unable to hold his sleepy attention.

When Julie laid his head back on the pillow, she found the fingers of his left hand entwined in her hair. The memories of his caressing her neck and hair brought a spate of sentimental tears, coincidental with a broad smile of thanksgiving. Her husband was getting better every day.

Rick awoke at first light to a quiet house, confused when he reached across the bed to find it empty. Dragging the same hand beneath the covers, he rubbed his bewhiskered face before memories of his illness flooded his awareness. His eyes searched the room and found no one; even the rocker was gone from beside the bed. *Well, at least my arms are moving again. Hmn, I wonder if I can reach that mirror on the nightstand?*

His errant right hand fumbled the attempt and brushed a tin cup clattering to the floor. His "Oh damn!" sounded almost normal.

"Rick?" echoed his oath of frustration, followed by the patter of bare feet crossing the floor. A bedraggled and wide-eyed Julie rushed in the room to check her patient, mussed hair and sleep-wrinkled cheek at odds with her alertness.

"You're beautiful in the morning, Darling—half awake and half-dressed as you are," Rick murmured, sincerity and humor equally evident in his voice.

"Hee! Hee!" She giggled nervously as she searched her husband's eyes for confirmation of his good spirits. She sat on the bedside to respond quietly, "Well, my dear, I see you're much better today. Are you hungry?"

"Oh yes, starved! But how long have I been ill? Scott has grown so. It must be Christmas season by now," Rick guessed in a puzzled tone.

"No, Dear, you've been abed longer than that. Burton's bullet struck your chest and punctured a lung. You've been lying here for five months. It's April sixteenth today."

Julie sniffed and wiped tears of happiness from her eyes as she concluded, "Enough talk for now. Let me fix you breakfast. Are you ready for eggs?"

Rick nodded agreeably, and Julie scurried off to the stove, sounds of the kitchen lulling him back to sleep.

Julie's gentle but persistent words stirred him awake moments later. Upon opening his eyes, he saw that his wife was dressed, and there was more light in the room. He mused silently, *Maybe I slept longer than a few minutes.* He shook his head slowly and vocalized his next thought, "Where did the time go?"

"It's repairing your body, which has been a big job. Here, this food will help. Can you sit up if I help you?" Julie asked rhetorically as she propped pillows behind his head and shoulders. She hand-fed him as she had done many times before although he insisted on drinking a half-cup of coffee with his own two shaking hands.

He was struggling with the task of coordinating flaccid muscles into doing his bidding when his father and the boy showed up at the door. Rick greeted them with a smile, "Come on in, Dad, and you boys, too."

Julie took the cup from his hands and spoke to Albert, "Will you drag the rocker in here for Grandpa, please?"

To her father-in-law she said, "Rick's ready for a visit, but don't overdo it. Send the boys outside when they get tired of hearing your stories."

As his wife left, Rick complained, "I'm so weak I can't manage my nightshirt. Show me my wound, Dad."

The boys scrambled over the bed, their shrill voices echoing, "Yes, Grandpa, show us, too."

Scott rolled back the heavy covers and unbuttoned the flannel nightshirt, exposing a rail-thin chest, ribs plainly showing beneath both clear skin and the scarred tissue on his right side. A jagged tear and a straight surgical line overlapped just below his nipple, neat suture scars as evidence of a doctor's work.

"Who sewed me up?" Rick asked curiously as he inspected himself.

"Doc Green from Ellensburg patched you up. Did a pretty decent job after he got over his peeve. Johnny wasn't too gentle in dragging him up here. Doc didn't think you'd live through his surgery, but he went ahead. Repaired your lung, closed the hole in your chest, and cleaned you up. He even came back a couple of weeks later to see how you were doing. Sort of a professional courtesy and curiosity mixed together."

As his father buttoned the nightshirt, Rick grimaced, a muffled groan escaping his lips.

Scott sent the boys scooting for the door with a "Go outside and play, boys," and then asked his son, "What's the matter? Tired?"

"Yes, but…ah..Oh, for crying out loud, where's the bedpan? How've I man..uh..I see, how embarrassing," Rick muttered as his pale skin flushed.

"Ha! Ha! Don't you even remember last evening with the pan? And I thought you were half awake. Don't worry, Son, your modesty is intact within our family. Only your wife, sister, and I have been your nurses through the winter months."

The next time Rick was awakened, it was by tiny fingers pulling on his beard, accompanied by the cooing of a baby. He turned his head as he opened his eyes and found his daughter studying him intently, right thumb in her mouth. She gurgled abruptly, reaching forward with slobbery fingers to touch his face again, seemingly fascinated by facial hair.

"Janie, what are you doing standing up? The last time I remember you were a wee baby. My, how you've grown," Rick said in conversational tones to his daughter, her reply a series of coos and gurgles punctuated with a gleeful shriek.

Julie laughed approvingly from the doorway, "Ha! Ha! I wondered where Jane had gone. Is she bothering you, Dear?"

"Not at all. My daughter and I are getting reacquainted. Come sit on the bed and join us for a while," Rick entreated.

Julie leaned over the bed to kiss her husband but declined with an apology, "Sorry, Dear, but Johnny and Lew are here for supper. Anne took them to your dad's cabin while I cook. Marshal Ashton wants to talk to you about the gunfight—an official report he said. Are you up to it?"

"Of course, and kind of eager to hear what I've missed. Can I have visitors before supper?"

Julie nodded and offered a deal, "Yes, I'll call the men while you watch Jane, but I get to listen, too. Anne can finish cooking our supper."

Rick half-lifted and half-dragged his daughter onto the bed beside him without physical twinges although the effort sapped the little strength he had. With his arms encircling Janie, he talked nonsense to her, getting reacquainted with his younger child. She shrieked her reply, kicking her legs excitedly into his chest. He grunted in alarm but relaxed when he felt only mild discomfort from the blows, realizing his wound really was healed.

Several voices reached his ears as the front door banged open, Julie's cheerful laughter leading an entourage of friends into the bedroom. She picked up the baby and stepped into the background as Lew and Johnny showered Rick with their attention. Scott returned order to the sickroom by suggesting, "Lew, why don't you tell your story and ask questions. Rick doesn't remember much of that affair, but maybe you can jar his memory."

"Well, to start with Rick, do you know who shot you?" Lew queried in an official tone.

"Yes, Ray Burton, and I think I shot him. The last thing I remember is falling backward and thinking it was a bit slow. What happened after I fell?"

Lew smiled as he answered, "You and I both put a bullet in Burton. Hmph! Don't know which one killed him, but he's dead. Oh yeah, one of us hit the fellow behind him. He and his partner lit out for Myrtle Point, where they claimed they'd been in a hunting accident. The doctor bandaged his shoulder, put his arm in a sling, and told him to come back in a couple of days. Naturally, both disappeared without a trace—good riddance, I say."

Scott completed the narrative with a shrug, agreeing with the marshal, "Yeah, same with those two yahoos Jack and I caught up with. They didn't put up any argument, being too scared to hold a gun, let alone shoot it."

"Ha! Ha! Our Indian friend's sense of justice and raw humor proved to be unconventional but effective—your good riddance philosophy, Lew. I took their weapons while Jack Sixes honed his hunting knife and began a Tutuni chant. He managed to wink at me before he got really worked up, and I played along, translating his gibberish into dire consequences like 'scalped', 'skinned alive', and 'castrated'.

"Of course, I didn't understand a word of his tirade, but I answered in kind, using the few good Tutuni words I could remember. Ha! Ha! Those yahoos broke and ran at first opportunity, and we let them escape by firing our rifles into the air. Jack agreed to chase them out of the valley, giving pursuit across the Sixes ford. George Hermann confirmed their departure through Port Orford on lathered horses. Hmph! Didn't stop or even slow down and haven't been seen since."

"Of course, I felt considerably less tolerant when I heard your shots and arrived to find you half-dead on the ground."

Rick smiled with his approval as his father concluded his story, murmuring in his muted voice, "Just as well they're all gone. Burton did all the shooting. How is Ezra?"

"He's just fine, Son. He and Phil have company up in the Sixes Valley. Half a dozen other prospectors have moved in. Jack and I have been selling them supplies," Scott answered.

Lew chuckled at the latter comment, ribbing Scott, "You two farmers are making more money than those miners, I swear. Phil told me no one is even making wages on their claims. Well, I guess Jack can stand a little profit, what with his wife pregnant again."

Rick sought his wife's gaze, and she volunteered, "Sandy's fine, Dear. She helped nurse you during the winter. Mother was here for a couple weeks, too."

"That Indian girl helped save your life, Rick. Your father carried you home in his arms, and that girl ran beside the horse, tending your wounds. You sure did lose a lot of blood," Lew concluded, his tone of wonder suggesting it was a miracle Rick was alive.

Scott was watching his son's drooping eyelids, and suggested, "We'd better let Rick rest. Are you through with your questions, Lew?"

"Yes, thanks. Rick, you get well. I expect to see you down in Ellensburg when you get healthy. I got me a promotion to Chief Deputy of Curry County and Town Marshal of our county seat," Lew announced with a touch of pride.

Rick nodded, muttered a "Congratulations!" and felt his eyelids drop closed of their own volition. *Hmph! I'm too weak even to listen to a good conversation—let alone say anything. I hope I'm stronger tomorrow.*

* * * * *

Feeling a soft warm body against his left hip and hearing Julie's gentle breathing beside him, Rick opened his eyes to find the gray light preceding sunrise illuminating the bedroom. He remained still as he gazed into her lovely face, features quiet in repose.

When she turned toward him and placed her hand unconsciously across his chest, he kissed her arm, teasingly nibbling her fingers until one of her eyes squeezed open to regard his. His wife playfully snuggled against him, bit his shoulder through the cotton fabric and kissed his cheek languidly.

"Hmn, Darling, are you strong enough to be amorous early in the morning?" she teased in a soft voice.

"Ha! Ha! Only in my dreams, Sweetheart. Mmm, but do you feel good. Did you sleep well?"

Julie answered contentedly, "Well, you didn't move all night—not an inch. So I counted my blessings and slept like a log. Shall we eat breakfast together? I can have coffee, eggs, and toast ready before anyone else gets up, if I'm quiet. Then we can visit for awhile. I'll tell you about your sister and your best friend."

Becoming a bundle of energy, albeit a very quiet craftsman, Julie started a fire under the coffeepot and dressed as she jury-rigged a breakfast tray across the bed. Soon she was cooking their breakfast, Rick's nose twitching at the pleasant aromas wafting in from the other room.

She delivered a mug of steaming coffee and a plate of toasted bread slices, announcing, "Eggs sunny-side up on their way, Master, and a bowl of canned peaches, if you're hungry enough."

Rick propped himself up, stuffing pillows behind his shoulders, sipping coffee as he waited for his wife. When she brought the rest of the meal and crawled onto the bed beside him, he fed his ravenous appetite to complete satisfaction. As both sipped the last of the coffee, he leaned back and asked, "Well, talk to me, Dear. How is my sister's love life?"

Julie chuckled silently, reporting winter news as best as she remembered, "You can read the *Port Orford Post* when you feel stronger. I've kept all the back copies for you. By the way, I hear Mister Upton is selling the newspaper. I suppose he's going broke in such a small town.

"About Anne and Johnny, I believe they'd be married by now if you'd been well. They have an understanding, but Anne wouldn't leave your side all winter. Then, too, George's bad leg has been acting up, particularly during the winter's cold and wet weather. Johnny told us his father could hardly walk in February, and he's been filling in for him.

"Anyway, there was a side benefit to Johnny's being in the store. He saw more people and landed a score of wills and deeds to write. You know how he dislikes being a clerk, and yet he's agreed to go partners with his folks. He's already moved in his lawyer's desk back into his 'niche' and works behind the counter or at the desk almost every day."

Rick nodded approvingly, "Yes, we talked about the Hermann store one day. He realizes legal work is limited in Port Orford, and he knows that George and Mary need help. He remembers John and Annie Larson, his natural parents, but he loves his foster parents and feels a strong family obligation to them. Angie has offered her folks a home in Salem, but they are an independent couple—and both love Curry County."

Julie concurred before changing the subject, "Johnny told me he would never leave Port Orford again. This country is his home.

"Captain Tichenor asks about you regularly. He still sails to San Francisco to visit Ellen and his granddaughters but has taken to spending more time at home. It seems he has a ladyfriend. Mary told me she expects them to get married this summer."

"More power to him, I say," Rick offered with a smile, adding, "How's Louie Knapp? And Grandma Knapp?"

"Both are fine, Dear. Louie was out to see you twice this winter, and he sent his best regards through Johnny yesterday. And Rachel was her perky self when your father and I ate dinner at the hotel last month. Scott, bless his heart, insisted I take a break, and as usual, he was right. I needed a day off and was almost relaxed by the time we got home."

"I visited the Hermanns and stopped by the Tuckers' place to see Beth—she's expecting in the fall. On the way home I congratulated the father-to-be at Girard's mill, and then we rode over to say hello to the Hughes family. Scott was a bit flustered, but pleased I believe, when I gave him a big kiss and a 'thanks, Father' in appreciation of his thoughtfulness."

"Dad's mightily impressed with Julie—as we all are. Is this a personal visit, or can I talk to the two of you?" a robed and freshly awakened Anne asked from the doorway.

"Come on in, Sis. I understand you've been nursing me these past weeks. Thank you," Rick stated formally, grinning devilishly as he added in sotto voce, "I reckon that stymied your love life a little bit, eh?"

She laughed with tongue in cheek, "Well, I could hold up my end of this conversation with stories of how big a boy your nephew is becoming, a description of that shipwreck off the dunes this winter, or tell about the new fish cannery in Umpqua. But what I really need is your advice about my so-called love life. Are you up to being a big brother?"

Realizing Anne was serious despite their light-hearted banter, Rick nodded soberly, assenting, "Of course. I can listen pretty well, but I'm not sure about being wise enough to give advice. Has Johnny proposed marriage?"

Smiling at her brother's usual bluntness, Anne answered, "You do get right to the point, don't you? Let's just say we've discussed the subject at length. We do share a lot of common likes, values, and memories, and I do love Johnny. Albert was my first and only true love, and although Johnny doesn't discuss Sarah freely, I suspect he felt the same way about her."

Concurring with a thoughtful nod, Rick said, "You're right, I'm sure. Even though he's never told me in so many words, Sarah is a memory of the past, which he won't or can't forget. But if you are both open and sharing, such memories shouldn't be a hindrance to a happy marriage."

"I told him that, and Dad's expressed his approval to both of us, but you and Julie have never said anything. You know Johnny's strong feelings about his Indian heritage. It gets in the way of his common sense. You're his best friends, and he's worried because you haven't said a good word to him about our seeing each other," Anne paused before asking a favor, "Would you talk to him this evening, Rick?"

The gleeful voices of children playing in the afternoon sun were a balm to a recuperating young farmer rocking on the porch with his daughter in his lap. Rick and Jane were watching Albert and Scott throw a stick away from Laddie, who fetched it to them with a repetition worthy of only boredom to an adult. However, the boys' enthusiasm ensured the collie's rote task was continued without pause.

Rick had gained strength over the past several weeks, his old robust self replacing the gaunt invalid following his return to consciousness. He'd been fishing this morning, catching enough trout for their midday dinner. *At least I'm of some use again,* he thought, *fishing and then tending the children while the women prepare for the wedding.*

Ha! Ha! Johnny didn't waste any time proposing marriage after we had that chat about his being my brother-in-law. Of course, they had to wait until I am recovered enough to stand up for him as best man. I reckon Anne will set the date when Johnny comes to supper this evening. I wonder if...hmn! Why's Laddie acting up?

The watchdog had deserted the boys' game and began barking. As he advanced across the yard facing the knoll, his hackles raised and flashing fangs showed as he challenged an approaching stranger.

"Laddie! Stay! And be quiet, we've all heard you," Rick ordered, calling up the trail, "Come on down, stranger. Welcome to the Myrtlewood Grove."

He peered through the trees lining the pathway, seeking to identify the dark shadow visible in the rays of sunshine breaking through the canopy of firs. No shape or color was distinguishable as the figure walked down the trail with a strangely familiar gait.

It was but a moment later that Rick leaped from his rocker, startling Jane as his left arm held her tight. Realization that the approaching man wore a black habit of a priest caused him to croak excitedly, "Georgie! Is that you coming home, Georgie?"

Aware of the sudden silence in the house behind him and with full recognition of his brother rushing toward him, Rick shouted, "Anne, come quick, Georgie's home!"

He met George in the yard with a firm embrace, his brother being careful not to squeeze his niece in the greeting.

"Rick, am I ever glad to see you on your feet. Johnny told me you were much better, but I've been worried. I've said many prayers for you. Say, is this young lady my niece Jane?" George prattled on as he took the baby into his own arms.

Anne rushed forward with a screech of joy, hugging her brother as she said, "Georgie, you made it. It's so good to see you, Little Brother."

The three siblings stood in close embrace for several moments, no further words necessary as tears appeared in their eyes.

"Are you Uncle George?" Albert queried in a serious tone, breaking the sentimental moment.

George knelt to give each boy a hug, affirming his relationship, "Yes, I am. You're Albert, and you just had your fourth birthday. I have a gift for you from China in my luggage. Johnny will bring it up later. And you are Scott, almost two years old, aren't you?"

Both boys nodded in turn, somewhat tongue-tied by their uncle's demeanor and appearance, Albert finally stating, "Laddie's our watchdog."

"And a fine one he is, Nephew. He heard me crossing the old bridge," George responded, turning to greet the waiting Julie with a bit of Celtic-Gaelic blarney, "Hello, Julie dear. I see my brother had the good sense to inveigle you into marriage—he's a lucky man. Who thought a couple of rough Oregon backwoodsmen fighting in the streets of San Francisco would ever meet with your approval."

Rick giggled happily as Julie and George embraced, teasingly saying, "Hee! Hee! I told you George has some Irish hidden in his Scots ancestry—more than Anne or I. How do your superiors put up with you, Father George?"

Julie protested, "Oh, Rick...", but George merely laughed, quickly retorting, "That's all right, Julie. It's good to be home and find my brother's sense of humor intact. To be truthful, I thought I might be coming home to a funeral instead of a wedding."

Turning to his sister with a twisted grin, he continued, "You and Johnny will have to set the date pretty soon if I'm going to do the honors—Johnny's already asked. I'm due back in San Francisco by the end of the month."

"Oh, that's wonderful, Georgie. I mean that you can marry us. Are you going back to Shanghai soon? Actually, I'm surprised you could make it home. China's a long way off," Anne responded.

George gazed fondly at his brother as he explained his visit, "My superior, Father John, remembered both Rick and my father. When Dad's letter arrived at the mission he was very sympathetic but still denied my request to return home. I made a few choice comments when he said no, the gist of my argument being that I was going with or without the church's blessing.

Father John was very forgiving of my effrontery and actually found a way to send me home. He transferred me to a mission being established this summer near Canton and then sent me to San Francisco to help Father Francis organize the mission."

Rick interrupted with a question, "Does Dad know you're coming?"

As George shook his head no, Rick suggested, "Dad's working in the east pasture. Why don't you go see him? He'll be so glad to see you. And besides, you can tell us the whole story when we're together at supper."

★　★　★　★　★

Scott's booming laughter punctuated George's humorous story, delight in his son's unexpected presence matching a father's pride in this man of the world. George was not yet twenty-one years of age but already a well-traveled scholar.

George's expression of subdued glee became somber as he studied his brother's tired countenance across the table. With a slight grin he asked, "Golly, Rick, how can we go hiking tomorrow if you don't get your sleep?"

Nodding agreeably as he rose from his chair, Rick returned the gibe, "Little Brother, you've always wanted to make such a statement but had to wait for just the right occasion. Next you'll remind me of our voyage to San Francisco when you ate constantly while I was forever seasick at the rail. I do believe there's a bit of the devil in our family priest, folks."

"You're right, as usual, Rick, although Father John called it 'being playful'. I'll have to be old sober sides in Canton. Father Francis is quite prim and proper and takes life very seriously. Even the bishop reacts to his dedication to the church. Ha! Ha! That may be why Father Francis is being sent to China. Oops, there's another irreverent thought," George concluded with a carefree air.

Scott smiled as he asked, "I'm glad you can relax at home with your family. How do you behave with the other priests?"

"About the same as with my friends, but I work hard not to offend the traditionalists in my order. Not too different than life in a small town like Port Orford," George responded and then addressed his brother; "We're off for Slide Ridge at eight. Get your rest!"

Three days of exploration and reminiscence had restored some of Rick's physical and mental endurance, his aching muscles demonstrating good strength. On the fifth day the brothers set off to locate the site of Buzz's heroism—and death. Laddie was allowed to take Cougar's role as companion as the trio ventured forth, first to the Sixes and over its broad gravel bed to the south side. George insisted on leading the way, concentrating on the still vivid memories of the great fire of 1868 when he'd accompanied Buzz on a hunting trip to this region. Gone were the massive firs forming a canopy overhead, and gone too were the towers of flame and smoke that had so terrified the young lad.

When Rick began gasping for air in his effort to keep up, George paused to look about them, commenting, "We're in the right spot, but the firs are so much smaller. Still, it's a lot greener here than the last time I saw it. Buzz and I hunted this ridge, and Cougar found water in the creek. Isn't the pool located just over that knoll up there and down in a ravine?"

"I think so, although I haven't been up here since the last time we came together. Carry on, Georgie, I'll stay with you," Rick promised.

Moments later they topped the heights and began their descent, crossing a rocky hillside. Laddie raced ahead, sensing their destination as he began barking from the bottom of the ravine. Both brothers spotted the collie lapping water at a pool, remarkably changed over the years, but still theirs.

"I reckon a couple of rock slides have reshaped the creek bed, but here's where Buzz saved your life, Georgie."

Crouching low amidst crumbled boulders and fingering the gravelly debris, George picked up a button, turning it over in his palm as he asked plaintively, "Wasn't Buzz wearing a plaid shirt with bone-colored buttons like this one? Golly, my memory is lousy."

The brothers stood side by side gazing over Georgie's nostalgic site, Rick finally suggesting, "Why don't we say a silent prayer for Buzz and head home. Dad will be waiting to hear about our adventure even though he never comes up here."

The trio returned to find Scott and his grandsons beside the gravel bed river crossing, fishing and waiting for them. Their father was happy to hear their hiking tale and pleased to see Rick with ruddy cheeks and a second wind.

"Well, Sons, I'm glad you had a chance to re-explore the valley together during the week, but this weekend belongs to our women. Rick, why don't you take the boys back to the house while George and I do some serious fishing. Why, we might even take a dip in the river, it's sure warm enough."

Chapter Fourteen

Johnny's Saturday night bachelor's party was a lively affair until a swirling summer mist combined with darkness to end the revelry. Billy Tucker and Jack Sixes had pregnant wives to pick up at the Hermanns' and Louie Knapp had to see the hotel guests and light his famous "mariners'" lantern in his highest window, Cape Blanco Lighthouse or not. Lew Ashton helped him carry a stack of cooking utensils back to the hotel.

Captain Tichenor and John Madsen headed for home and bed, as did the Sixes group of Patrick Hughes, James Girard, and Rod Bishop. Soon only the overnight guests and Uwe Gerbrunn were left at the Larson house. Uwe and Angie had arrived with their four children earlier in the week by ship and were staying at the crowded Hermann home, site of tomorrow's wedding.

Johnny offered, "Why don't you stay here, Uwe? We have plenty of floor space left."

"Sure, Johnny. I don't relish the idea of spending the night listening to women plot your wedding. Now I know why Johann insisted on staying with Dad, who wanted to come despite his frailty. Anyway, both send best wishes and a gift, along with all of Anne's furniture and knickknacks from our attic. Besides, what's good enough for my father-in-law is good enough for me."

Scott chuckled humorously as he gibed, "Ha! Ha! That's not quite right, Uwe. George is sleeping in the bed, and I've claimed the sofa. Age has its prerogatives, you know."

Rick joined the teasing repartee as he nodded to Fred Madsen slipping through the door, "Well, Phil usually sleeps on the ground, and George is supposed to abstain from luxury, but Fred here seems to be walking on air. How is that women's party going? I suppose Delores chased you out?"

"Oh no, her mother made her…," Fred retorted spontaneously, blushing as he faced Uwe and concluded more thoughtfully, "Angie said she had to wash dishes and men weren't welcome in the house. We were being very proper sitting on the porch."

A sympathetic Georgie consoled the young lover, "Of course, you were. You were both responsible youngsters. Don't let your brother kid you. Delores is a lovely girl—looks like her mother. Wasn't Angie about her age when you met her, Uwe?"

"Ha! Ha! A point well taken, Georgie!" Uwe agreed readily but added a father's correction to Fred, "Of course, Angie was older than fifteen, young man."

As George yawned and disappeared into the bedroom, Scott lay back on the sofa, ousting his sons unceremoniously as he bid goodnight, "I'm for bed, and George needs his rest. Who's cooking breakfast?"

A refreshing off-shore breeze made the summer sun bearable to the wedding guests congregated in the Hermanns' yard to celebrate the recent rite of marriage performed by Father George. The bride and groom had socialized with their family and friends before cutting the cake. With the afternoon wearing on, Johnny's patience was growing thin, and he whispered an aside in Anne's ear.

Her answering giggle reached Rick and Julie on the porch, and as the newlyweds separated to maneuver toward the harbor, best man and maid of honor followed discretely. Johnny and Anne came together to join hands and lengthen their strides down the street, the bride lifting her long hem high in the air. Rick and Julie led a cheering crowd of well-wishers while tactfully impeding their pursuit.

Seemingly before anyone realized it, the couple was entering the Knapp Hotel where their "honeymoon suite" was waiting—Louie's best room.

Mary's voice could be heard in the doorway, telling everyone to eat up or the food would go to waste. True to character, Scott led the second helpers into the dining room for one last meal. He had volunteered to help George's "moving crew" exchange complete households with the honeymooners.

The newlyweds were off to San Francisco for two weeks, thanks to a wedding gift from the McClure family. Johnny and Anne had entered into a formal partnership with his parents while Angie was in town. They would pay the Gerbrunns the agreed upon purchase price over the next five years, thus buying out Angie's "inheritance" rights in the store. As a wedding present, the Hermanns had traded houses with the Larsons, their place being better suited for the young family.

When George explained the arrangements to Scott and Rick, his old friend replied, "Whew! That is complicated. You're lucky your son is a lawyer. How can I help?"

"You can stay with us for a few days and move furniture or mind the store or whatever. That is, if Rick has recovered enough to manage ranch chores," George replied, casting a quick glance at his young friend.

Rick laughed and nodded agreeably, "Ha! Ha! As long as I'm not included in all that lifting and toting, I'll take care of chores at home. Besides, Dad, you're staying over to be with George on his last night, and then see everyone off tomorrow. You need a good break."

"Did I hear my name mentioned?" George said as he joined them, adding more soberly, "I've said my good-byes to Julie and the children. They're ready to return home when you are, Big Brother. Can we walk down to Battle Rock and watch the gray whales playing along the coast?"

"Good idea, Georgie," Rick said as he threw his arm over his brother's shoulder with comradely affection, and the two sauntered down the street to the bluff facing their landmark isle—the tide being high at this hour.

Breathing a sigh of contentment as a whale and her calf cavorted offshore, Rick recalled, "Remember when we were boys and watched the gray whales from here? Sometimes Father would let us play in the sands by Battle Rock. We had a lot of fun re-enacting that Indian fight."

George grinned in nostalgia, reminding his big brother, "Yes, and you insisted on being Captain Kirkpatrick, while I ended up as the poor savage who lost the fight. Then Dad told us the Tutuni had won, with his friend Charlie's tribe on Hubbard Creek chasing the white man away. Afterward you played Charlie or his father 'Chat-al-ha-e-ah'. How times have changed in thirty years. I saw Old John the other day and realized how badly the Tutuni have been treated."

"I wonder if the white man is going into China is any different. I know God's word must be spread, and I believe in the importance of my church's work in the heathen country, but the opium traders and gunboat diplomacy I hear about are ruining an old and vulnerable regime—and its people. That's really why I was able to come home from Shanghai. I volunteered for that new mission we're establishing in Canton, and white men are neither welcome nor safe in that province."

Rick turned pensive with understanding and rephrased his brother's statement, "So your work in China is far away and perilous, and you'll be staying there for awhile. How long, Georgie?"

"I'm committed to Canton for many years, maybe longer than our father has left in his life. I trust you to care of him in his old age. Anne will support you, I know, but Father and you are the Myrtlewood Grove. He'll never leave the ranch," George prophesied.

"Nor will I, Georgie, and I hope at least one of my children cares for it as Father and I do," Rick stated hopefully.

Turning with George to begin the short walk back to the Hermanns, he offered best wishes in a halting, yet serious tone, "God bless you and your work. I'm proud of you, and I love you, Brother."

Two pairs of eyes misted as the brothers felt their strong emotional tie reach a peak, no further words necessary as they completed their brief sojourn, still arm and arm in a comradely fashion. Julie and the children came out the door to kiss George farewell.

A glance from his wife reminded Rick of one last piece of business, and he extracted a leather pouch jingling with gold coins. Ignoring George's frown and negative shake of the head, Rick handed him the purse, announcing, "For your Canton mission, Father George, from your family and the Myrtlewood Grove."

✻   ✻   ✻   ✻   ✻

Turbulent rain clouds filled the western sky, a gusting wind rocking the ladder beneath the apple picker's feet. Teetering amid the lofty branches and holding a frail limb with a crushing grip, Rick grabbed one last apple before scrambling to the ground. The weather had abated before noon, the hiatus of half a day, all the time needed to complete their fall harvest.

Scott rose from the muddy field with a shout to his son, "Come on, slowpoke. This drizzle will become a downpour any minute now. I'm ready to call it quits as soon as I stow these potatoes."

Father and son proceeded to run for cover, their progress hindered by the spongy soil and flapping gunnysacks. Both farmers were soaked by the time their task was finished.

Rick burst into the house dripping wet, but relaxed and was looking forward to dry clothes and a warm fire. Julie left her iron range with its pot of stewing apple butter and helped him dump the apples into a wooden tub, offering a boon, "Should I bake a couple of apple pies for dinner, Dear? The Sixes family came over for a visit and to show us little San-ah-te, almost two months old now. Sandy says they can stay for supper."

A baby's wail came from the bedroom, followed by a muffled burp, and Sandy spoke, "Julie Anne is full. Good girl! Hello, Rick."

The young mother came out of the bedroom buttoning her shirt and carrying her baby wrapped in a blanket. Rick dutifully inspected the tot and praised mother and daughter, making a comparison designed to satisfy Sandy, "Your baby is growing faster and getting as pretty as you. Julie Anne is bigger than the Tucker boy by far."

"Oh, Rick, Billy Junior is only five weeks old," Julie interrupted with a sigh of exasperation.

Sandy was undeterred by the correction, happily boasting, "My baby is strong and healthy. Eat good, sleep good, and ever happy."

"All the children had a good summer. Both Jack Jack and Jane are walking now, and little Scott is talking," Julie remarked, adding, "And Albert keeps telling his mother he is ready for the Port Orford School. He's only four and a half years old, so Anne is teaching him to read at home."

Sandy's cheerful expression sobered with perplexity as she muttered, "How children go to school? Jack say Jack Jack and Julie Anne need school."

"Why, I'll teach our children right here in this house, at least until they're old enough to ride to the Blanco School," Julie volunteered as Jack and his son entered the room.

"Good, Julie. You are smart and can teach our children much. We pay with venison, like the quarter of meat I just hung in your meat house," Jack stated assuredly, a deal being struck as far as he was concerned.

Rick smiled acceptance, his covert glance silencing his wife's objection to accepting pay from their friends. Jack was happy with his swap of services, and a classroom was three or more years away.

Autumn days shortened as the sun approached the winter solstice, and dismal gray clouds hovered over the Oregon coast, so that the McClures elected to stay homebound and tend to the ranch chores. Scott caulked his cabin's drafty windowsills, Rick added two-by-four trusses to strengthen their barn's creaky hayloft, and Julie began sewing new curtains for the windows. Occasionally Girard had a load of lumber for the McClures to deliver, and once Scott sneaked off to visit the Hermanns and play checkers with George.

One atypical day after Thanksgiving, sunshine brought the Sixes family to the Myrtlewood Grove for a visit, Jack talking Scott into riding to the mill to see Girard about another log run in the spring.

Rick chose the clear weather to track down a buck he had seen foraging in their haystacks. He traipsed back and forth across the valley floor, following the deer's cloven sign, unconcerned that he never spotted the beast. In early afternoon a thickening layer of cirrus clouds moved eastward to dilute the sun's warming rays, and he joined a trio of prospectors leaving the Sixes diggings, swapping stories with them on their trek out.

The men accepted Julie's offer of a warmed-over dinner thankfully and soon moved to Port Orford while the weather held. Jack and Scott passed them on the knoll, arriving home just in time to finish the tepid stew before the Sixes headed back to their lodge.

By now a few cumulus clouds appeared about the sun as it sank behind the south ridge, a sure sign of more rain during the night. Rick and Scott were sitting on the corral fence, heavy coats wrapped about them though still unbuttoned, enjoying the last of the beautiful day. Little Scott waved from the doorway and called, "Supper's ready."

As Scott climbed off the fence behind his son, he marveled, "Your son is some talker these days. He said that real clear, even with his head cold."

Both men came to an abrupt halt as hoofbeats echoed from the log bridge. Someone was coming upriver late, and Rick guessed, "I bet that's Fred. He said he'd be over for a visit after the holiday."

No more said than done, Fred Madsen rode Ariane into the yard, sober-faced as he leaned forward in the saddle to hand Scott a letter, announcing, "A letter for you from Salem, Scott. I got one from Delores also." He dismounted and watched Scott open the letter silently.

Rick had a foreboding when his brother-in-law said nothing and maintained a serious demeanor. His father read the short message quickly, a pained expression crossing over his face as he glance at his son, explaining, "Kurt had a stroke and is dying. Uwe writes that he asked for me, his best friend. I have to ride to Salem," and in a snap decision, concluded, "Saddle Berlin for me while I pack a saddlebag. I'm leaving right now!"

Rick hesitated, worried about his father's riding so far at his age and suggested, "Maybe I'd better saddle Rhine, too. Traveling together would make a safer trip."

"No, Son. We can't leave Julie alone. She needs you, and besides we've got a contract with Girard to honor," Scott retorted, fully understanding Rick's concern.

Fred barked a single laugh, and stated, "Ha! I packed a bedroll so I could ride with you, Scott. Delores wrote me the story of Kurt's collapse. She invited me to come calling, with her folks' approval yet. I figured now is a good time to go courting. You know the way, and I'm a good worker. We should make Salem in four or five days."

And so it was that Scott and Fred became partners on the ride north, one to seal an old friendship, and the other to rekindle young love.

*　*　*　*　*

One indistinguishable rainy afternoon in early December, a number of neighbors congregated at the Myrtlewood Grove. All had different reasons for their visit, the Madsens coming to see their grandchildren, the Sixes leading the McClure bull back to his home corral, and Johnny meeting Phil Smythe with a load of supplies for the diggings. Julie's ingenuity with venison and her kitchen range were tested, since everyone quickly accepted her impromptu offer of supper. Then the mill crew arrived, James Girard, Billy Tucker, and Rod Bishop, each apologizing for the hour but readily taking a plate of stew from their hostess.

Jack politely burped his appreciation for the delicious meal, remembering too late the white man's manners. Girard eased his discomfort at the gaffe, stating his own agreement, "Just the way I feel, Jack. Thank you for your hospitality, Julie. Is it permissible to talk business now?"

Receiving her smile and nod, he continued, "I'm in need of fir logs for my mill. I know we planned a February log drive, but I hoped we could round up a crew and float a bunch downriver this week."

Eagerness lighting his stolid features, Jack responded immediately, "Good idea, James. Don't you agree, Rick?"

"Sure, I'm willing. I know you've been logging all fall, Jack, but Scott and I haven't cut a single tree. I'll need help to be ready so soon. Phil, can you and Ezra work for a couple of days? Johnny, do you have time?" Rick asked around, finally looking to his father-in-law.

Amidst a chorus of yeses, John nodded slowly and qualified his agreement, "With Fred in Salem, I can't give but one day. When will you float the logs out?"

"Let's do it in three days. If we can use Scott's cabin for sleeping, and Julie would feed us, we'll be ready," James declared.

*　*　*　*　*

By mid-month the log drive was behind them, and the McClures still hadn't heard from Scott or Fred. Rainy weather continued, and as it grew cooler an occasional snowflake could be seen in the drizzle. One misty morning Billy Tucker rode into the yard, delivering payment for Rick's logs and a letter from the post office.

"I know you're waiting to hear from your dad, Rick, so I came right out. The mail rider floundered in the mud up by Marshfield. Fell into Coos Bay itself, I heard. I hope your letter is readable," Billy explained as he leaned forward in the saddle to hand a smeared envelope and a pair of gold eagles to his friend, concluding, "See you later. I'm late for work."

"Thanks, Billy, and thank James for the money," Rick responded, raising his voice as Billy rode out of the yard, "And give my regards to Beth and Junior."

Tearing open the envelope as he joined Julie inside the warm house, he scanned the damp sheet of paper, inked words smudged badly but still legible. "Kurt died over two weeks ago. Dad writes that he and Fred made the trek in four days, and he visited with Kurt every day until his old friend passed quietly away in his sleep. Hmn, Dad mentions he's in the will. Horses and cows, it looks like, but this ink is all but washed out."

"Does he say when he'll be home?" Julie asked.

"Hmn! No, but he and your brother should be here any day if Kurt died two weeks ago. I wonder how Dad is taking his death?"

After two days of her husband's pacing about the house, Julie suggested, "There's a break in the rain, Dear. Actually, it's sun shining on the hillside behind us. Why don't you ride up to Langlois' store and see if Scott and Fred are coming home."

Grinning irrepressibly at his wife's understanding offer, he promptly acceded, "Thanks, Julie. Can you manage all right if I'm gone overnight? I may go up to Bandon."

"Of course. I'll be just fine. But you have to dress warmly and take care of yourself. I don't want to be your nurse again this winter," Julie retorted with a knowing smile.

An hour later he rode over the knoll, his wife giving him a good-bye kiss and a sack of biscuits and slices of roast venison.

His attention turned to planning the trip north, and as he cleared Slide Ridge, he kicked Rhine into a gallop. *If I hurry, I can buy a sarsaparilla at Langlois' to wash down my lunch,* he thought. *Maybe I can stay at that new inn north of Bandon tonight. That way I can ride as far as Coos Bay tomorrow before turning around. It's a nice day for a ride.*

Gray clouds obscured the patches of blue sky by the time Rick saw tendrils of smoke rising from the houses of Bandon a mile or so ahead. His daydreaming ended as he refocused on the trail he was riding, his casual glance spotting a sign of a large body of horses and cows traveling south. The tracks in the rutted soil were less than an hour old by his best guess. He hadn't seen anybody, but then he recalled the smell of smoke in the air a half mile back.

Reining his horse about, he followed the animals' spore into the forest, along a familiar path his father had used on more than one occasion. Soon the smell of smoke titillated his olfactory sense, and he paused to look about the area in a fading twilight. Spotting the quivering flame of a campfire through the dense undergrowth, Rick called out in a stentorian voice, "Hello, the camp! Is that you, Dad?"

"Yes, come on in, Rick. Fred and I were wondering who our noisy visitor was. Did you come out to lend us a hand with the cattle drive?" his father's teasing voice moderated as Rick rode into camp.

Laughing in relief and happiness, Rick acknowledged his quest, "Ha! Ha! Yes, we wondered where you two were, so Julie sent me out to rescue you from the throes of Mother Nature. What do we have here? Hello, Fred," he queried slowly, his gaze moving along the picket line.

"Come on over and sit by the fire. Fred will tend to Rhine. Do you have any meat with you? Beans without bacon are kind of tasteless," Scott said as he stirred a cooking pot over the fire.

"Yup! There's a little venison left over from my noonday meal," Rick replied, lifting his voice to carry to the edge of camp, "Bring that roast venison in my saddlebags, will you, Fred?"

Looking askance at his father, Rick waited patiently for an explanation. Scott related his story of Kurt's passing and funeral, finally pointing casually to the picketed animals as he continued, "My inheritance! Three of Gerbrunn's yearlings and an older mare Fred owns for helping me out. Those youngsters are hardly big enough to pack that furniture Johann gave me for the Larsons' home."

"Delores likes the mare because we rode a lot after she got home from school," Fred recounted, his manner proprietary when talking about the girl.

Scott smiled tolerantly, having heard about Delores for days on end, clarifying the young people's relationship with tongue in cheek, "I do believe the love bug has smitten our friend here. He is 'almost' engaged or so he tells me. Angie and Delores will visit the Hermanns next summer to discuss a formal engagement. Say, Fred, how are you going to pay for a ring to give Delores?"

"Oh Scott, quit teasing me. I'm serious, and you said I could work for you when you sell these steers to the butcher in Umpqua," Fred said a little anxiously.

Rick chuckled in empathy with his brother-in-law, keeping his peace as he recalled his suit for Julie's hand.

Fred relaxed enough to state, "Delores will be sixteen years old next year, and I'll be twenty. I reckon that's old enough for us to know our minds."

With that declaration even Scott's humor was stifled, and the conversation got around to Port Orford news items, the three men chatting well into the night.

★ ★ ★ ★ ★

The weather continued to be dominated by southwest rainstorms, with rivers running over their banks all along the coast. Plans for a large family Christmas at the ranch were scrapped, and Scott and Rick braved the elements the day before Christmas to deliver gifts and good will. They saw no one else on the trail, or even in the street when they reached Port Orford. Crossing the Sixes and Elk Rivers was a struggle safely won by the two riders even though the presents exchanged showed considerable wear and tear from contact with river water and rain. The two men were happy to return to the warm and snug house before dusk, and they watched little Scott and Jane fall asleep amidst their gifts, damaged or not.

Julie picked up Jane and carried her to bed, Rick doing likewise with his son. After tucking their children beneath the covers, both returned to sit beside Scott, Julie asking, "What's new in Port Orford? Oh, did you invite James to Christmas dinner?"

"I saw him at the Tuckers while Dad was visiting with Louie and his mother at the hotel. James is spending the holidays with Billy, Beth, and Junior. She confided to me that she's pregnant again, and when I told her that you were expecting in July she was excited that our babies would be the same age," Rick reported.

Scott added quickly, "And remember that Johnny announced last week that Albert will have a brother in May. Anne looked good when we dropped by the house."

"How interesting," Julie commented happily, pausing to speculate aloud, "If Sandy is pregnant again like she thinks, all four of us will be having babies next summer. I'll have to ask her tomorrow when the Sixes come to dinner. I wonder if Phil and Ezra will make it?"

"They wouldn't miss one of your chicken dinners because of a little flooding," Scott promised Julie with a paternal smile, giving her a hug and a kiss on the cheek as he wished her a hearty "Merry Christmas!"

Rick put an arm around the two of them, giving his wife a buss as he murmured, "and a Happy New Year!"

✶ ✶ ✶ ✶ ✶

Rick twisted about in the saddle to wave good-bye to his family in the sunlit doorway. He turned Rhine loose on a pair of cantankerous steers, and the herd closed up as it crossed the knoll. Good weather during the last week in February had allowed the rivers to drop about the same time Scott received a letter from the butcher in Umpqua City. He offered to buy four healthy steers at the going price, delivered to his shop by mid-March. He'd give Scott a bonus, a case of locally canned salmon for prompt delivery.

Since one of them had to stay on the ranch, Rick volunteered Fred and himself, his brother-in-law eager to be a cowboy again. The Madsens had two steers for sale, so the partners decided to trail seven steers to the cannery town, selling three beef cattle along the way—maybe at Gardiner and then sharing the proceeds.

Fred remained on point as the small herd crossed Slide Ridge and passed through the gap.

Trailing steers through familiar country made the early going easy with fair weather. One of Rick's cantankerous steers seemed to be the leader, moving to the point beside Fred. When the herd reached Coos Bay and crossed the flats successfully, Rick sold the other ornery steer to a lumber camp cook. The beast had slowed them down with his spirited antics, and his absence made the job easier. However, that steer may have been their lucky charm, because the next day stormy weather struck the coast.

The lead steer bolted into the dunes during a particularly nasty gust of wind, Fred able to hold the other five steers bunched together while Rick spurred his horse in pursuit of the frantic animal. Before he caught the steer and literally dragged him back to the herd, a half-day had been lost. It was a wet and bedraggled pair of herders who reached the Umpqua with a tired herd intact.

With a rising river and tired steers, Rick was forced to pay the atrocious fee demanded by the ferry operator to carry his herd to safety on the north side. Fred was riding point as they left the river landing, when the trouble-making leader broke ranks and darted into the forest. This time Rick bunched the others and let his partner do the chasing.

Suddenly the elusive troublemaker burst out of the underbrush ahead and ran into a muddy slough, coming to an abrupt halt haunch deep in muck and river water. Fred rode to a peat hummock near the steer and tried casting a lasso over its short horns, receiving no cooperation from the animal.

The red-faced cowboy finally dismounted and waded into the mire to rope the troublemaker, only to have the beast rear up the hummock, thrashing in the slime and knocking Fred head over heels into the muck.

Rick laughed uproariously at the sight of his mud-plastered partner crawling out of the slough on all fours. Even Fred was laughing as the caterwauling steer fell again, but when a stray hoof chopped his legs out from under him, Fred screamed in pain. Forgetting the five quiet steers, Rick raced his horse to the hummock and lassoed the steer, pulling him from the slough before he dismounted and helped Fred ashore.

Grasping Fred's canteen of fresh water, Rick washed the dirt away from a gashed and bleeding skin, already turning black and blue from the bruising. He let the wound bleed itself clean as he moved the leg about, testing the joints as he felt the bone itself. Securing a bandana over the wound, he wrapped Fred's belt around it, applying firm pressure as he talked to his friend, "Fred, you have a nasty gash there. Probably needs a few stitches, but your bones appear sound enough. Let's get you on your horse and into Gardiner to a doctor."

The youngster gritted his teeth and groaned as Rick lifted him bodily into his saddle, answering his partner's unasked question, "I'm all right, Rick. I can manage the drag if you'll lead us into town. Better keep your rope on that yahoo."

An hour later Fred was being stitched up on the doctor's table, and Rick was pocketing the sale price of the troublemaker and one other steer.

"I'll deliver the other steers to our butcher friend in Umpqua City and return by dark. Doc'll help you over to our room in Harvey Masters' old hotel. You stay off that leg tonight, you hear?" Rick ordered sternly, leaving the office as his brother-in-law nodded wearily.

The following afternoon the doctor called on Fred in their hotel room to change the dressing and afterward pronounced him sound and ready to ride.

Rick figured differently however, announcing, "We deserve a holiday, Fred, and so do our horses. Here, throw your right arm over my shoulder and hang on. We'll hobble over to that saloon across the street for a drink or two. I hear they're serving steak for supper tonight— 'old trouble-maker', I hope."

"Sounds good to me..er..Dad doesn't approve of my drinking," the young man replied in confusion.

Rick grinned in response, suggesting, "Whatever you do is all right with me partner. You're nineteen years old and a full-grown cowboy. Besides, a little medicine for your injured leg is in order."

"That's right, Rick," Fred brightened as he spoke, "The doctor said a drink wouldn't hurt, and cowboys have been known to have one or two after a cattle drive."

✶ ✶ ✶ ✶ ✶

Iridescent apple blossoms shimmered against the Oregon greenery in the west acreage, father and son planting potatoes and onions in the plowed soil. Stripped to the waist, their pale white skin was reddening under the bright midday sun, and they joked about washing the tint off in the river waters. Rick finished his tedious chore first, and without a word raced toward their old fishing hole, his father following suit a moment later.

Running beneath the shadowy myrtlewoods, Rick re-emerged into sunlight on the gravel beach and dove headlong into the eddied pool. He burst to the surface at midstream, head and shoulders above water as he cried, "Yeow! It's like ice in here. Come on in, Dad."

Scott merely smiled as he seated himself on a gnarled stump at the river's edge and ladled water over his face and shoulders, teasing, "Brrr! You're right, Son. It's mighty chilly water. That's why I let you beat me at our planting chore. I wanted to see you turn blue. It's prettier than pink."

Rick cupped water in his hands and splashed ashore, Scott cheerfully retreating out of reach as he donned his shirt. The sound of hooves stilled their horseplay, Johnny's form visible riding down the path.

Calling out as he pulled his reins, Johnny joked, "Brr! You look frozen, Rick. Isn't April a little early for swimming?"

Rick responded by dousing his friend with handfuls of water, the twinkling globules startling the horse and forcing Johnny to grab the saddle horn with his free hand.

"All right! All right! I surrender. Here I do you the favor of delivering a personal message to Scott, and I'm attacked by my childish brother-in-law. Anyway, Captain O'Keefe's schooner is loading lumber at Hubbard Creek, and he has issued an arm-wrestling challenge to Scott. Winner buys drinks for all of us."

Johnny visited with Julie and the children while the McClures saddled their horses, then the three men rode down the road to the coast trail. Out of earshot of the house, he commented, "Julie's baby is showing, but not like Anne's. My wife is as big as a house. Of course, she's due next month."

"Is Anne feeling well? And how is Beth Tucker?" Rick queried.

"Anne is uncomfortable but healthy, and Beth is over to our house regularly, trading baby secrets with the missus. By the way, Bill gave us a hand salvaging that shipwreck off Cape Blanco last month. I even managed to be attorney of record for the shipping company while Dad bought the salvage. Their agent didn't see any conflict of interest in Dad and me being partners. You know, this lawyering thing is paying off since I've located my office back in the store."

Scott chuckled at Johnny's cheerful enthusiasm but changed the subject as he muttered rhetorically, "How does O' Keefe look? As big and brawny as ever? Let's get moving."

Spurring Berlin into a gallop, he led the entourage into town, a gathering of men in front of the tavern awaiting their arrival. Word of the rematch between McClure and O'Keefe had spread even though only a handful of men from the fifties during their original match still lived in Port Orford.

Scott dismounted quickly and met the Irishman in the doorway, both graying old-timers eschewing any enmity by coming together in a grand bear hug, O'Keefe roaring in a stentorian voice, "By God, you look fit for an old man, Scott. That's good, I wouldn't want to take advantage of you, my friend."

"Ha! Ha! And where have you been sailing these past five years? Why, Rick here has married Julie Madsen, and I'm a grandfather many times over, but I'm ready for your challenge. Sure you don't want to reconsider and just buy a round for the fellas here?"

Several gamblers protested his offer with a chorus of "Noes", and O'Keefe grinned broadly as he boasted, "Oh no, Scott McClure. I've bested everyone in the tavern, young and old. You're next. In fact your own son-in-law, Judge Larson here, can referee. That's fair, isn't it, lads?"

After an ever more resounding chorus of approval, Johnny motioned the men to the table and stood watching as they settled into position. When both were seated with right elbows on the table edge, he ordered, "Not yet, gentlemen. I want your left hand tucked in your belt behind you," and after compliance, he concluded, "Best of three matches is the game. Now lock your right hands together. Good, on the count of three...one, two, three!"

Muscles tautened perceptibly as both men strained to force the other to put the back of his hand on the surface, Scott grunting in disgust as O'Keefe slowly overpowered him, Johnny's hand slapping the table to proclaim the sea captain's victory on the first match.

Scott conceded in good humor, assuming his position for the second without a rest, remarking, "Congratulations, Captain! Now that I'm loosened up, let's try it again."

Johnny checked positions and first grip, announcing "Advantage O'Keefe, second match on the count of three...one.., two, three!"

Remembering their contest years ago when Scott's bold quickness had won the day, O'Keefe was prepared, matching speed and guile with brute force, the two grunting men struggling without fault in the silence of the crowded room. Slowly the local hero's arm fell from the vertical, eliciting a low groan from the crowd behind him, a gasp of hope generated when Scott shifted his direction in a feint and brought the forearms to a vertical position. However, it was to be his last offensive move as his old friend's massive strength gained momentum. The groans of losers preceded Scott's hand to the table as Johnny slapped his hand on it a last time, and declared, "O'Keefe wins by two pins."

"Want to try three out of five, mate?" O'Keefe graciously offered, ignoring the objections of the winning gamblers.

Scott laughed merrily, as good a sport as his friend had been thirty years before, declining any reprieve, "Ha! Ha! No, my friend, you won fair and square. Come to think of it, I remember how surprised I was that my trick won that contest years ago. Drinks are on me, Captain O'Keefe—as they should be."

Digging deep into his pocket for a few silver coins, he turned to his son, asking, "Do you have any money, Rick?"

"Not any more, Dad. I bet every dime I had on you. However, Johnny must have a few dollars on him. Being judge kept him from betting."

And so Judge Larson paid his father-in-law's bar bill, starting a long evening of partying. After a single beer, Johnny slipped away to relieve his father behind the store counter, so George could visit with his old friends. Shortly afterward Rick followed suit, Scott nodding happily at his son's suggestion that he spend the night in town while Rick went home to begin their hay harvest after chores the next morning.

Chapter Fifteen

Life on the Myrtlewood Grove settled into an active summer mode after the first hay crop was in, different from many previous years by an ethereal attitude of anticipation—a waiting mood. Even when Mary Anne Larson was born on the last day in May, it seemed a far-removed event because Julie was too far along with her pregnancy to ride into town. Isolated as she was from her female friends in Port Orford, she refused to rely on second-hand reports from the men of her family, instead sending her mother in to visit Mary and Captain Tichenor's new wife, both of whom had helped at Anne's delivery.

Phil and Ezra plodded up to the corral where the McClures were working out one of their Gerbrunn horses. Huge backpacks straddled their shoulders, lending them the air of being a beast of burden. With identical grunts of disgust at their plight, the partners dropped the bundles on the ground and leaned against the pole corral.

Scott climbed the fence like a ladder to perch on the topmost bar, smiling friendly-like as he inquired, "Where are you two going?"

Phil answered for the partners as usual, "Our claim has played out, Scott, and we reckon it's time to move on. One of our neighbors told an interesting story of the Skagit River up in Washington Territory, and then I hear the Fraser River in Canada is still producing gold. Thought we'd see for ourselves."

"You're packing a load of equipment for a long journey. Are you sailing to the Puget Sound or trekking overland through the Willamette Valley?" Scott queried.

For a change it was Ezra who replied, "Thought it might be cheaper to trail up there, but we'll need a packhorse—my back is killing me. You fellas want to sell that horse?"

★ ★ ★ ★ ★

The week after their friends had headed north leading the packhorse, Patrick Hughes came visiting, spending more time in idle conversation than was usual for the busy man. Neither Rick nor Scott was surprised when their neighbor brought up the subject of horses, expressing interest in Berlin and then in Rhine, which he knew were not for sale. Both McClures surmised correctly that he wanted one of the Gerbrunn horses. Winking at each other, they played dumb as Patrick worked himself into a bartering fervor.

Finally understanding the meaning of Scott's giveaway smile, Hughes muttered forlornly, "I suppose you've figured out that I need a horse. What's it going to cost me for that one in the corral, neighbor?"

"Ha! Ha! It took you long enough to get around to what's on your mind, Patrick."

Scott paused to consider a bargaining position and offered a steep price, "We can use a good young milker and one of your bulls."

"Well, I've got a nice cow you'd like, and I might trade you bulls. Your Mason bull would help my stock's bloodline. That seems fair," Hughes countered.

"Sure it's fair as far as it goes. I see you have a few sheep at your place. Throw in a couple of lambs and you've got a deal," Scott bartered.

Hughes finally gave an affirmative nod and compromised, "You can pick your milker and bull except Old Muddy and one lamb when you deliver your bull. I'll take that horse now if we have a deal."

Scott held out a hand to his neighbor, their shake cementing the deal, commenting, "Always good to do business with you, Patrick. My son will fetch your horse while we say hello to Julie. She'll want to send regards to your family."

Scott, the volcano builder, sat at the supper table shaping a mound of mashed potatoes, punching a crater into which his grandfather ladled steaming brown gravy.

"Oh, Dad! You shouldn't encourage such table manners," Julie fussed, telling her son, "No more playing with your food, Scott. I expect a clean plate before you get a cookie."

Jane giggled as she copied her brother, her fisted spoon not as controlled as her brother's. A glob slopped on the floor, the girl's eyes opening wide in innocence.

Julie reacted angrily, tapping the table several times with her fingertips and scolding, "No! No! Jane. Eat your food properly, or you'll go to bed hungry."

With tear-filled eyes the girl looked at her father, who shook his head briefly, ordering, "Eat! You know Mama means what she says."

Grandpa ignored her and her brother and was suddenly busy eating, so Jane did as she was told, her fondness for mashed potatoes outweighing any thought of a tantrum.

Soon the children's plates were clean, and Scott asked for his cookie, Jane's hand going out, too. Grandpa led them outside to play in the setting sun while Rick cleared the table.

"This damned pregnancy! I'm as grouchy as I am fat," Julie complained as she attempted to rise from her chair, doubling over in pain and moaning sharply.

"Are you all right, Dear?" Rick asked solicitously and rushed to her side to support her.

"Ohhh! No, Rick, my water burst. I'm so embarrassed. I think my labor has started. Get Mom over here, ohhh…".

"Sit still, Dear," he counseled, stepping outside to shout, "Scott, Jane, come inside and get ready for bed now. Dad, fetch Hazel. Julie says her time is near."

By the time Scott had Berlin galloping down the Sixes road, Rick had his wife comfortably in bed and the children in their pajamas and at work helping him clean up the kitchen. Actually, he was keeping them busy until bedtime and calming their excitement, which had motivated the clean-up.

When Scott asked seriously, man-to-man look on his face, "Will I have a brother to play with, Daddy?" Rick knew it was time for them to be abed. His answering, "I don't know," only elicited more questions.

✸ ✸ ✸ ✸ ✸

Rick's head snapped back against the rocker's headrest, his eyes opening wide as the coffee pot banged on the stove top, Hazel murmuring quietly, "I'm sorry to wake you, Rick. I guess I'm getting careless with all this waiting. Julie's back to sleep again."

"That's all right, Mom. What time is it anyway?" He yawned in asking.

"About four o'clock in the morning. It should be getting light soon. We'll all be tired out by the time Julie's baby decides to come. Why don't you lie down in the children's room?" Hazel suggested.

"Nah, actually I think some fresh air would be good for me, and I can start doing morning chores. Call me if you need help."

Rick was feeding Julie's chickens an hour later, dawn gradually erasing the stars from the night sky, when the cabin door opened and Hazel called out, "Rick, your baby's coming. No hurry, but I can use more hot water and towels."

"Coming!" he retorted eagerly, casting the remaining feed about the enclosure and hurrying to the wash basin on the porch to clean up.

Rick stoked the fire and brewed fresh coffee, keeping busy as Hazel's low voice soothed her groaning daughter in the bedroom. He would have gone to his wife and given comfort, except he'd learned during Scott's birth that he wasn't any help. His mother-in-law was a competent mid-wife.

Hazel brought out a handful of crumpled towels to Rick, informing and instructing in one breath, "Julie's fine, although the baby is slow in coming. Wash these towels and wring them as dry as possible."

Moments later Julie's delivery began, her piercing screams followed by a series of ululating moans, and finally by a grunting sigh of relief. A slight slap could be heard before the cry of a newborn baby.

"Rick, come hold your daughter."

Rushing to the bedside to accept the blanket-wrapped bundle with a proprietary air, Rick was amazed once again at how small Melissa Anne was. He cooed to the sleeping baby, startled abruptly by a shrill scream from Julie. He saw her body was rigid with effort as she pushed hard again.

Hazel announced, "Yes, Julie, you're having another baby-a twin girl."

Julie's strained body collapsed as her second baby emerged, her unfocused eyes seeking her husband as she asked, "Are they healthy, Dear? What will we name Melissa Anne's sister?"

Rick was caught off guard by the latter question, turning thoughtful as he said, "Yes, they are wonderful, Julie."

Hazel placed the second bundle in Rick's free arm with a gleeful if somewhat weary smile, and he announced, "They're like peas in a pod, Honey—twins. We'll name her Anne Melissa. How does that sound?"

He looked up to see that Julie was asleep and turned to Hazel for instructions. She suggested, "Go sit in the rocker with your daughters, Richard. They'll be screaming to be fed soon enough. I'll clean up here."

Settling into his chair with a tiny babe on each arm, he espied Jane's head peeking at them from behind her bedroom door. Speaking in gentle tones, he said, "Come see your twin sisters, Jane. Did they wake you up?"

Scott joined his sister, studying the new arrivals doubtfully, concluding tactlessly, "Ugh! They're homely."

Jane nodded in agreement but gave her less critical assessment, "Uh huh, but they're my sisters."

Scott entered quietly, coming to look at his new granddaughters with an observation, "Twins, heh? They'll grow up as lovely as their mother, children. Besides they are very special because today is Independence Day, and Fourth of July babies are exceptional."

Rick dismounted in front of the post office, greeting the Tichenors strolling away from the building, "Good morning, folks! Out for your constitutional?"

"Yes, the Missus and I came looking for a letter from Ellen and found one from a granddaughter instead—graduation announcement. We just might sail down to San Francisco for that occasion, eh, Dear?"

His wife was less than enthusiastic as she cautioned, "You're not as young as you used to be, William. That voyage down to Ellen's will be the death of you yet."

The Captain retorted with a condescending smile, "I'm an old sailor with no fear of the sea, just a healthy respect for it. I'll take my chances as long as Ellen and the girls will put up with me."

His wife smiled in exasperation and changed the subject, "Did you hear that Beth Tucker had a girl last week? Elizabeth Anne is so cute."

"Yes, the Larsons were out for dinner on Sunday, and the women compared babies. Sandy Sixes had hers the week before. Imagine five girls born over the last two months. What kind of odds is that?" Rick marveled.

Tichenor laughed as he boasted and joked simultaneously, "Ha! Ha! That's nothing. Ellen has nine daughters and no sons."

"Richard, when you see Beth, tell her I'll be over to see her this afternoon with that comforter that I knitted for Elizabeth," Missus Tichenor said.

"Yes, ma'am, and a good day to you both. Captain, give my regards to Ellen," Rick concluded as he stepped into the post office.

Reading a long letter from his brother in China, Rick bumped into Louie Knapp, quickly apologizing, "Oops! Sorry, Louie, I should look where I'm going. How's construction going on the new hotel building?"

"Just fine, Rick, but I think it was easier to rebuild after the fire of 1868 than while this old building is still in use. Mother will show you around if you have eggs for our kitchen in that packsaddle on your horse."

"I do, and Julie sent along a bag of fresh vegetables from her garden. Sort of a thank you to the Knapps for the knit booties your mother sent to our babies," Rick paused and chuckled before adding, "Ha! Ha! Julie hates being house-bound, I'm her eyes and ears on this trip to town, with instructions galore on who to see and what to do."

"You're a lucky man, Rick, and you have the good sense to know it. Maybe I should find myself a good woman and start a family," Louie remarked wistfully.

Rick gibed, "Ride out for dinner Sunday, and we'll give you a taste of family life. You can tend the children while Julie and I sneak away for a moment alone. We don't see many of those romantic times anymore."

Both men chuckled as they parted, Louie agreeing to the invitation, "See you all on Sunday, Rick."

✳ ✳ ✳ ✳ ✳

Trading milk and eggs for a wheel of golden cheese was a deal Julie and Jane had made during the recent visit by the Hughes to the Myrtlewood Grove. Rick was delivering his side of the bargain when he saw Patrick running on foot toward the gold diggings on the Sixes bar.

Spurring his horse into the farm yard, Rick unloaded the two cans of milk inside the dairy cooler and called out to Jane walking toward him, "Where's Patrick running off to?"

A note of concern could be heard in her reply, "A prospector rode by the house with the news that a miner was killed in the gold camp and told Patrick. He was going into town to report it. Would you go over and help my husband?"

Rick remounted quickly and raced Rhine down to the sandy beach to find Patrick bending over the collapsed miner. The landowner felt for a pulse before conceding the man was dead. To the side sat the hunched-over figure of a sobbing man, visibly shaken by his death. A miner Rick recognized from an earlier visit told the new arrivals that the dejected man was the guilty party. Bystanders agreed that the two friends had disagreed over a money matter, a fist fight resulting.

The unlucky loser fell backward into a woodpile, his head striking a double-bladed axe wedged in the chopping block. He was killed instantly, albeit accidentally. Patrick was a recognized authority since he owned the adjacent land, and he began questioning everybody on site.

By the time Johnny Larson rode into camp, the full story was known, and the repentant killer had corroborated his guilt, claiming it was an accident. The other miners obviously empathized with their friend, passing the hat to raise funds to hire Johnny to represent the man. He accepted the case, pulling the man onto the horse behind his saddle and riding for town.

A week later, Johnny showed up at the Myrtlewood Grove to collect his visiting family and shared his story, "My client was found 'not guilty' of murder, but he was convicted of assault and battery. Thirty days in jail is more than a fair sentence, don't you think? Anyway, he claims he'll be back digging gold by late September."

"How'd the other miners take the news?" Rick asked curiously.

"They seemed happy enough with the verdict. In fact, I've been getting a lot of lawyering business from those men. All of a sudden, I'm downright popular. Ha! Ha! My client put it in proper focus for me when he said his friends trusted me even if I was a backwoods lawyer."

Everyone laughed at the self-deprecatory bit of humor, and Johnny quickly announced, "But the real news is that my sister and her daughter are due in port tomorrow or the next day. Uwe stayed home with the rest of the family. He and his brother are investing in railroad stock. What with the Northern Pacific all but into Portland and several local communities anxious to have a branch line to their area, the Gerbrunn brothers see lots of opportunity. There's talk of a railroad over to Tillamook or Florence—even along the Umpqua."

Anne interrupted impatiently, "Enough of railroads and investment opportunities. Tell us more about Angie and Delores. Will they be staying with us? Does Fred know they're coming? Romance in the offing is much more interesting than our nation's industrial revolution."

Leaning back against the sun-drenched white masonry of the Cape Blanco Lighthouse, a bemused Rick stared sightlessly at the blue Pacific. His thoughts were shaped by the written words of his brother in far-off China as he reminisced about their shared youth. *Georgie and I had a good time as children of the Sixes, although he recalls our adventures better than I do. Probably because a lot of memories were stirred up during his visit last year. His long letter was directed more to me than to Dad, nostalgia and all.*

With a sudden clarity of understanding, Rick envisioned his brother's message as a final good-bye. *Perhaps clairvoyance is a better term for what I see now, Georgie spending the rest of his life in that Canton mission serving his church and its Chinese congregation. He said as much that day we parted company near Battle Rock. "Take care of Dad," he implored. I will, Georgie.*

His attention was called back to the present by the sound of hoofbeats approaching. Rick straightened his frame and turned to meet his father who had been visiting with Patrick Hughes. To his surprise, his father was not in sight, and the noise came from behind him.

"Hello, Rick," called Fred from a distance, "Did we disturb your daydreaming?"

Spinning about on one heel, the dreamer laughed as he returned the greeting, "Afraid so, Fred. Basking in the sun is very comforting to this tired farmer. Welcome back to Curry County, Delores. How was your voyage to Port Orford?"

"Just fine, Mister McClure. Mother and I are good sailors," the girl replied.

"Mister McClure? My God, I'm not that old yet. Save the Mister for my father and call me Rick."

A smile belied his complaint as he nodded to the girl's mount, observing, "I see you renewing your acquaintance with that Gerbrunn mare."

Delores laughed and leaned forward to scratch the horse's ears, agreeing affably, "Ha! Ha! Hilda remembers me well. Fred promised to keep her for me when Grandpa died and gave all his horses to your father—Mister McClure."

"Oho! Your girl has a sense of humor as well as her mother's beauty, Fred. Have you popped the question yet?" Rick teased the young couple.

Delores blushed, but Fred just smiled at the gibe, answering seriously, "Several times, but her mother won't let her say yes. Angie thinks she's too young."

"But I'm almost sixteen, and my answer is yes. I just hope mother agrees before we fight about it," the girl averred, eyes flashing and jaw firmly set.

Rick smiled sympathetically at the young lovers, offering Delores some sound advice, "Talk to my father, he's like an uncle to Angie and Uwe. He may able to help."

With those words he mounted Rhine and suggested, "No time like the present. Let's ride into the Hughes place and pick up Dad."

✷ ✷ ✷ ✷ ✷

Scott called out loudly, "Last one to finish has to cut firewood," and promptly cast his last pitchfork full of hay onto the stack. As he trotted across the pasture, he shouted playfully, "I get to go fishing!"

A half-hour later Rick joined him at their favorite fishing hole, finally able to voice his complaint, "You left a whole row of hay for me to finish stacking, and half of it was yours."

"Oh well. I'm senior partner, someone needed to catch supper. Of course, you could eat another omelet tonight if you want. I'm going to eat trout, and in the morning, I'm going to track down that young buck we saw today. We've been so busy with harvesting that we're out of meat, and I'm not going to eat my own beef—that's money on the hoof," Scott prattled on as he pulled in another trout.

Rick just smiled as he caught a fish of his own, finally agreeing with his father, "All right, Dad, I'll spend my Saturday picking apples for Julie while you hunt deer, but remember, we're all having Sunday dinner at the Hermanns'. You promised to talk to Angie about our young lovers."

"Well, Son, I'm not sure it's our business," Scott replied with a doubtful tone of voice.

"Since when have you started worrying about whose business it is? You're always involved with everything going on in the north end of Curry County. Besides, it's my wife's business, and she'll nag you worse than I ever can, if you back out."

✶ ✶ ✶ ✶ ✶

Sitting in the shade of the porch with a gentle breeze blowing off the ocean was tolerable for the Hermanns' guests, certainly more comfortable than the steaming house. Rick heard Angie whisper to her daughter, "Not now, Dear!"

She opened a letter from Uwe and read part of the second page, "The Northern Pacific reached Portland on September seventeenth with a big celebration at their new terminal. Johann and I invested two thousand dollars in stock, after which several sales men approached us promoting local railroad projects. All of those fellows offered fly-by-night schemes based on future prosperity and whatever (?). Johann found one company actually building a roadbed in the Willamette Valley, but its price per share was too high. Then I found a company planning a route to Lincoln County on the coast, which would be contingent to my hauling business. We invested another two thousand in that company. It's a gamble, but I figure I can make money from the region either way. Tell Scott we saw no reasonable proposal for Coos or Curry County."

After a short pause, Scott commented, "Thank Uwe for his news, Angie, and wish him luck on becoming a railroad magnate. I wonder if we'll ever see a track laid along the coast?"

"I kind of like our frontier style of life," George chided, complaining, "All these modern machines take away men's initiative. Of course, I might think differently if I could travel by train up to Salem to see my grandchildren every year."

"Well, if Mother would stop saying no, one of your grandchildren would live in the area," Delores stated boldly, meeting Angie's angry stare with a combative stance. Silence wore thin as the two women maintained that posture.

Scott sighed loudly, keeping his promise to Julie as he recalled a previous such family confrontation, "As I remember, Angie, your folks and the Gerbrunns sat in my house and argued the same points I've heard all month. Let's see, you were sixteen, and the two families lived far apart. Seems to me your marriage has been quite successful."

"Oh, Uncle Scott, you're against me, and you've always been my good friend. Delores isn't even sixteen until December," Angie lamented with the hint of tears glistening in her eyes.

George cleared his throat as if to speak, but Scott retorted quickly, "I'm still on your side and always will be, Angie. You were a sweet child, a lovely bride, and a wonderful wife and mother. I'm proud of you and know you'll always stand in fair judgment for your children. It's just that Delores is the spitting image of you on that day years ago."

Angie's mood softened perceptibly during the ensuing silence, her smile finally breaking the tension; as she looked at her daughter, reminding Scott, "Uncle Scott, you meddled that day just as you are doing now, but I loved it. I know you've always been my friend and never given me bad advice."

"Does that mean that I can marry Fred, Mother?" the question fairly bursting out of Delores' mouth, her eyes filled with hopeful tears.

"Yes, but not until you're older. I'll agree to a wedding next spring and let Fred give you that engagement ring he found in Gardiner."

"How did you…?" Delores broke in.

"Your friends, Rick and Julie, have been working on me all month. I wondered when Scott or Daddy would have something to say. Your father and I wish you the best but think that you should wait awhile," Angie explained.

Delores hugged her mother and then Fred, accepting the ring, which came from his pocket with an enthusiastic, "I can hardly wait, but spring will be here in no time. Mother, we can start planning a March wedding tonight."

Angie rolled her eyes and laughed, countering with, "How about May?"

* * * * *

High seas and torrential rains blanketed the Cape Blanco area over the Christmas holidays, no ships venturing into Port Orford except a lumber schooner perilously riding out the storm. Trees fell helter-skelter in the forests, blocking trails as the rain-swollen rivers tore at their banks. There was a little leeway for travelers along the coast, even the mail rider unwilling to hazard a trip north.

The McClures rode out the storm with a satisfying level of comfort, having prepared for the wintry weather following harvest. Rick had even moved two haystacks near the corral, so feeding the penned livestock presented little challenge.

Christmas night the children finally wore down from their exciting day and went to bed, falling asleep before their mother could tuck them in properly. The adults sat around the table chatting in the afterglow of the family gathering, festive in mood despite the threatening weather.

Scott was sharing his last bottle of brandy, and with mock sadness, toasted the holiday, "Merry Christmas! And drink up, I'm all out of spirits, unless you count the jug of homemade blackberry wine—vinegar by now, I bet."

He listened for a minute to the howling wind and then prophesied, "That miserable wind is louder than ever. We're in for a hum-dinger tonight."

Rick stepped to the door, tenaciously gripping it with both hands as he peered into the darkness and listened to the night sounds. Closing the door, he grimaced at his dilemma as the shrieking gale counteracted his strength. Wind-blown and partially soaked during the brief interlude, he suggested, "You'd better sleep here tonight, Dad. I bet that wind is blowing a hundred miles an hour out there."

Rick was awakened by a rush of air through the house and the sound of a door closing, reckoning to himself, it's getting light and the wind has died down considerably. Dad must have gone outside to inspect the farm, and with that thought, he quickly rose from bed and dressed. Rekindling red embers with pieces of pitchy kindling, he stoked the firebox of the stove before following his father into the yard.

Scott was standing amongst the myrtlewoods, looking up at their whipping branches, oblivious to the continuing storm. Plodding down the path toward his father, he saw an old giant with its bole scarred by a fracture, one of its massive limbs lying at Scott's feet.

His father signaled to the limb, and Rick picked up the nearest end, the two men struggling to tote it up to father's cabin. Puffing from exertion, Scott announced, "There's enough wood here to craft a rocking chair or carve a half-dozen rifle stocks. I hope that myrtlewood isn't seriously damaged. It was Buzz's favorite, and he claimed it was over five hundred years old."

"Uh huh, it appears to be the only serious result of last night's wind, although your cabin roof needs a shingle or two replaced. The barn's fine, so I guess the livestock were as comfy as we were. You know, if that tree has survived Mother Nature all those years, it'll probably be here long after we're gone."

Mild weather returned the week after Christmas, skies clearing and streams abating as life returned to normal along the Oregon coast. The Hermanns paid the Myrtlewood Grove a rare visit, accompanied by the Larson family, Johnny insisting on being his folks' escort whenever they rode out of town. The entourage met the Madsens at the Sixes River crossing and came on to the ranch together.

The men wandered down to the river to fish while the women cooked a New Year's Day chicken dinner, both parties talking about the Madsen-Gerbrunn wedding, now scheduled for the Easter weekend in Salem. Everyone was going to the ceremony except Scott and the children, the patriarch deciding early that he could manage both ranches and the youngsters with a bit of help from the Sixes family and Billy Tucker.

As they sat around the table counting their blessings, George saying grace, they silently appreciated the old year and their good fortune. Quiet pervaded the mealtime as appetites were sated, Scott finally rising to his feet. Holding his glass high, he spoke, "Thanks for refurbishing my supply of brandy, George," and then proposed a toast. "God bless our family and friends, near and far. May we anticipate the New Year, 1884, with as much gusto as Fred here, and may we prosper in good health till our next New Year's festivities. Skoal!"

Epilogue

The completion of the Northern Pacific Railroad as a transcontinental route in 1883 brought the Industrial Revolution to the Pacific Northwest, Portland and the Willamette Valley thriving during the next two decades. A network of connecting rail lines brought civilization to central Oregon despite the great depression of 1893, but had only a minor impact on isolated Curry County.

The deaths of Captain William Tichenor in 1887, "Mother" Rachel Knapp in 1888, and Patrick Hughes in 1901, concluded a pioneer chapter of Port Orford history, but each of their roots was sunk deep in this frontier land, a legacy of children and grandchildren abounding.

Jane Hughes bridged the generation gap, living until 1923 in the Victorian mansion, which Patrick had built for the family in 1898. The Hughes home was restored as a museum in 1989 and stands today as part of the Cape Blanco State Park. The late Patrick Masterson, grandson of Patrick and Jane Hughes, and son of Alice and P. J. Masterson, chronicles these pioneer families in his book, *Port Orford, a History* (copyrighted by the Friends of Cape Blanco).

Louie Knapp married Ella Stagg in 1893, all three of their sons being born in the hotel, later to be known as the Historical Knapp Hotel. After Louie's death in 1929, Ella lived with her eldest son, Louie Jr., on his large Elk River ranch. Orris and his family took over operation of the hotel until the United States Highway Department bought the site to make way for Route 101. Orris married Hazel Brown, and their union produced three children, Harold, Orris, and June. The youngest son Lloyd married Laura Reed, daughter of W.P. Reed, founder of Reedsport, and they had one daughter, Margery.

To this list of real people and events described in history books, the reader should add the Quah-to-mah Chief Te Cum Tom (Old John). Other Indian characters join the McClure family, their friends, and their occasional foes in the author's fictionalized version of the period.